"I was born in 1888.
Jack the Ripper was my father."

Thus speaks Lord Grandrith, Apeman of the Jungle, whose agility and youth are the result of an unholy alliance.

Stalking him through the savage jungle is Doc Caliban, a magnificently huge man, superbly proportioned all over...

Their meeting is an unforgettable climax of blood and lust, as shocking now as it was then.

A decade ago the unspoken question was: Why don't superheroes have a sex life—or, indeed, sex organs?

"A Feast Unknown is Philip José Farmer's rip-roaring answer."
— Theodore Sturgeon

PHILIP JOSÉ FARMER
A FEAST UNKNOWN

PLAYBOY
PAPERBACKS

an Evolution
Strange
two tongues Touch
exchange
a Feast unknown
to stone
or tree or beast

Evolution
May Swenson

Editor's Note

Lord Grandrith has written nine volumes of auto-biography, totaling close to a million and a half words. Yet this volume, the latest, covering only a part of 1968, is the only one published. Lord Grandrith had planned to publish all the volumes some-day, when it became possible to reveal his true identity and true story. However, Grandrith turned against the Nine who had given him the elixir of prolonged youth.

The first eight volumes are hidden in a place only Grandrith and his wife know. He made arrangements through the editor to publish Volume IX after he had failed to get it published in England, France, Sweden, South Africa, and at several houses in the United States. Grandrith states the Nine were behind the rejections and the various "accidents" to and "losings" of the mss. he sent out.

Fortunately, he had met the editor at the home of a common friend in Kansas City, Missouri. The editor did not then know the true name of James Claymore, as he was calling himself at the time. A letter sent from Lima, Peru, told the editor of Clay-more's actual name and identity. It also outlined the danger that Grandrith, his wife, and several others were in. The next letter came from Dublin, Ireland. The third had no postmark and was left in the editor's mailbox between midnight and six a.m. The editor sent his reply to a man in Stockholm,

Sweden, as requested. The ms. of Volume IX was mailed from Western Samoa.

The editor has Americanized various English terms, changing bonnet into hood, petrol into gas, lorry into truck, etc. The locations of various places in Kenya and Uganda were purposely made vague by Grandrith. This was not done to protect the Nine but to protect those foolhardy people who might try to seek out the Nine or the now-buried gold mines of the valley which Grandrith named Ophir.

In addition, the incident of the landing at Penrith is not quite accurate. Penrith has no airport. The events after the landing did happen as described, but the airport was created by Grandrith to obscure the actual event. He wants to protect a friend who set out lights on a meadow so the plane could land there. Grandrith refuses to change the incident to bring it closer to reality. We can only respect his reasons without understanding them.

In his last letter, Grandrith says that "almost nobody will believe this. Not at this moment, anyway. But events conceived and brought forth by the Nine will soon convince the world. I hope then that it will not be too late for the world. Meanwhile, we are all alive and fighting, though doing more hiding than fighting. And I have added another book to the autobiography."

—*Philip José Farmer*

Foreword

Since the first eight volumes of his memoirs have not yet been published, Lord Grandrith has written a special foreword which encapsulates the early part of Volume I. Without this, the reader would be puzzled by some of the references in this volume.

I was conceived and born in 1888.

Jack the Ripper was my father.

I am certain of this, although I have no evidence that would stand up in court. I have only the diary of my legal father. He was, in fact, my uncle, although he was married to my mother.

My legal father kept a diary almost up to the moment of his death. Shortly after he had locked it inside a desk, he was killed. His last written words recorded his despair because his wife had just died and I, only a year old, was wailing for milk. And there were no human beings within hundreds of miles, as far as he knew.

I alone have read the entire diary. I have never permitted anyone else to read any of the diary preceding the moment when my uncle and my mother sailed from England for Africa.

My "biographer" would have been too horrified by the truth to have written it if I had been unkind enough to reveal it to him. He was a romanticist and, in many ways, a Victorian. He would have made up a story of his own, ignoring the real story, as he did with so many of my adventures. He was interested mainly in adventure for its own sake, although he did describe my psychology, my *Weltanschauung*. However, he never really transmitted the half-infrahuman cast of my mind.

Perhaps he could not understand that part of me, although I tried to communicate it as well as I could. He tried to understand, but he was human, all-too-human, as my favorite poet says. He could never grasp, with the human hands of his psyche, the nonhuman shape of mine.

That part of the diary which I had forbidden others to read describes how my mother happened to be with her husband in Whitechapel on that fog-smothered night. She had insisted on going with him to look for his brother, who had escaped from the cell in the castle in the Cumberland County. Private detectives had quietly tracked John Cloamby to the Whitechapel district of London. His brother, James Cloamby, Viscount Grandrith, had joined the hunt. My mother, Alexandra Applethwaite, related to the noble family of Bedford, had insisted on accompanying him.

My uncle objected to bringing his wife along for several reasons. The strongest was that his brother had attempted to rape her when he had broken out of his cell after bending several iron bars and uprooting them from their stone sockets. Only her screams and the prompt appearance of two manservants armed with pistols had saved her. Alexandra, however, persisted in her insane belief that she alone could make him surrender voluntarily when he was found. Also, she said that she alone could locate him exactly. There was, she claimed, a psychic bond between them, "vibrations" which enabled her to point toward and track him as if she were a human lodestone.

I use the word "insane" in describing this belief because later developments (described by my "biographer" and by me in Vol. I) revealed her mental instability.

She also said that if she were not allowed to go with her husband in the search, she would inform the police and the newspapers of what had happened.

My uncle gave in to her. He had a horror of publicity of any kind and especially of this kind. Also, he might have been arrested for concealing evidence of murder. He was, in fact, an accessory after the fact of murder, if, indeed, there was a fact.

My uncle believed that his brother was responsible for the disappearance of two whores from villages only a few miles from the estates. A severed breast was found on the shore of a tarn; this was all. The locals presumed that somebody had done away with the two women and buried them somewhere. My uncle connected his brother to the murders because of his ravings while in the cell about killing all whores, including his mother. Especially his mother.

His mother, of course, was safe from him. She had killed herself when James, John, and Patrick, her three sons, were quite young. Her husband had killed himself because he suspected that a Swedish gentleman was the father of the boys and that she may have killed herself because her conscience made life unbearable. Their aunt raised the three boys and was much loved by them. But John Cloamby never forgave his mother, although he had never spoken of her until his madness took him.

Later, my uncle believed that John was Jack the Ripper. Before his breakdown, John had been a medical doctor. His real motive in becoming a physician was not in curing the sick. He wanted to know everything about the human body because he intended to find out the secret of immortality. To this end, he had meant to learn much more of chemistry and botany than any medical doctor had ever known.

This obsession was supposed to be the cause of his sickness. Instead, it was the symptom.

It was ironic that he did not find that secret but that I, his son, did. I supposed this, only to have to change my mind.

If my mother and uncle had not gone to Africa primarily to put my father behind them, I would not have become immortal (have a very long prolonged youth, to be exact). Or so I thought.

I am immortal in the sense that I will be thirty-two years of age in body for a very very long time. However, accident, murder, and suicide can reduce me to the rotting corpse which others usually become before their hundredth birthday.

I omitted disease from the fatal list. The same elixir that gives me a potentiality of 30,000 years or more also preserves me from disease. This does not, however, explain my seeming immunity from all the diseases so common in tropical Africa before I became thirty-two.

My uncle's diary recounts in an elegant style, reading like a prose Racine, a ride through the dark fog of the night on March 21. He glimpsed his brother after hours of driving through the mists, and he leaped out of his carriage and ran shouting after him. My mother sat shivering with cold and fear in the carriage while she tried to peer through the wet grayness. A gas lamp nearby shot a ghastly half-light through the swirls. She was alone. Her husband had not wanted a coachman because he might report the peculiar occurrences of the evening to the police.

For a while, there was silence. Then she heard the clicking of hard heels on the stones. A man appeared like a ship sailing through the fog. He stopped and turned, and by the dim light she saw her husband's mad brother.

When James Cloamby returned, he found his wife unconscious on the seat of the carriage. Her skirt and petticoats were up over her face, and her undergarments had been cut off, probably with the scalpel that later took apart the bodies of the White-chapel whores in such grisly fashion.

My uncle was to reason that his brother had not killed her because she was not a whore. But John did hate his older brother, and he may have raped Alexandra for revenge, or possibly because she was not a whore and so was better than his mother, whom, in one part of him, he must still have loved. Also, since John loved Alexandra, or had said he loved her, it was possible that this was his act of love. Who knew what the madman was thinking?

My uncle lit a match when she did not reply to his cry of alarm. He saw the white legs, stripped of the black stockings, and the black, exceptionally hairy vagina out of which oozed my father's sper-matic fluid and some of her blood.

The strange thing, to me, anyway, was that this

was the first time my uncle had seen any of his wife's body below the shoulders.

Although they had been married for a month, the two had not had any sexual intercourse beyond some kissing and slipping his hand down her bodice and over her breasts. The day of the wedding, she had begun menstruating and would not stop. He, being a Victorian, could not bed her while she was "unclean." (Although there were plenty of Victorians who would have done so.)

The day before John broke loose from the cell, Alexandra had ceased to flow. My uncle (as recorded in his diary) was ecstatic. He could quit masturbating now and could stop eyeing his wife's maid.

Then my father-to-be got out of his cell in the north tower of the half-ruined Castle of Grandrith. He and his wife were too upset for some time to consider sexual intercourse. At least, she was.

Now, in the London fog, James Cloamby pulled his wife's skirts down and revived her. She became hysterical, and not until the next day did he discover that his brother had attacked his wife.

His wife seemed to recover. A few months afterwards, they sailed for West Africa, where James was to conduct a secret investigation for the Colonial Office. (This was not the investigation which my "biographer" described, however. He knew the true reason, but he chose to give a spurious one.)

Alexandra now refused to have intercourse with James. She said that she was too "ashamed," felt "too unclean," and, besides, wanted to make certain that she was or was not pregnant. If she was to have a child, she wanted to be certain of its paternity.

Before they sailed, the first known murder by

Jack the Ripper occurred on Easter Tuesday, April 3rd, 1888, on Osborn Street. My uncle heard about this (it was not reported in the *Times*) and wondered in his diary if it could be the work of his brother. Later, he was certain that it was. Yet, so great was his dread of the shame and disgrace if John should be caught, he did not inform the police.

He did continue the search on his own through private detectives. When he sailed for Africa, he sent an anonymous note to the police, describing his brother but not naming him. This note is not in the official records. Research has convinced me that it was suppressed by politically powerful influences.

My father disappeared when Jack the Ripper disappeared. It was not until 1968, the year of this narrative, that I found out what had happened to him.

Alexandra Grandrith was finally able to accept her husband in bed. But by then she was too big with child. My uncle continued to suffer and then backslid, as he put it, to masturbation and, once, a few days before sailing, to the maid. These necessary discharges caused much breast beating in private and many mea culpas.

The events that led to the Grandriths being stranded on the West African coast are familiar to the readers of my "biographer." The reality was somewhat different, but the result was much as depicted in the romances based on my life. James Cloamby built a strong house on the shore near the jungle, and they survived the first 20 months.

I was born November 21, 1888, at 11:45 p.m.

My mother's mind was never thereafter quite in Africa. She spent most of her time in a dream

England, a country much better than the one she knew in reality, I'm sure. Despite this, she was very competent in taking care of me, if I am to believe my uncle's diary. James could not make love to her then because it would have been too much like taking advantage of an idiot. So my poor uncle suffered, and I think he may have been glad when death came at the hands of the chief of a tribe of The Folk. Any horror he felt would have been for his nephew, a 12-month-old baby crying for food and for his mother's milk.

I was to get no more of that because she had died in her sleep a few hours before my uncle was killed. I did get a mother's milk, though it was not quite human milk.

1

The morning of March 21, 1968, was a fine morning. I was seventy-nine years old and felt, and looked, thirty. The sun woke me up that morning. Or so I thought. Sometimes the African sun sneaks over the horizon like an old lion on the prowl, the mists diffracting its rays into a mane. I awoke as if I had been tickled on the nose with a hair from that mane.

The silence was like a breath on my face. It was the silence that had quietly awakened me.

The whinnying of horses, the bellowing of cattle, the squawking of chickens, the chittering of the monkeys were compressed within lungs and sealed by mouths afraid to open.

The voices of the cooks, house servants, and yard men were there, but noiseless. They hung in the sky, turned to cold blue air. I could sense them fluttering the windpipe.

Fear?

Or stealth by some and fear of others?

Treachery.

Perhaps.

Jomo Kenyatta had said that I was the only white man he had ever respected. What he meant was: feared.

During the so-called Mau-Mau revolution, he told his men to stay away from me. My own tribe, the blacks who had initiated me with blood-letting and buggering into their tribe and who had selected me as their chief, hated the Agikuyu. And they loved me. Not as a brother but as a demigod. They would have died to a man to defend me.

Besides, Kenyatta knew that though I was white, I was even more African than he. After all, I was adopted and raised by The Folk.

My blood-brothers and warriors, the original tribesmen, had almost all died off. The survivors were creaking-boned whitehairs. I had been given the choice of becoming a citizen of this African state and declaring the source of my wealth or getting out. Old Kenyatta felt strong enough now to send me that ultimatum. Even though he was no longer the titular head of state, his voice was behind the order.

I had refused to do either. And so I had waited. But I had waited so long for action to be taken that I had become a little careless.

The sun was no longer an old lion. It was the red eye of Death, the drunken always-dry sot who had thirsted for me for almost 80 years.

Now the red eye was bisected by my penis, which reared with a piss hard-on. I was lying on my back, naked, and the scarlet ball climbed up the shaft and was on its way to being balanced atop it.

From some distance, there was a click.

The sky was ripped as if it were rotten old cloth.

The sun was on top of the head of my penis, seeming almost to spurt out.

I knew what the ripping sound was the moment I heard it, and I knew what the click had been.

As if it were red seed, the sun burst open from my penis. It disappeared in smoke. The walls flew apart as if they had become a flock of cranes disturbed by an eagle. The smoke poured into me and filled me to the backs of my eyeballs. The noise was squeezed out of me.

I was turned inside out like a glove. I was a tuning fork trying to find the correct resonance.

The first shell may have struck just outside the bedroom window. The second shell may have exploded at the end of my bed. By one of those freaks and coincidences that have caused many to mock my biographer, but have actually happened to me, the blast lifted my spring and mattress and me upwards and backwards and out the window behind me.

I must have landed in a pile of wood and plaster and bricks. I was still on my mattress, which was by what was left of the veranda. I crawled slowly out of the pile, like the naked body of a tortoise working through its shattered shell. I felt but could not hear other shells. None of these came close enough to damage me; they must have been striking other parts of the house. Through the smoke, I could see the stone foundations and these were sending off chips of stone and also pieces of wood were breaking off and flying into the air. Machine guns and rifles were trying to shred away all the stone and brick and mortar and wood and anything of flesh which the shells might have missed or failed to utterly destroy. Rock fragments struck me in many places.

I was half-stunned, but I had one thought. That was to get to the refuge prepared for such an emergency. More smoke poured over, obscuring my vision and making me cough. I had, however, seen that the thin stone shell which was actually a doorway, an exit, to the refuge, had split open. I reached inside the portion of foundation still standing, felt the steel handle, turned it, and slid inwards.

Even as I closed the door it swung in hard, propelled by a bullet. I was in darkness and utter silence. I groped around until I found the oxygen bottles and cracked them to make sure they had a sufficient supply. I couldn't hear the hissing, so I felt out the nozzles. Cool air struck my palm.

I decided to use the lamp for a moment and examined the room. It was a box 12 feet by 12 by 8. It was double-walled steel with fiber glass insulation between the walls. It contained the oxygen bottles, five gallons of distilled water, medical supplies, some cans of food, pistols, 2 rifles, and ammunition. The main entrance was through a trapdoor in the bedroom above, but the two small exits could be used as entrances. The refuge had been built thirty years before and updated now and then, hence, the fiber glass stuffing. I had built it at my wife's insistence, who had pointed out that we would have been safe a number of times if we had had the refuge. So I had built it and it had not been used until now. In fact, I had almost neglected replacing the empty oxygen and water bottles and over-aged cans.

I hoped that no one outside there knew about the box. Since it had been built, I had taken great pains to get the stores into it unobserved and to never speak of it to anyone besides my wife. If the enemy got hold of an old Bandili who remembered it, and the old one talked, I would be as helpless as an elephant in a pit.

While I crouched in a corner, I discovered that

I had spouted jism over my right leg. This probably occurred when the first shell exploded.

Hemingway and his imitator, Ruark, are usually full of shit when they speak of Africa. Or, as the Yankees say, they didn't know shit from shinola. But they were sometimes accurate in their observations of animals, particularly leopards, shooting sperm at the moment of violent death. Ejaculation is a form of protest of the body against death. The cells want to live forever, and they will try to impregnate the air in desperate copulation, to perpetuate themselves when faced with the end.

That is my explanation. I, personally, do not fear death, but my cells are not as rational as I.

What women do at the moment of suffering a violent death, I do not know. I never heard of a woman shooting out an ovum. Perhaps they do this, but the egg is so small it's unnoticed. Of course, there are so many days when no egg is available, and a man always has sperm. It's possible women substitute voice for sperm; their ejaculations are screams.

I waited in the corner. The box was dark now because I had turned out the lamp to conserve the battery. The silence continued for a long time. I had a sharp headache which I endured for some time and then took two aspirins to relieve. The relief did not come. From time to time, I felt the vibrations of explosions against my back. These, I imagine, were direct hits. The enemy certainly believed in overkill. To use a cannon against one man seemed superfluous, but it was also guaranteed to destroy me entirely. Like so many guarantees, it was worthless. So far.

One or more of the direct hits must have blasted away part of the outer steel wall. Another direct hit removed the fiber glass and the inner wall. I felt as if I were buried under tons of dirt, and I lost consciousness.

2

When I came to, I could hear somewhat. My sense of smell was as sharp as ever, that is, much more effective than a human's but not quite as good as a bloodhound's. (The reasons for this are explained in Volume I along with another explanation, in the appendix of Volume I, of my YY chromosomal mutation.)

There was, stronger than anything, the knife of gunpowder smoke. There was the needle of widely scattered food. There was the saw-edge of pulverized plaster and rent wood. Faint, the odor of human sweat and of a dog.

I opened my eyes. It was high noon. The sun blazed through a small hole in the mass of wood and bricks covering the ripped open upper corner of the box. I was covered with smoke, ashes, and dirt. The five gallon bottles of water had broken and spilled their contents over the room to make a fine mud. The cans were broken open. I think shrapnel had bounced off the walls and struck them. The weapons were buried under dirt that had fallen in.

On top of a pile of mud was a hunting knife. This was the knife I had found on my uncle's skeleton in the house he had built. I was ten then and had found out how to gain entrance. There were bones over the floor; The Folk invading the house had eaten my uncle and mother before leaving it and taken some legs and arms with them. I had used the knife much; hence, its thinness. It was now more of a stiletto than a hunting knife, but I cherished it and kept it in my bedroom, though I had not carried it for many years. A shell had lifted it up and cast it through the opening in the box before the opening was covered up again.

It seemed like a gift to me and cheered me up, despite my headache and earache.

I was also thirsty. I chewed some of the mud to get moisture, and I collected a thimbleful of food from the cans. Then I pushed the mud into the corner opposite the opening, smoothed out my tracks, and pushed the mud over me. Hours passed. My hearing sharpened. Drums beat. Voices shouted and laughed. I smelled liquor, faintly. I heard cattle mooing and bellowing and then smelled blood. After a while, smoke drifted to me and the odor of cooking flesh.

Once, I heard footsteps and the rattle of wood being pushed aside. Several men spoke in the tongue of the Agikuyu. I could imagine them looking down into the box. One said something about going down to see what it was and what was in it. Another said something about tossing a grenade into it just for fun. I did not move.

They talked among themselves in a much lower voice and agreed to come back tonight when no one would notice them and climb down. Perhaps the Englishman had hidden money down there, or the gold he was rumored to have in great quantities.

It became darker. The drums and shouts and stamping feet of dancing men became louder. The moon paled the night and made a skeleton of the wood laid over the opening. I arose, stretched and bent until my muscles were loose again, and then stepped on a ledge and opened a little door.

This was hidden by more debris, but I could see well enough through it. Capering figures in front of great bonfires were lifting bottles from my liquor stores or shooting at the empties when they tossed them into the air. Those who still wore their clothes were in the uniform of the army of Kenya. There was also a number of my own tribesmen, all young fellows.

At the nearest fire, 60 feet away, three men were holding down my pet bitch, a German shepherd named Esta. A young Bandili, Zabu, naked except for an ostrich feather headdress—which he had no right to wear according to tribal law—was holding the bitch by the flanks. His hips moved back and forth rapidly while the soldiers and Bandili laughed and clapped their hands in rhythm with Zabu's strokes. The dog was howling in agony and struggling frantically.

Zabu was a leader of the youth of the villages in this area. He hated all whites, and most of all he hated me. I don't bother to explain my position or views very often, but I had done so with the young racists of my tribe. I tried to explain that the color of my skin was not relevant. I was not as other men, black or white. My rearing by The Folk had resulted in a lack of conditioned reflexes concerning skin color among men.

Nor had I exploited the blacks, as other whites had. Actually, the Bandili had no cause to complain about any whites. I had kept whites from possessing, or even living in, this relatively broad territory. I had also kept the Agikuyu from attempting to run the Bandili out. And I had spent much money to establish local schools, bring in qualified teachers, and send young Bandili, male or female, to colleges as distant as England and America.

All of this made no difference to Zabu and his fellows. I was a white. I must go.

I don't like to be forced into doing anything. On the other hand, it would have been a great relief to get away from my duties and obligations as the owner of the Grandrith plantation and as chief of the Bandili. Especially, it would be a relief to get away from the overcrowdedness, noisiness, bickering, and hatefulness of the humans here.

Once, there were only a few small tribes here and much room to roam and great herds. Now . . .

I was stubborn, and I stayed.

I had recently sent my wife off to England to shop, visit friends in London, and inspect the ancestral estate in the Lake District. Thus, I did not have to worry about her. I had only myself to take care of, and that is the way I like it.

Zabu was not content with my death. He had to revenge himself on the poor dog because she was mine. There was nothing I could do for the moment to help her. I did, however, crawl out to hide behind a pile of bricks and stones. I did not want to be caught in the box if the three who planned on searching the box did return. I was covered with dirt and mud, so my white skin did not show. And I had the hunting knife in my hand.

After a while, an officer pushed the onlookers aside and violently yanked Zabu off the dog. Zabu arose and staggered back, turning, and I saw, by the light of the fire, that his belly and genitals were covered with blood. The slit of the animal had not been large enough for him, so he had used a knife.

The officer shouted at Zabu in his tribal speech and then in Swahili and drew his pistol. I thought he was going to shoot Zabu, but he turned and held the muzzle a foot from the bitch's head and fired. She jerked once.

Zabu had held up his hands in a pleading gesture, evidently thinking that the officer was going to kill him. The officer was a Mugikuyu and so hated the Bandili.

Seeing that he was spared, Zabu laughed and took a bottle from a man and swaggered off. The officer spat at Zabu's back. I didn't know whether he interfered with Zabu because of humane feelings or because he wanted to bug a Bandili.

I waited. I was hungry and thirsty, but I would be stupid to try to stroll out through that crowd in the light of the bonfires. If I could get past the fires, I might pass for one of them. I was taller than most, but a few were the equal of my six foot three, and at a distance, in the dark, I was muddied enough to look black-skinned. There was no chance just then, however.

I fixed my eyes on Zabu and hated him. After a while, as if he were hypnotized by me, he lurched very near. He was mumbling to himself, his head swinging low. I rose up behind him and chopped him on the side of the neck with the edge of my palm and dragged him back behind the pile. Nobody had noticed us. Everybody was looking at a group of young Bandili dancing a spear dance around the dead dog.

3

Zabu awoke on his back with my hand over his mouth and my knife at his throat. His eyes widened like water boiling over. He shook. With a rip of gas, he shot out a long turd. His breath stank of my whiskey and of terror. The blood on his belly and genitals stank of the terror and agony of the bitch, and of the sperm he had loosed.

"Tell me how this happened, Zabu," I said. "Otherwise, I kill you right now."

He was willing to buy a few minutes of life, although his grandfather and father would have died rather than tell an enemy anything. His lips spewed Bandili. His eyes rotated as if he were looking for some device to appear from the air and give him a handhold whereby he could be whisked away from my knife.

Perhaps he thought I had been killed and my ghost had come back.

He had gone through school and college with my assistance. He had denied believing in ghosts. He was an educated man, he had said. *But he believed.* The hindbrain is almost always stronger than the forebrain, though in a subtle fashion.

Zabu said that the Kenyan army had moved in with the assistance of some of the young Bandili. At the last moment, the older Bandili in the nearby village had found out about the attack. They were told to keep quiet or die. Three of the old men had tried to warn me. One was Paboli, the Spear-Launcher, Zabu's grandfather. All three did die.

A strange thing happened then. Zabu, speaking of his grandfather's death, wept.

The army units had moved in on three fronts, leaving the western open because I was returning from a hunting trip in that direction. After I got home, the units quietly closed the gap.

During the night, with utmost care, a cannon and six .50-caliber machine guns were hauled in by foot soldiers. The trucks were kept far out in the savanna to avoid noise. The young Bandili had told the army officers that the stories of my supersensitive hearing and sense of smell were not exaggerated.

Zabu talked on and on, as if enough words would build up a wall thick enough to bar my knife. He tried to justify his treachery, although he did not call it that. He called it patriotism and Africanism.

Humans are always labeling deeds. No doubt, he thought he was right. But he was moving his thoughts around in two boxes labeled BLACKS and WHITES, just as the whites he hated—with the exception of myself—moved their thoughts around in their two boxes.

What happened next surprised me. I did not intend to do it and had no thought of doing any such thing.

Looking back, I see that the treachery, so unexpected in those who had been my people for 60 years, combined with the shock of the explosions, had literally loosened something in me.

Rather, *loosed* it.

It had always been in me but shoved down as deep as deep was.

I stunned him with the knife hilt. While he lay half-unconscious, I cut his tongue off close to the root to keep him from screaming. The pain brought him to his senses. He tried to sit up, and his mouth gaped. The blood shot out.

I kissed him. One, to drink the blood, which I needed because I was thirsty. Two, to stop any sound he might have made. Three, I was compelled to do so.

The blood was salty and unpleasant, as if it contained the essence of a sea-bottom built up from the decomposing flesh and bones of a million poisonous fish. It contained a trickle of tobacco, which I hate. In other words, his blood was like most of the humans from whom I have drunk.

But the blood was strengthening, and I began to feel an excitement similar to that which I felt when in battle or making a kill. However, when it became more intense, it was obviously sexual.

Quickly, before I climaxed, I cut Zabu open with a stroke down his belly. It was not deep enough, however, to cut into the intestines. I know my anatomy well.

As the knife sank into the flesh, I spurted over his belly and the knife.

For a moment, I lost control. My arm straightened, and the knife went in to the hilt.

He writhed briefly as he died. I shook like a tree in a storm.

I sat back, gasping. I wiped off my knife on his hair. I wondered what had made me behave thus. I had intended to stick my penis into the wound and do to him what he had done to my dog.

4

Finally, I quit trying to explain to myself my strange compulsion. I am a relentless hunter but only if there is a scent or track to follow.

I waited. The noise increased, and the celebrators staggered even more. When the moon had quartered the sky, the inevitable fights broke out between the Agikuyu and the Bandili. The few officers not thoroughly drunk separated the fighters and sent them on their way. Some soldiers, however, staggered into the village, a hundred and fifty yards away. They were after women, of course. The older men in the village were Bandili, as proud as ancient Romans and as courageous. They had been imprisoned by their youths, who had surprised them. Now, they were free, and they fought. And the Bandili youths could not stand aside while their sisters and mothers were raped and their elders killed by Agikuyu. They attacked the soldiers. Presently, the two factions were killing each other and innocent bystanders, as in all wars, and the village huts were ablaze.

The battle gave me a chance to leave the ruins of my house unobserved. In a few minutes, I had worked my way through the shadows to the cannon. It was a British gun-howitzer of World War II, a 25-pounder or 88 mm, set on a two-wheel carriage and carrying a shield. The caisson held some shells and point-detonating fuses. These were inserted just before the shell was loaded into the gun and would explode on striking.

The crew of four were moving the cannon to a slight hill to fire upon the village. They were drunk and probably would have hit their own men as well as the target.

I took a semiautomatic rifle from a stack near them and killed each with one bullet. With the first shot, my penis began to rise. At the fourth shot, it was in the state where, usually, the orgasm was within ten seconds of arriving. Then it slowly subsided, and the pleasurable sensations diminished.

The cannon was too close to the soldiers. Before I could have fired two rounds, they would be at me from three sides. I picked up the end of the carriage and towed it off across a level of forty yards and then up a 25-degree incline for perhaps fifty yards. Past the top of the hill, I turned the cannon around on the wheels and inched it down the other, which was a 30-degree incline. I had to dig my heels into the dirt to keep it from getting away. The next hill was steeper and higher. Twice, the 900-pound cannon and carriage almost got away. A small flat space on top of the hill was large and broad enough for my purposes, and it commanded the side of the smaller hill and the village and the area around it.

I ran back and pulled the caisson, into which I had loaded the dead crew's rifles, ammunition, and some grenades, up to the hilltop. I then cached three of the rifles and ammunition behind trees at various places. I lined up the cannon, depressed the muzzle, inserted a fuse, loaded in a shell, and took one more look at the situation.

It was then that I saw dark figures coming out

of the woods on the east side of the plantation, behind the soldiers. They advanced in an arc, and several times the moon struck something metallic. There were about forty men on foot, and two groups carried bulks which could be recoilless rifles on tripods.

Behind them, something big emerged from the woods. A long barrel of a cannon projected from a platform. It was a half-track, self-propelled cannon which I estimated to be a 90 millimeter.

The foot soldiers and the half-track reached a line of trees and stopped. They were out of my sight when they were behind the trees. Four dark figures ran out from the trees towards the cover of other trees near the village. They were scouts.

By then, the Kenyans had discovered that their cannon was missing. Four men followed the wheel tracks towards the smaller hill and soon were hidden by its bulk. The flames from the village were searing the skies. There were many bodies, men, women, children, sprawled between the burning huts. Machine guns were still shooting, but the rifle fire had died down.

5

Suddenly, all firing ceased. The soldiers began to regroup on the east side of the village. I supposed that the officers had sobered up enough to bring the men under control. They were beginning to realize the consequences of their actions. It might be possible to get the government to consider this just an unfortunate incident, but justified, because the mission had been successful. It had obliterated me. But if the other Bandili villages revolted because of this massacre, the government might shoot them to satisfy the Bandili.

On the other hand, they might be re-forming for another attack on the Bandili survivors, entrenched in the woods on the west side of the village.

The newcomers were moving back. Their haste gave me the impression they intended to remove themselves at a great distance from the Kenyan army. It was evident that they were surprised to find the soldiers. I supposed they had come to attack me. For Revenge. For Wealth. For the Secret of Immortality. Perhaps for all three.

Their appearance here at the same time as the army attack was one more of the many coincidences which some readers of my biographer's novels have found incredible. These people do not know that some men are not only endowed with "animal magnetism," but some men also have what I call a "human magnetic moment." That is, some men, of whom I am one, are the focus of unusual events, of mathematically unlikely coincidences. They radiate something—a quality, a "field," which pulls events together. The field slightly distorts, or warps, the semifluid structure of occurrences, of space objects intertwined with the time flow.

Whatever the reason for their being here, the newcomers were now leaving. I could, however, directly influence them now. I picked up the tailpiece of the carriage, turned the cannon, unconsciously estimating the distance and trajectory as if I were firing an arrow. I depressed the muzzle and then got down off the operator's seat and jerked the lanyard.

I had been vaguely aware that I was sexually excited. Now, as the cannon went off, so did I.

The orgasm, however, was not nearly as intense and ecstatic as when I had thrust my knife into Zabu's belly.

Thereafter, I was all action, intent on the "red business," as Whitman so appropriately and beautifully phrases it. If I had a hard-on or came during the next few minutes, I did not know it.

My first shell landed about ten feet ahead of the half-track. It stopped, backed up, and then turned to the left. My second shell landed on its right and drove it still more leftwards so that it was heading towards the village again. The third shell exploded in the middle of a group of the newcomer foot-soldiers, which had hit the ground when my first shell struck. The three survivors got up and ran. About eight bodies were on the ground.

At this time, as I had expected, the four trackers came over the smaller hill. My rifle fire got two, because they were such fine silhouettes against the fires. The other two dived back behind the hill and began firing at me. I ignored the bullets, although some hit the cannon and some spurted dirt near me. My fifth shell blew up the top of the hill. The two men may not have been hit, but they were discouraged, because they quit firing. Perhaps they were working around the hill to flank me.

By this time, the Kenyans had seen the half-track and were firing at it from behind the line of trees. The vehicle replied with shell and three machine guns. The other newcomers turned and advanced across the field towards the Kenyans.

My next three shells went down the line of Kenyans on the left, middle, and right, and put an indeterminate number out of the fight. They ran away then, some towards the distant forest to the north and some towards me. The half-track went at full speed to the north end of the line of trees and caught a number of the soldiers trying for the forest. The newcomers on foot cut towards my hill.

I turned the cannon and fired two rounds to the right on the lower slope of the smaller hill. This was to discourage the Kenyans from coming around that side.

I was working furiously and sweating and beginning to feel tired because I had had almost no food or liquid for 20 hours. I was loading the shell, slamming the breech block shut, turning the cannon by lifting the tailpiece of the carriage, revolving the wheel to depress or elevate the barrel, and yanking the lanyard, though not always in this order. I had glimpsed the two soldiers scuttling across the level ground between the two hills, one on each side of me. I had to take care of them before I got rid of the last two shells.

One emerged from the shadows into the moonlight briefly, and I tossed a grenade his way. It fell a few feet from him; he froze; then he dived away from it. The explosion caught him in mid-air. He did not get up. I ran a stream of rifle fire across him to make sure he stayed down.

The other soldier was a brave man. He came up the hill at a run, zigzagging, and firing. I shot once; he fell backwards. I approached him warily and put a bullet through his head.

With each death, I was numbly aware of my swelling penis and the rising tide of seminal fluid,

During this fight, the other soldiers came around both sides of the little hill and started up the big one towards me. They were desperate to get the cannon. With it, they could decimate the newcomers. They would, however, have to get me first and then bring up other caissons, because there were only two rounds left. I did not have time to fire these. I pushed the cannon over the lip of the hill and had the satisfaction of seeing a number running and screaming to get out of its way. Then I lobbed five grenades down the hill and took off down the other side with a BAR, a magazine belt, and three grenades.

Ten minutes later, I came up from behind one of the soldiers looking for me. I slit his throat, cut out his liver, and ate while I walked away from the others.

The cutting out of the liver finally evoked the orgasm that had been threatening, if I may use such a word. It was exquisite, but it was also disturbing.

(Those who have not read Volume I of my Memoirs, but who are familiar with the first of the romanticized biographies, will object that I am not a cannibal. My biographer, when describing how I had killed the first human I ever encountered, said that I had first thought of eating him. Then I had rejected the idea because of an *instinctive* horror of cannibalism. This is one of the several cases of romantic nonsense and genetic misinformation that he believed in. The truth (which he did not know) is that I devoured the killer of the only being I had greatly loved. I did not like the taste, but I ate him as a matter of revenge. I have eaten other human beings since, but only when I could get no other food.)

Strengthened, I set out to torment the soldiers. These had pulled the cannon back up onto the hill and brought another caisson of shells up. The half-track, meanwhile, had taken a station behind a tree. The artillery duel began. A number of shells exploded around the vehicle, and one blew the tree in half. But eventually the recoilless .88 succeeded in hitting close enough to the Kenyan cannon to kill its crew and to blow up the other shells. The vehicle waited a moment, and then, probably receiving orders via walkie-talkie, started across the level ground towards the hill.

At that moment, I threw a grenade onto the platform. The crew died, but the shells failed to go off, as I had expected. Two men fell out of the cab and staggered away. I shot one and stunned the other with the butt of my rifle. It was easy to catch up with the vehicle, which was still rolling, and stop it. I put the two unconscious men on the platform and drove across the plain and as deeply as I could into the forest.

One man looked as if he would not recover. The other gained his senses with nothing but a headache from the blow. He was a muscular Arab, black-haired, clean-shaven, eagle-nosed, with two large but close-set eyes. He seemed to be about 30 years of age. He was dressed in khaki but wore no military insignia. He looked bravely enough at me, but he was shaking and was pale under his sallow skin.

The cannon and the grenades had again deafened me. However, I am an excellent lip reader in French, English, Arabic, Swahili, and a number of Bantu languages and dialects (if the latter are not tone languages).

I questioned him in Egyptian Arabic. He replied in Syrian Arabic. He said his name was Ibrahim Abdul el Mariyaka. He did not know what he was doing here or anything else. He felt brave enough to call me a dog of a Nasrani.

He ran his gaze up and down me and then licked his drying lips. He was standing with his back against a tree, both of them gray in the dawn. He was about six feet tall, but I was three inches higher and outweighed him about eighty pounds. I was naked, and my skin was smoke-blackened, but my gray eyes must have gleamed palely and wildly out of my dark face. Dried blood covered my mouth and chin and splotched my chest and hands, and there was dried blood and spermatic fluid on my belly and genitals. In addition, as I gestured at him with my knife, my penis rose slowly like a leech swelling with sucked blood.

Being an Arab, he must have been sure I was

going to sexually assault him. In a way, he was right.

I kicked him in the stomach, and while he writhed, retching drily on the ground, I drank from a canteen of water I had taken from the cab. Then I removed some rope from the platform and tied him up. After propping him against the tree, I dragged the other man from the platform and sat him up against a wheel. He was gray-blue and breathing shallowly, but his blood pressure was high enough to drive a geyser into my face when I cut off his penis. I stuck it in his mouth and then drove his knife up through his chin to keep his jaw from falling open. Eyes open, limp bloody penis protruding from his mouth, he sat opposite the other man.

I cut out the liver, chewed off a piece, and swallowed it.

The Arab by the tree turned as gray-blue as the dead man when he saw me ejaculate on slicing into the man. He tried to retch but was unsuccessful. I waited. I had made no threats. None were needed. When he had quit trying to throw up, he leaned his head against the tree. His black eyes were dull below the half-closed lids. A snake of spittle ran down his chin.

I said, "I will ask. You will reply."

He knew, probably from experience in torturing others, that very few men can hold out against prolonged torture. He was willing to settle for a quick death. He answered my questions fully, and his information seemed to be valid.

The leader and organizer of this expedition was an Albanian. He went under the Arabic name of

Muhmud abu Shawarib. His real name was Enver Noli. The others were mostly Arabs, although a few were Bulgarians who had fled to Albania because of their Red Chinese sympathies.

Noli had promised every man in his army that he would have enough gold to support him and four wives for the rest of his life. That is, if the Englishman, John Cloamby, Lord Grandrith, were captured alive.

"He talked only of gold?" I said.

"Yes. Was there anything else?"

Noli was not likely to promise his men the secret of prolonged youth, even if he believed that I possessed it. They would think him crazy and would not follow him. It was possible that he had no thought of the elixir, but I have encountered other men, all dead now, who believed, with good reason, that I had an elixir and were prepared to do anything to get the secret from me.

The Arab said, "You can kill me, Nasrani. But Noli will find you and inflict great pain upon you until you tell him where your gold is hidden. He is a very determined man, very cunning, and very strong."

"That may be," I said. I stabbed him in the solar plexus. Now I failed to have a sexual reaction, and I hoped that the aberration was, for some reason, gone. I doubted it. The truth was that I had only so much jism, and it had been used up for the time being.

I booby-trapped the vehicle with some wire and grenades so that three shells—one by the gas tank —would go off if the cab doors or the hood were opened. Then I went into the woods and up a

tree and waited. The sounds of battle had died out.
Presently, as I knew they would, the invaders came
on the track of the vehicle. Two jeeps drove up;
behind them straggled a mob, the survivors of the
battle with the Kenyans.

6

Enver Noli was a huge man with a large belly, a shaven head, and great drooping moustaches that fell to his chest. His nose was immense, curved like a scimitar. He wore green coveralls and paratrooper's boots. He held his kepi in one tremendous fist and whacked it across the palm of the other hand. When he gave an order, he bellowed.

A soldier ran out from the main body of the troops and warily approached the vehicle. When he looked into the cab, he saw the wires I had gone to some pains to hide. He reported this to Enver, who stood up in the jeep, which was about seventy feet from the half-track. The soldier raised the hood to check the motor for traps there, and the grenade exploded and then the three shells. The vehicle and the soldiers disappeared in smoke and flame. Noli was knocked off the jeep, but he bounded up and ran away with the rest. Unfortunately, nobody was hit by the shells or splashed by the gas. I did shoot two during the noise and panic.

Noli stopped running and managed to halt the twenty or so of his men. He got them to line up and to begin firing with two machine guns and fifteen rifles into the woods. While the bullets were flying around me, whipping the leaves and knocking off chunks of bark, I shot two more Arabs. Immediately after, I descended the tree and ran off in the direction opposite the invaders and then curved around until I was some distance behind them. The field, where the main fighting between the Kenyans and newcomers had taken place, was now being held by the jackals, hyenas, and vultures.

The two hills yielded more dead. The wounded had either been taken away or put out of their pain. The carrion eaters were busy here, too.

The village was entirely burned down, and of the survivors there was no sign. I knew they were hiding in the forest. They had fled to the forest more than once from Arab slave-raiders, though not until after great losses. I had been the one who had led them to victory against the Arab invaders and then led them across the country to terrorize the slavers so much that they never again dared enter Bandili country. I had led them against the Germans in World War I. I had led them in a great raid into Gekoyo. Now they were hiding again, and if they came out once more and fought they would do it without me.

For 60 years I had been a Bandili and the great father, the elephant who charges, for the Bandili. Now, I was truly exiled. This was no temporary loss. It was forever.

I wept then. I had loved these people as much as I could any group of humans. I was far more Bandili than I was English. I had had true friends among them. But all that was ended. Although this village was the only one of the ten Bandili villages that had betrayed me, the others would be no better. The young were too hating and the old too feeble and too few.

Moreover, the Kenyan government had made it plain that I could no longer live in this country. Not in the open, at least.

I made a sentimental gesture. I waved my rifle

at the ashes of the village and then at those hidden in the forest. It was the only good-bye I could give, and doubtless no one saw it.

Then I turned and began to trot across the savanna, towards the hills to the west.

My destination was the mountain range that lay far beyond the hills, approximately a hundred and fifty miles away, and twenty miles into Uganda. I trotted all night. The false dawn, the wolf's tail, was graying the savanna when I began to think about holing up for part of the day. The acacia trees in the distance looked like black cutouts of the monsters of Bandili myth. Then the sun leaned against the night and swung it away, and day padded in. A lion roared in the distance. The air was cool, moving gently from the mountains in the west. A wart hog trotted out of the tall grass, his tail held stiffly up. The sun gleamed on a yellow tusk.

I ran along easily with the savanna on my left and a clump of hills to my right. I carried the rifle in my right hand. I stopped for a moment because I saw the grasses move against the wind. Something big enough to be a lion or a man was approaching through the cover about thirty yards away.

The rifle soared up out of my hand, torn away by a blow like that from a crocodile's tail. It spun off, and then the sound of the shot came from the hills.

7

My arm was paralyzed by the transmission of shock through the rifle, but I did not find that out immediately. I dived towards the tall grass and rolled towards it. Dirt and grass flew up so close they fell over me. There were four gouts of earth and flocks of tiny pieces of grass, each followed by a shot ringing across the savanna.

I jumped up, and, zigzagging and bending low, ran. There was a growl, and a big yellowish brown body moved away from me. I smelled a lioness. She was gone, and I had the grass to myself except for the brief company of two bullets which cropped stalks only a few inches from me. I dived once more, and I stayed where I was.

Several minutes passed. My arm lost its numbness. More shots. More stalks cut in half, falling on me. The bugger had superb vision. I started crawling, though slowly. It was impossible to keep the grass from signaling my progress. More bullets slashed the grass.

When I had crossed about 35 yards, I was at the edge of the grass. I leaped up and ran away, still crouching. There were no more shots. Not for a second had I thought that the sharpshooter was a member of the Kenyans or of the band of the Albanian, Noli. A third party had dealt himself in.

I heard a roar behind and looked over my shoulder. A male lion was charging after me. I did not know how he could be in this neighborhood or why he was chasing me. He must have been very near but somehow hidden from me. The stimulus of seeing me run away from him had evoked the reaction of running after me. I knew every lion for 40 miles in any direction from my plantation. This one was a stranger and should not have been here out of his own territory.

He was the largest lion I'd ever seen. He weighed 650 or more pounds, and his mane was so thick that I knew at once that he had not been in the brush for long. He looked as if he had been bred for the purpose of eating me. He also looked as if he had not eaten lately; his ribs were getting close to the outside air.

I'm not often amazed, but this was one of the times. In my seventy-nine years, I've fought at most twelve lions, considerably less than my biographer records. Usually, a male lion is as eager to avoid a battle as I am. But I have killed them with only a knife, as my biographer records, though there have never been any of the face-to-face encounters shown in those very bad and lying movies. If I got into the situations those actors did, my bowels would have been scooped out or my back muscles plucked out or my head bitten off.

I crouched, waiting for the lion with my knife in my hand. The next thing that happened told me that the hitting of my rifle had been no lucky shot.

The knife was jerked out of my hand. Like a bright bird, it flew up and away. I heard the distant report of the rifle before the knife struck the ground.

My moment of shock almost cost me my life. The lion launched himself towards me on the final bound. I got to one side just in time; a paw flashed by, brushing the skin of my chest.

Getting onto the lion's back when he is in full charge requires very swift and unhesitating movements. If the slightest thing goes wrong—slipping a little, estimating the trajectory and speed of the final leap by too little or too much—it's over for the man. I had jumped to one side while he was still on the downcurve of the arc of his leap and stomped one foot and was bounced back in again and had grabbed the mane with my left hand. A savage yank pulled me along with the beast and also up into the air. Usually, I had to use one hand because my knife was in the other, but this time I had both free. And so I had a better hold and was on its back even more quickly than usual.

He reared up and then fell to one side. I went with him but twisted to keep from being crushed. Up he came again. I had my arms under his front legs, and when he rose I had my hands around the back of his neck and locked together.

His roaring had been loud. Now, from somewhere in that cavernous body, he got the force to double the noise. He rolled again—making me feel as if I were being spread out like a turtle under an elephant's hoof—but I managed to keep my legs locked around his belly. His hind feet moved up to tear my legs, but he could not get them under me or even touch my legs.

Then, as we lay in the dirt, slowly, slowly, his bones creaking, his head went down under the pressure of my arms. I realize that this is difficult to believe. A lion has truly enormous strength in those massive neck muscles. But I am not as other men, in degree or kind. Not in many things, anyway, and this was not the first time I had broken a big cat's neck with a full-Nelson, though the other had not been as huge as this one.

It was not easy. For a long time, the lion, growling much more softly now, resisted my utmost efforts, and his neck refused to bend any more. But the time came when the bones creaked again like a wooden ship in a heavy sea. My head was buried in the mane as I sweated and strove. The hairs stuck in my face like little spears. The green-yellow lion odor was strong, and, beneath it, was the stench of awareness of death. Not fear of death, awareness of its inevitability. The end had come for him, and he knew it. Everybody born in Africa—antelope, lion, black man, Arab, Berber—knows when the time has come. The awareness is a legacy from this ancient land, the birthplace of mankind and of many many species of beast. Mother Africa lets her child know when he is about ready to fertilize her soil with the body she gave him. Everybody knows this except the descendants of Europeans—myself excepted.

As I felt the neck muscles weaken with this awareness, and my arm muscles gain in strength for the same reason, I became conscious of an approaching orgasm. I don't know when my penis had swelled and my testicles gathered themselves for the explosion. But my penis was jammed between the lion's back and my belly, and it was throbbing and beginning to jerk.

At that moment, the lion's neck gave way. As the muscles loosened, and the bones broke, I spurted, sliming the fur and my belly.

The lion moaned with a final outgoing of air, kicked, and himself spurted. I rose, unsteadily, after dragging my leg out from under him. I scooped up some of the lion sperm in the dust and swallowed it. This was a custom of The Folk, one which my biographer avoided describing. It is supposed to bestow the potency of the male lion upon the eater. I believe it does; no amount of European education has convinced me otherwise. Besides, I like the heavy big-feline taste and odor of it. It is, more than almost anything, African in its essence. There is everything in it. Let him who would envision the soul of this ancient continent, eat lion sperm.

Always, after making a kill of a beast of prey, I stand with one foot on the carcass and give a great yell of triumph. This, too, I learned from The Folk. But this time, the orgasm and the knowledge that I was a target for a sharpshooter, chopped off that cry.

8

Although the knife bore the dent of the bullet near the hilt and also had been twisted by the impact, it was still serviceable. Moreover, I would not have thrown it away if it had been useless. Though I am not sentimental, I could not bear to get rid of it. It had been my real father's in England, and he had given it to my uncle before he became mad. My first sight of the knife was my first knowledge of metal. And it had served me for 70 years and killed 10 times that number of prey and enemies.

I put it in the sheath and looked towards the hills. The sun flashed now and then. The reflection of binoculars or cameras, possibly. Or of a telescope.

A puff of dirt struck immediately in front of me as I stooped to pick up the rifle; the sound of the shot came about a second later. The shooter was approximately 1125 feet away. The second bullet struck a few inches to my left; the third, to my right. The fourth went between my legs. I was being told to run away onto the savanna and leave the rifle behind.

Instead, I cut the lion open and removed a piece of his heart and chewed on it. Four more shots, very close, enabled me to discern the exact location of the rifle. I also saw four men through the bush on the hill.

I left at a slow walk. I abandoned my rifle because its barrel had been bent by the bullet. I was angry because of the ease with which the rifleman was herding me and the contempt I felt he had for me. If he thought I was really dangerous, he would have killed me with his first shot. His actions seemed to say: Try your best, my dear Lord Grandrith. It won't be nearly good enough.

When I had walked a quarter of a mile, the shots ceased. From time to time, as I strode to the west, I looked back. Two miles away, a cloud of dust followed. When I stopped to bathe in a waterhole, the dust settled. I caught and ate several almost mouse-sized grasshoppers which inhabit this region. I threw a stone at a kingfisher but missed it by a wing's length. There are many kingfishers in this region, where there is little water except during the rainy season. But the kingfishers have abandoned an aquatic diet; they have adapted to catching grasshoppers and other insects.

When night came, I backtracked. Twenty minutes later, I had found the camp of the sharpshooter. It was on the flat top of a small hill in a clearing around which was an unusual growth of bush and number of trees. A depression beside it held some water, which accounted for the dense growth. In the clearing were two large trucks, one of which carried a very large camper, and two jeeps. Three tents were pitched; two fires had been built. Some blacks were cooking over one fire, and coffee was boiling over both. There were six blacks and two white men in sight. Then I saw a white man move behind the half-opened flap of a tent. The weak light from the lamp within gleamed on a bronze back for a moment.

I had smelled the coffee a long way off and had been salivating. I love coffee. If these people had not been shooting at me that afternoon, I would have been tempted to join them.

I moved around until I could get a better view of the man inside the tent. I still could not see much of him, but I got the impression of a very large and very solid man. He seemed to be doing some peculiar exercises. I caught glimpses of bronzed biceps, bunching and smoothing over and over again. The muscles looked like mongooses slipping back and forth in a wild play under a blanket woven of bronze wires. I know that that is a rather fanciful description, but that is what occurred to me.

The other two whites, old men, sat on folding chairs with their backs to me. The smaller was thin, quick-moving, wary as a bird, and had a face sharp as a neck of a broken-off bottle. He was dressed as if he had just stepped out of the most expensive safari outfitter's store in Nairobi. As he talked, he gestured frequently with a silver-headed black cane.

The other old man was so wide and had such abnormally long arms, thick neck, simian features, and low forehead, and his arms were so hairy, he could almost have passed for one of The Folk.

The blacks had talked among themselves in Swahili, so I knew the names of all three whites. The man in the tent was a Doctor Caliban. The dapper old man was a Mr. Rivers. The apish old man was a Mr. Simmons. All three were from Manhattan Island.

I suspected that the old men were talking so loudly because they hoped to entice an eavesdropper—me of course—to come closer. I found the trip wire which would have set off some kind of alarm and got over that without disturbing it. I also detected the two rocks, made of papier-mache, which held electronic eye devices inside them. I had come close to wriggling between them, because that was the natural route to a depression in the ground behind a bush, an excellent place to hide while listening. Only because I happened to rub up against the false stone did I discover what it was.

I became even more cautious then. And I noticed that the flap of the tent in which Doctor Caliban had been exercising was now closed. For all I knew, he might be slipping out the rear of the tent to catch a spy.

If the two old men were part of a trap, they certainly took no care to keep silent on matters that an enemy should not know. And they talked about Caliban as if he were deaf.

I crawled around to one side where I could see their lips. This was not as informative as listening, because I missed words now and then, but it was safer.

". . . really know what's got into Doc?" the dapper Rivers said. "Something sure as shit is wrong."

"Looks as if he's gone ape," Simmons said.

Rivers laughed and spoke so loudly I could hear him. "Ape! Ape? You old Neanderthal, you're throwing stones at a glass house!"

"Listen, you sick legal eagle, you," Simmons said, "this is no time or place for your tired old bullshit. This is serious, I'm telling you. Doc has a screw loose somewhere. I think it's the elixir; it has to be. The side effects are finally coming through. I warned him years ago, when he offered it to us. I ain't one of the world's greatest chemists for nothing."

I had been intrigued before. Now I was caught, a crocodile on a hook. Elixir!

"You really think he's crazy? After all these years of doing good, combating evil, fixing up all those criminals we caught, and reforming them?" Rivers said.

The apish old man said, "That's another thing . . ."

I missed what he said next, then his cigar left his lips. ". . . operated on them, he said. Cut out the gland that made them evil, he said at first. Then later on he quit talking about that gland, because there ain't no such thing, and he started to talk about re-routing and short-circuiting neural circuits. Now, I ask you, do you really believe that shit? It was all right in the old days, because we didn't know much about the causes of crime then. But it's different now. We know it's caused mainly by psychosocioeconomic environments."

"Do we?" Rivers said. "What really do we know now more than we knew then, besides some things in the physical sciences and a little progress in the biological?"

"O.K., so they ain't as smart nowadays as they like to think they are," Simmons said. "But in the '30's, we could believe anything Doc told us because he told us it was so. But did you ever see him operate on a criminal? Not that I doubt he did something to them, handy as he is with a knife. But this crap about curing criminals with surgery . . . know as well as I do that a criminal is the product of genetic predisposition plus environment."

"Doc isn't the man we knew, that's for sure," Rivers said. "I don't know. It's like seeing Lucifer fall. Well, that's stretching it. Doc's no evil angel, but

. . . if you want to get right down to the honest-to-God-call-it-shit-not-peanut-butter-reality, Doc may be right about the causes and cure of criminals."

Simmons looked as if he were grunting. He said, "Maybe. And maybe Doc was getting his kicks . . . well, I shouldn't say that, wouldn't, if it wasn't for his funny behavior now. You gotta admit he's been acting kinda peculiar lately. Now, I ain't saying he's become a Doctor Jekyll-Mr. Hyde . . . but . . ."

They were silent for a while. Simmons puffed on his cigar. Rivers lit a long cigarette in a long cigarette holder. After a while, Simmons pulled some rectangles—photographs, I presumed—from the pocket of his bush jacket. He held them up so that the firelight illuminated them.

He said, "Looka the whang on that wild man! Did you ever see such a prick on a white man?"

Rivers took one of the photos and studied it. "My tool is longer," he said. "Used to be, anyway. Eight inches. But it's skinny. I never saw such a shaft on a man except once."

"The son of a bitch is queer," Simmons said. "I was looking through the glasses when he got up after breaking that lion's neck. He had a hard-on you wouldn't believe outside a zoo. And he was coming like a Texas oil well."

"Yes, I know," Rivers said. "My choppers about dropped out. I saw Doc once, just once, and he's the only man I ever saw, black or white, with a dong as big as that Englishman's. In fact, I'll swear his was even thicker and longer."

"You saw Doc's cock?" Simmons said. "When the hell was that?"

". . . adventure of the Tsar of . . ." Rivers said. "You remember, Doc and I'd been a long time hiding . . . had to piss . . . my eyes about flew the coop, believe me."

Simmons looked around uneasily. "Maybe we shouldn't be talking like this. Doc might . . ."

"You think he hasn't heard us a million times before? He knows how curious we've been. Personally, I think he's been listening to us for years. But what we said never seemed to bother him. You know what a button-down lip he's got. And he's the most self-controlled man in the world; he couldn't admit that anything we said would stick in his craw. And maybe it doesn't. He *knows* he's the superman's superman!"

"After what I seen today, I ain't so sure," Simmons said. "I've never seen anything like it! But I can understand now why Doc is so hot to tangle with him. He wants to test his mettle on somebody who looks as if he could give him a hard time!"

The little man said, as if he hadn't heard Simmons, "You know, I used to put it out of my mind, or tell myself that Doc was just keeping his private life entirely to himself. But he never lied to us, as far as I know. And he always said he led too dangerous a life and was too busy and always off on some quest or other. He couldn't afford to get married; it made him too vulnerable. That's understandable. But he went further. He said he didn't want to get involved with any woman because it wouldn't be fair to waste her time. That's understandable. But then he claimed he had nothing at all to do with women. Nothing at all! Now, didn't you ever think that was peculiar? No ass at all! No pussy, no nothing, for God's sakes!"

"Well," Simmons said, "he coulda been jerking off. But it just doesn't seem like Doc to be doing that. I always thought maybe he wasn't so perfect, after all. You know, maybe he was paying for his mental and physical superiority to the rest of us— to every fucking man in the world—by not being able to get a hard-on. Could be. Jesus Christ! There has to be some sort of compensation in this world!"

"There does?" Rivers said. "Who told you that, you shoddy imitation of a philosophizing orangu- tan!"

"One of these days, I'll orangutan it all the way up your decrepit asshole," Simmons said.

"No, you won't. I don't allow anything but high- quality shit up there," Rivers said.

They talked for a moment with their hands over their mouths as they held their smokes in their mouths. Then I saw Rivers' lips.

"You know, Doc and . . . as if they were brothers . . . coloring . . . black hair and gray eyes and a darker skin, but Doc has . . ."

They talked on, rambling much. I got the impres- sion that these two octogenarians had known each other intimately for a long long time. They had been through much with each other, and they were very fond of each other. The abuses and insults they loosed at each other were good-natured, indeed, their second natures. And as I listened—read, rather—I understood that they were here on The Last Great Adventure. There had been three other men who had shared their exploits and dangers in the past. But these were dead now. The two old men expected to die soon, but they had insisted on coming to Africa with Caliban, and he had re- luctantly agreed.

Now, they were sorry they had come. Or, at least, disturbed. Something had happened to the good doctor. He was here to hunt me down and to kill me. Not with guns. In barehand combat. This was not at all like Doc. He had always been averse to killing. He had only done so when he absolutely had to. And he had maintained that every man, no matter how evil, was worth saving.

Something had changed his mind. They knew what it was, but so far they had not named it. They referred to it circuitously.

Doc Caliban had told them that I was an abysmally evil man who should be obliterated. The two were not convinced. From what they had learned about me from other sources, they did not think I could be the monster that Doc described. Yet, all their adult lives, they had trusted Doc. They had regarded him as an oracle, as the fount of wisdom, as a doer of great good.

Doc had been born in 1903, I learned when the two were quarreling about the best sign in the zodiac. He was now 65 years old, but he looked as if he were still 30.

They did not seem bitter that he had not shared his secret of prolonged youth with them. They spoke as if he had offered it to them, but they had turned it down.

I could not believe this. I assumed that I misunderstood them. There was the possibility that they had been over fifty when the offer was made. In that case, the elixir was only able to slow down aging somewhat. By the time they were ninety, they would have aged physically to about seventy. Perhaps, on considering the price they must pay for this slight prolongation of life, they had rejected it. What, after all, was an extra thirty years or so of life?

But when a man was offered a chance to live at least 30,000 years, then the price looked small.

I liked to think so.

But listening to them, I was forced to dwell a little on that which I had pushed away because it was too painful. Had I, by becoming a god, become less of a man?

9

Now I knew what Doc Caliban's ultimate goal might be. He meant to kill me, for some reason, but the end of his journey could lie in the mountains to the west, where I also intended to journey.

I began to get more uneasy. Not that I expected him to try to kill me now. It was obvious that he was "toying" with me. Also, it was obvious that the old men had instructions to talk as freely as they pleased. Caliban wanted me to learn much about him. The more I knew, the more "equal" would be the hunted and the hunter.

I felt angrier. Up to now, every enemy had done his best to make the situation as unequal as possible. But Caliban was treating me contemptuously.

Very well. Let him have his contempt. If he really intended to fight me to the death with only his bare hands, he was not going to frighten me.

I would leave now for the mountains, where I had an engagement for which I would be late if I did not start now. Doctor Caliban, if he was to make the same destination on time, would do better to start on the journey at once.

I inched backwards. Then I stopped. A bronze cloud had scudded into the light of the campfire.

There were empty shadows. A second later, as if stepping from the wings of a stage, the man, the bronze cloud, was there.

The two old men started, even though they must

have experienced this noiseless unannounced jack-in-the-boxery many times before.

Doctor Caliban was at least four inches taller than I. His body was superb, massive yet beautifully proportioned. The bones of skull and torso looked very thick, and his skull was long-shaped. He was the only other man, besides myself, and some of the Nine, who had such heavy bones. Which meant he had more foundation for muscular attachment and for larger muscles than most men.

His skin was a pale bronze. His hair, which was of medium length and parted on the right, was a darker bronze. It looked like a metal cap that had been welded onto his skull. And though he was too far away for me to determine accurately his eye color, I got the impression they were light-green.

His face was extremely handsome and regular. It was masculine, yet almost beautiful. It also looked familiar, though I had never seen him before.

He spoke in a deep resonant voice, like a bronze bell's. His speech was even and regular with none of the hesitations, pauses, vague exclamations, or broken off sentences and phrases that distinguish the speech of most humans.

"Lord Grandrith, the Noble Savage, the titled man-ape, is watching you two," he said.

He looked into the shadows at the exact spot where I lay. He laughed and pulled from his belt a round object I recognized a moment later as a grenade. He pulled the pin and with a swiftness that might have dazzled a leopard, tossed it at me.

It would have landed just out of arm's reach if I had not moved forward. I caught it and hurled it back at him and then was gone into the bush. I looked back. He was standing with his hands on his hips, his back bent backward, head thrown back, and laughing. The grenade was at his feet, and the the two old men had dived away—very swiftly for 80-year-olds—and were hugging the ground.

The blacks were standing up and asking questions, but they could not see the grenade and so did not know what was causing the commotion. A big Negro stepped out of the tent with a rifle. I had not seen him before. He looked as if he were a Yankee.

Doc Caliban said, loudly, "It's a dummy! I just wanted to test his reactions! They're very good! The best I ever saw outside of my own!"

Simmons, getting up, spoke in a squeaky voice that was comical issuing from such a squat long-armed brutish man. "Doc! When're you going to cut out this crap! If he killed Trish, why don't you kill him and get it over with?"

10

Usually, I don't think in the human categories of good and evil. Those who would kill me are enemies. Just that and nothing more. I kill them without having to justify the deed by classifying them as evil.

But seeing this very handsome man, I experienced a feeling of genuine evil, of the antigood. The hairs rose on the back of my neck as if a demon of a native African religion had pulled them up with his cold hands of wind.

It was a feeling I did not like.

I decided to leave for the mountains. However, about twenty yards from the camp, I came across a large aluminum-sided wooden-floored cage lying on its side, the door open. I sniffed at it, and I knew not only that it had held a lion, I knew which lion. I also knew why I had been attacked by a hungry lion that had no business in this area. Doc Caliban had not only loosed it at me, he had probably spent some time conditioning it to attack human beings.

If he had wanted an estimate of me, he now had it.

I lifted the cage above my head—it only weighed about 200 pounds—and carried it to a tree I had noticed a moment ago. This was tall and thin and had all the characteristics required for my sudden plan. I never learned its English name—if it had one—but knew it by the Bandili word, *ndangga*.

After lassoing its top with my rope, I pulled it

down with much straining until its top almost touched the ground. After securing the rope around the trunk of another tree, I wove the branches of the bent tree into a rough net near the top. This required the breaking of a number of branches, which might bring Caliban running. That was a chance I not only would take but welcomed. He, however, did not appear.

The net of branches held the cage as well as I had hoped. I looked through the trees and saw that the two old men had returned to their chairs. They were talking so loudly that they covered any sound I might have made while constructing the catapult. A black brought them glasses with some dark liquid in it, and, between sips, they shouted what must have been insults at each other. The blacks were squatting on the other side of their fire and talking. The fire gleamed on their rolling eyeballs and teeth.

I waited a while. Caliban stuck his head out of the tent once to say something to the old men. At that moment, I whacked the rope in two with the knife. There was a hum, a crack as the rope snapped past me, another hum, deeper, and a loud whish as the tree straightened. The cage flew up and out in a trajectory that came from accident and hope more than skill. But the result was admirable.

The cage, turning over slowly, flew down towards Caliban's tent. He burst out of it like a bronze shell from a 17th-century cannon. The two oldsters jumped up from their chairs, their drinks flying and their smokes falling out of their mouths as they looked around for the source of the noise. The blacks scattered, some running towards Caliban's tent.

Caliban kept on running and disappeared into the darkness, undoubtedly looking for me. The blacks were behind bushes and trees and looking at the crushed tent. Simmons was jumping up and down like an enraged chimpanzee and howling, "Oh, my God! My God! I shit in my pants! I was so scared, I shit in my pants!"

Rivers was on the ground and rolling back and forth and laughing hysterically.

For a moment, I thought of ambushing Caliban and getting this conflict over with. I was restrained by knowing that he probably had the same goal as I and that I would meet him there. I wanted to find out if he could continue to track and harass me. I also wanted him to be even more convinced that he was dealing with a buffalo in the bush, not with an antelope.

11

The dawn was as gray as an old lion's hopes for fresh meat. It quickly enough became bright and quick and sent its golden roar out over the savanna. The gold melted over the world, and the day was hot and sluggish.

I trotted across the plain for an hour after the sun rose. I had been trotting all night and was thinking about holing up until late afternoon. The mountains, light-purplish and getting taller, were about thirty miles to the west now. Perhaps, if I pushed on, I could get there before dusk and even be part way up the flank of the nearest one.

I kept on going. After a while, I was within a half-mile of a Kitasi village, a collection of about thirty huts, round, double-domed, and built of sticks, grass, and dried mud. The Kitasi were cattle herders, drinkers of blood, many-wived, and of ancestors who had mixed their Negro genes with dark Caucasian somewhere in the north a long time ago. In 1920, when I first encountered them, they wore bark-fiber loin coverings which projected fore and aft, looking from a distance like the paper boats that schoolboys make. In the old days, the Kitasi had killed their king as soon as gray appeared in his hair. The British had forced a halt to this custom, but the king died by "accident." Then a white man had given the new king a bottle of hair dye, and the latest king might yet die of old age.

At one time the Kitasi had been a powerful

people. They had warred with the Masai, the Agi-kuyu, and the Bandili. The thirty villages of 20,000 population, as a result, were now six with about a thousand inhabitants. The Kitasi hated many people, but they hated me most of all, and with good reason.

The men in the old stake-bed truck heading out from the village may have been told about me by radio and were looking for me. It was going south-west. We were about a mile apart. Then they spotted me, and the truck swung around and raced towards me. I ran towards some acacia trees, a half a mile away, and got behind the nearest one as the truck pulled up, brakes screeching. It had stopped about a hundred yards away.

There were three men in the cab and six on the bed. All got out of the truck. Three were armed with rifles that looked, from my distance, like pre-World War I Enfields. One carried a heavy spear and a machete in a sheath. Two had bows and wore quivers of arrows on their backs. One had a revolv-er, and the other two carried big axes.

They talked awhile and then spread out in an ever-widening arc, the ends of which curved out towards me. A rifleman was on each end; the third rifleman was in the center. The two bowmen flanked him, and the spearman and the axeman were equi-distant between the center man and the end men. The arc advanced slowly while the men shouted encouragement to each other or shouted insults and threats at me.

So far, they did not know whether or not I had a revolver, but they did know I had no rifle. There were nine of them, and they should have charged me in the truck, swung broadside when near me, and then let loose with a volley. Afterwards, they could have jumped off the truck and charged me on foot. If they were brave and determined, they probably would have gotten me, even if I had killed a number of them.

They preferred to take it cautiously. My reputation probably made them extra careful. When they were within 60 feet, they stopped. I remained on the other side of the tree. The riflemen on the ends ran even further outwards and then cut in so they could get behind me. I waited. I was naked and had only the knife, which had been worn down so much that it no longer had a good balance for throwing. I was going to have to depend upon speed, and I was not at my freshest after having run all night without eating and with little water.

Nearby were several stones, two of which were of the right size and shape for throwing. I put the knife between my teeth and picked up a stone in each hand. The riflemen on both ends, seeing this, shouted the news to the others. Then they started shooting at me.

A bullet ricocheted off the tree. I darted around to the other side and started running at an angle from the men in the center of the arc. The rifleman there started to fire at me, and the bowmen shot their arrows. They missed. Immediately after the arrows were released, I cut back in the opposite direction. The second flight of arrows missed also, and though I heard some bullets, I was not hit.

All of these men had been raised on tales about me and so regarded me as some sort of demon. They were very excited and apprehensive, and the fact that I ran towards them instead of away additionally rattled them. Moreover, under these conditions, my zigzagging made it even more difficult to hit me. And

I am swift; I have been clocked at 8.6 seconds in the 100-yard dash, and I was barefooted.

Yet they were brave men and stood their ground. (The Kitasi still eliminate their cowards before they reach 18, despite the watch that the British had kept on them.) They kept to their stations and fired at me, and the spearman and the two axemen ran towards me, shouting Kitasi war cries.

I stopped briefly and cast a stone. It caught the rifleman on his head. He fell backwards, and I ran again, this time straight towards him. The youth with the revolver ran towards me, firing. I paid him no attention because he would hit me only by accident while he ran. The bowmen aimed again at me, while the axemen and spearman ran in towards me. I threw myself down and then jumped up and hurled my second stone. It struck the bowman on my left in the neck, and he fell down.

The riflemen on the ends were running back now and firing as they ran. One of their bullets struck an axeman, and he was out of the fight.

It had been nine. Suddenly, it was six. The spear went over my shoulder and thudded into the ground before me. I yanked it out, paused as bullets screamed by, and cast. The spear went through the shoulder of the youth with the revolver.

I dived for the rifle by the first man I'd hit, rolled, and came up with it. It still had an unfired cartridge in it. I took my time and aimed, and the rifleman on the right threw up his arms, his weapon flying, and fell on his face. I picked up a cartridge off the ground beside a spilled box and inserted it in the breech and jumped to one side, went to one knee, and fired again. The last of the riflemen clutched his leg and fell down and kicked and screamed. I removed the bandolier from the corpse and slipped it over my shoulder.

Sun flashed off an axehead as it turned over and over with me at the end of its arc through the air. I leaped to one side, inserted another cartridge, and killed the man who still had his axe. He fell a few feet from me; another two seconds and he might have split my skull.

The others ran away. Since I was between them and the truck, they went on foot. I drove off in the truck. The fuel meter was broken so I could not know how much gas I had left. It did not matter. I would drive until it ran out.

I was happy. The fight had lifted me up, and I had a means for putting more distance more swiftly between me and my pursuers. I also noticed that I had not had an orgasm during the killings. This meant that the exertion and excitement had been too much for even that powerful aberrated behavior to appear, or it meant that I was still drained of seminal fluid, or it might mean that I was rid of my aberration. I was inclined to favor the second speculation.

But I had water in several canteens in the truck and could rest for a while. The bumpy ride was, to me, a relaxation. And I was headed at a speed faster than I had hoped to attain this morning towards the people who could give me an answer, if anyone could.

12

The shadow slashed across the truck like a knife cutting apart my hopes of escape.

The roar of the jets followed the shadow. Overhead, by 30 feet, the jet sped ahead, pulled up and around, and then came back in. In the brief look at it, I saw that it was a Kenyan Army plane, an English Huntley-Hawker.

The jet came back only 20 feet above the ground and about fifty yards to my right. The pilot was trying to see if I was in the truck. He shot by, his black face turned towards me. He grinned. Well he might. He carried rockets under his wings, pods of napalm, and, if these failed, or he did not want to waste them on one man, he could use his machine guns and the cannon.

I began evasive action. It looked, however, as if my evading days were over. I had no cover near. Even if I had, I would have been burned or blasted out.

The jet passed me and continued near the ground for perhaps 2000 feet. Then it pulled up to about a thousand and circled so that it would come in straight at me. Undoubtedly, though I could not see his features, he was still grinning. He was happy to be obliterating the white man, the fabled Lord Grandrith. He probably did not know the reason for the Kenyan government's decision to destroy me. He may have heard stories about me, but, as an educated man, he would have been forced to laugh at the teller of them as an ignorant and superstitious man.

Whatever he believed, he must have thought he had me powerless. He was the absolute master in this situation, and none of my demonic abilities would help me.

He came down swiftly. I pressed on the accelerator, ready to swing the truck to the left the moment the rockets or napalm pods were loosed. They would be going so swiftly that even my reflexes would be too slow. But I was going to try evasion. Something . . .

Overhead, something did develop. It was tiny and blue as the sky. It looked as if it were a bolt in the big door of the sky and someone had slammed it shut. It was blue and then it merged with a glitter of the sun on the jet, and both became a great red and white ball, expanding as the tiny missile and the rockets and the napalm and the fuel supply exploded.

The truck was going west and on a level. The fireball was going east and at a steep angle. I drove at full speed ahead; I could do nothing else. The light roared overhead. Heat struck in through the open windows and the broken windshield, and then the ball smashed into the ground behind me with a great noise, many in one. The heat intensified. I smelled paint and wood burning. There was light inside my head. The skin on my right arm and shoulder reddened with the sudden sear. I was already holding my breath and hoping my skin would not crisp and curl off me. And then I was out of the blast.

Some distance away, I stopped the truck and got out onto the top of the cab for a better look.

The wreckage was scattered over a half-mile square area. A hole in the midst of the flames could have been ten feet deep. Bushes and trees burned, and the grass was beginning to blaze in a fire that would sweep the savanna.

Far to the east, two clouds of dust rose. They were approximately the same distance from me but separated from each other by three or more miles.

One cloud would be rising from either the Albanian-Arabic party or Kenyan Army vehicles. The other would be from Doctor Caliban's group. I was sure that it was he who had fired that tiny but deadly missile. One of the trucks carried a camper that was more than a camper. It concealed a missile launcher and only Caliban knew what else.

I felt no gratitude. Instead, I burned as brightly inside as the wreckage outside. I burned with fury and frustration.

After a while I cooled off, helped by the fact that the fire behind me would be frustrating my pursuers. It was racing across the savanna towards them, and they would be forced to run away from the flames—and so away from me. In the meantime, I would go ahead in as straight a line as the topography permitted. I would travel at 30 mph until the gas gave out or I reached the foothills.

I laughed. Caliban, momentarily at least, had checked himself when he had saved my life. A minute later, one of the worn old tires blew. I replaced it with an exhausted-looking spare, and ten minutes afterwards a stone went through that.

I continued on foot. Behind me, the world seemed to be going up in flames.

13

Six hours later, I was on the first of the foothills. Two hours later, I was on the top of the third large hill. The sunset was only two hours away. I felt tired and hungry, but first I had to survey the country behind me. The plains looked smooth from my altitude and distance, but I knew that they were very rocky for the last ten miles and crossed by a grid of wadis. Three dust clouds separated from each by about three miles, were slowly converging in the east. Dusk would fall before they got near each other, however.

I continued climbing through forest which was largely deciduous: oaks and maples. Though the savanna was dry, there was enough moisture here, mostly from underground sources, to supply a very thick growth. In fact, at many places, the trees were so close to each other that I could travel occasionally from tree to tree. Not in the fashion my biographer describes or as those lying movies portray. But adequately enough. My speed was faster in the trees, even though I went no faster than a slow walk, because I could avoid the almost impenetrable undergrowth. I could have made even better time if I had abandoned the rifle.

On the broad branch of a great oak which grew on an almost vertical slope, I waited for the dusk. I was tearing at the delicious meat of a scaly anteater and watching the dying dust from the three parties after me. They had gone as far as they could in their vehicles, and besides they had to camp for the night. Each was only about a mile apart from the next, but the hills barred their views. This did not mean that they were not aware of each other.

The Kenyan army personnel would stop where they were, if they observed national boundaries. I was now in Uganda. The Albanian-Arab party paid no attention to it, of course. Thirty tiny figures walked down a hill and then were lost. As nearly as I could determine, they carried no weapons heavier than rifles.

Doctor Caliban's party threaded down a narrow ravine. I counted them. Two blacks were missing. They had stayed behind, probably to operate equipment in the camper. It was then that I decided to go back down the mountainside. This took into account the strong possibility that Caliban anticipated just such a move and had taken measures against it. He was the most dangerous man I had ever encountered, and I've run up against scores of the most cunning and vicious of killers. Although I knew little about him, I felt that he was by far the most intelligent and the best equipped, technologically, teleologically, and physically (in a neuromuscular sense).

The shadows had flooded that side of the mountain and stretched out to cover the smaller hills and some of the plains. Despite the growing dark, I saw a party leave the Kenyan camp. They did not intend to stop at the border.

I passed them on the way down. They were struggling through the undergrowth in a very narrow path which then enlarged with machetes. An officer said something about stopping soon, and they went on by me. We were separated by a few feet.

I was tempted to approach the single file from the rear and cut a few throats before disappearing, but I resisted. To harass them for my amusement would spoil my plans.

In the darkness, I watched the Kenyans that had stayed behind. They were busy. Evidently others were going to follow the first party in the morning. And from what I could hear of the radio operator's conversation, planes—transports and helicopters— were bringing in other men and supplies. I did not know what they were after. Surely they would not be going to this trouble and expense, and risking unpleasantness with Uganda, just to kill me. No, it had to be the gold. And they were acting as if they knew where they were going.

I went on to the camp of Doctor Caliban. The trucks and jeeps were parked to form a square in a clearing inside the woods. No men were in sight, and the camper shed no light. A small dish-shaped antenna on top of the camper turned around and around. This was probably only one of the devices for detecting intruders.

I waited. The night stretched out and blackened. Clouds were covering the stars. The moon was a dim irregular shape, like the just-beginning-to-form body of a chick in the yolk.

The door in the rear of the camper opened and shut. No light shone. Undoubtedly the door was connected to an off-switch so that the light would not give them away when they passed through.

Only one man had come out. He walked around the inside of the rectangle formed by the vehicles. He was smoking but took care to shield the fire in his palm. It would have been easy to get him with the rifle, but I did not want to alarm the other man or attract the Kenyans. He was pacing back and forth in the square, stopping short of one jeep and turning and striding back to the other and turning. He carried a submachine gun in his hand, as nearly as I could tell in the dark.

I timed him for a while and then leaped over the hood of the jeep, without touching it, as he turned away from it. He heard me and whirled, but I crashed down on him. Before he could cry out or trigger the gun, he was dead with my knife in his throat.

While I was waiting to launch myself, my penis had risen up, and as the man's blood spurted out, I spurted over him.

For a moment, I crouched, trying to recover my breath and also to listen for sounds within the camper. The orgasm had taken such violent possession of me, it had made me drop my knife and writhe as if I had been electrically shocked.

The aberration was getting more dangerous. How could I kill more than one person in a fight if the first kill made me momentarily helpless?

The submachine gun was of a make unknown to me. It was very compact, and the slender muzzle could eject nothing larger than .22 caliber, if that. It was probably custom-made for Caliban, and probably shot explosive bullets. I took the gun, felt it, inspected it as best I could in the dark, found out how to operate it, and then approached the camper. The antenna was still rotating.

I placed my ear against the metal of the camper but could hear nothing. Its walls were well insulated. I left the camper and explored the other truck. It was locked, but the keys were on the body of the black. I unlocked it and went into the supply camper, and came out with several grenades. I pulled the pin on one and tossed it as far away as I could. I had decided I wanted to get the other man out as swiftly as possible, and I was not going to worry about the Kenyans. I hoped that the man in the camper would run out to see what the noise was. He could stay within and warn Caliban, of course, since I was sure he was in radio contact with him.

Immediately after the explosion, the camper door flew open and a big figure shot through. It landed on the ground crouching, a submachine gun in its hands. It called, "Hey, Ali! What's going on? Man, where you at?"

He may have sensed me. He whirled around. I chopped his neck as he was halfway around, and he kept on spinning but his knees were buckling and his body folding. I had not struck him with full force, however, because I wanted a prisoner. He was very strong; his neck was pyloned with muscles. He must have been partially stunned, but his fighting reflexes brought him back up and at me. I caught his wrist and turned it. His scream cut the night. Far off, a leopard coughed, but it may have been a coincidence, not a reply.

He dropped to his knees, his trunk bent backwards, teeth white in the darkness. I brought my knee up against his chin, not too hard. He fell back on the ground.

Afterwards, I noticed that I had a slight erection. Evidently my penis knew when I intended to kill and when I did not.

14

The man was the Negro I had thought was American. He was as tall as I and perhaps fifty pounds heavier. His shoulders were broad; his waist, narrow. His haircut was "natural," and he had a thick moustache and goatee. His skin was so light and his features so Caucasian, I suspected he was one-quarter white.

Tchaka Wilfred was born in Cleveland, Ohio. He had been a professional football player until he had been caught after holding up a bank to finance a militant black organization. He escaped from prison and joined another organization in Harlem. There he had run afoul of Doctor Caliban, who had taken Wilfred prisoner but had not turned him over to the police. Instead, he had sent Wilfred to the private sanatorium, where Caliban rehabilitated his criminals. By surgery.

This confirmed what the two old men had said.

I had little time for talk, but this information intrigued me. I have an M.D. and though my only practice has been among the Bandili, I read a certain amount of medical journals every year.

"What kind of surgery?" I asked.

"I don't know, honky," Wilfred said sullenly. "A cat under ether isn't too observant, you know."

"Obviously, he didn't tell you anything about his illegal tamperings with your brain. Didn't you ask him what he did?"

"Man, I asked till I was blue in the face, if you

can imagine that!" Wilfred said. "Old Doc said it was a trade secret, and he wasn't about to let it out. Unscrupulous men might get hold of it and do great evil! Especially the Communists! Doc's really uptight on the Reds the last couple of years. He thinks they're out to take over and just about got it sewed up!"

That did not sound like a man who served the Nine. Loyalty to the Nine comes first, and the servant will get along no matter what the government. However, they do not care what a man's political beliefs are, as long as he obeys the Nine.

Wilfred laughed and said, "I thought maybe the bronze cat performed a prefrontal lobotomy, but I'm no zombie. And those old honkies, Rivers and Simmons, they say no. They think the Big Bwana Honky maybe installed a microminiature circuit board—one running off the electricity of my nerves —inside my head. Man, that's spooky! But . . ."

"Caliban threw me weaponless against that hungry lion," I said. "That doesn't sound like a man of irreproachable virtue to me."

"If the doc says you're evil, you're no fucking good! A-1 rotten. Essence of putridity. Evil as Lucifer after the Fall. Evil as the soul of an Alabaman Ku Kluxer!"

"Do you know who I am?"

Wilfred grinned, though the grin was nervous.

"Yeah. Doc told me. And I said, 'I hear you, Doc, but you just hung up my sense of credibility.' Doc didn't answer. He seldom does. And he could care less if I believe or not. Doc doesn't lie. Only honky I ever saw who don't. But I still didn't believe. He had to be putting me on. Then we came to Africa and caught that lion and let him loose at you, and there you were, big as life, and bigger. I saw you break that big cat's neck! But I still couldn't believe that, and I couldn't believe that you were really you. But I guess you really are. Man, you're something else!"

"It doesn't matter," I said. "I wonder why he hired you? For your muscle?"

He rubbed his wrist and winced.

"Yeah, partly for my muscle. But I'm an electronic technician and a damn good one, honky."

"But Doc is still, as you put it, a honky?"

"He's the only honky I wouldn't dare call honky to his face. That bronze cat was what Nietzsche was dreaming of before he flipped. A genuine Sooperdooperman! Sure a shame he isn't black!"

He was leaning with his back against the rear of the truck. I said, "I can see you're thinking about rushing me again. Here."

I held out my right hand.

He said, "What do you want?"

"Take it," I said. "Do whatever you want with it."

Instead, he advanced swiftly and tried to thrust his knuckles into my solar plexus. I seized the hand and squeezed on it. He screamed and fell to his knees.

"Do I make myself clear?" I said.

He moaned while he held the injured fist with the other hand. He said, "You're still a big donkey-pricked dirty stinking honky."

I admired his spirit but deplored his lack of intelligence in this situation. Obviously, he could gain nothing by antagonizing me.

And there was no use trying to tell him that I was outside his conflict of white and black any more than there had been in telling Zabu. I was probably the only white in the world entirely free of prejudice towards men because of their color. Even if I could have convinced him of my attitude, I would not have bothered. What did I care what he thought?

"You will show me everything I want to see," I said. "Otherwise, I kill you."

We went inside the camper. It was crammed with equipment and instruments, most of it electronic. At the touch of a button, these sank away, and the top of the camper rose and split and folded to two sides. A pedestal with a bazooka-like tube rose up from the floor, and then the tube telescoped outwards. At the same time, a section of the floor opened, and a replica of the tiny missile that had destroyed the jet appeared. This was about two feet long, was rocket-shaped, silvery, and weighed about 40 pounds.

Wilfred adjusted the controls of an instrument with a cathode-ray screen. A section of the mountainside to the west sprang onto it.

A generator under the truck floor hummed.

The antenna turned southwards as Wilfred rotated a dial. It stopped when it pointed almost south, and I saw part of the Kenyan army camp as if I were looking from the mountainside from a distance. In the daylight.

The picture was wavy and broken with jagged streaks, and almost immediately became so pale that I could see it only with difficulty.

Yet I should not have been able to see anything at all. The Kenyans were behind a tall hill about a mile and a half from us.

Wilfred explained that the antenna shot a beam against the mountainside. This bounced down over the Kenyans and then bounced up and against the ionosphere and back to the antenna. Unfortunately, the dark green of the mountain vegetation absorbed much of the energy, and the many irregularities of the treetops made for a broken picture.

I noticed that his attitude seemed to have changed, though he was unconscious of the change. He acted as if he actually respected me, and in addition, was in awe of me. He had become so interested in his explanations of the devices, he had forgotten to act as if he hated me because I was a "honky."

"Doc said he invented this beamer back in 1943, believe it or not," Wilfred said. "Hey, we need another transceiver!"

He opened a cabinet while I watched him closely for a trick. He brought out a deflated sausage-shaped balloon about a foot long and attached the open end to a nozzle. The balloon filled up and became a blimp about four feet long. He fastened a small blue cigar shape to four eyelets along the blimp to make a tiny gondola. He released the airship, and it rose swiftly, carried eastward by the wind. Wilfred adjusted controls on a board, and the airship, visible in the light streaming from the open top of the camper, turned southwards.

I watched the picture on the screen. It was a bird's eye of the country beneath the balloon, as seen in the moonlight.

I asked how Caliban got such a bright picture in the dark.

Wilfred shrugged and said, "I don't know. He might use heat-radiation to help develop the images, but I don't know just how an ultra high-frequency beam could pick up heat images. I just don't know. I do know that the CIA and the Commies, Chinese and Russians, got wind of this device, and Doc was fighting his own people as well as the Commies. For some reason, he didn't want the U.S. to get it."

Apparently, Wilfred did not know about the Nine.

I watched the screen. Presently, the Kenyan camp was in view.

The balloon must have been directly over it.

"You mean it when you say you'll kill me if I don't show you how the missile-launcher works?" he said.

I did not reply, and he said, "You mean it." He grinned. "Doc doesn't care, anyway, if I get rid of a few Kenyans. He says they're interfering."

I said nothing. I had expected him to object because the Kenyans were blacks, but he seemed to regard them as enemies, which, indeed, they were, if Caliban did not want interference with his hunt.

Wilfred loaded the missile into the tube. Another appeared in the opening in the floor.

The tube rotated and elevated in response to Wilfred's adjustments of the controls. A grid appeared on the screen. A white dot danced out and went past the intersection of the X and Y axes and then shot back to it.

Wilfred straightened up. "It's all automatic now. If you want Little Miss Annihilator to land dead smack in the middle of their camp, press that button there."

"What about the hot jets from the missile?" I said.

He grinned. He had been standing in one corner, as far away as possible from the flames which would issue. Undoubtedly, he had hoped I would be caught and burned. Moreover, I did not put it past the doctor to have a dummy button with a poisoned or drug-coated needle to pierce the thumb that pressed the button. I suspected that there were many traps which Wilfred was aching to use.

I picked up a pair of pliers with insulated handles —watch out for electrical shock, too—and pushed the button with the nose of the pliers. The missile flamed and whooshed away. The truck did not even rock with the takeoff. The heat from the jet warmed my skin as I stood beside Wilfred. If I had been unwary enough to be closer, I might have gotten a bad burn and been off balance enough for him to attack me.

I was watching the screen but also flicking glances at Wilfred. He was staring wide-eyed at my penis, which had been rising as the rocket rose.

The missile shot up in a high arc which the eye might not have been able to follow if the jets were not burning so brightly. It curved over and behind the hill. I looked back at the screen. The missile appeared suddenly, and whiteness gouted and smoke roiled out and up. Bodies, pieces of bodies, a truck, a jeep, and pieces of vehicles and equipment flew out of the cloud.

I kept hold of my knife and my eye on Wilfred as I shook and groaned with the ecstasy. He moved away from me, his eyes on my spouting penis.

"Man, you got a beautiful setup!" he whispered. "But you're sure weird!"

I said, "Load another!"

He obeyed, while a third missile rose from the floor. He crouched beneath the tube, and I punched the button. The third missile completely destroyed the Kenyans.

Three times, I jetted. I writhed in powerful orgasms and waved my knife at Wilfred to keep away. He stared with bulging eyes, and, after the third ejaculation had ceased, and my penis had drooped somewhat, shook his head.

"You're sick, man, real sick," he mumbled.

I came towards him. He backed away, hands out, and said, "You don't want to fuck me with that knobkerrie, do you? Don't, man! It'd split me wide open! Doc didn't say anything about you being queer!"

"Quit talking and scan that mountainside now," I said.

Since he could get a direct beam against the mountain, he switched off the balloon's transceiver but left the balloon cruising around in a circle. At that moment, we heard the distant but unmistakable noise of a helicopter. It became louder in a minute. Wilfred switched the transceiver back on, loaded another rocket in the tube, and this time, at my order, punched the button. I felt nothing then. Apparently, only killings directly done by me brought on the aberrated reaction.

The Kenyan helicopter went up in a great bloom of fire.

15

The beam probed the mountainside. The slope looked like solid vegetation, but the view could be squeezed down with the beam so that we could see a square of two feet from a seeming height of ten feet. Thus, we could look between the trees. It took an hour before we located Doctor Caliban and his party. I could see the dark bronze head of the doctor near a tree. He was holding a metallic box with an antenna.

"All right," I said to Wilfred. "Blow the good doctor and his colleagues to kingdom come or wherever they're going after death."

Wilfred howled and leaped at me. He tried a karate hand chop. Again, I grabbed the hand. I clamped down on it and jerked him past me and slammed him into a bank of instruments. He fell unconscious.

The little white ball came out on the grid of the screen and stopped at the center lines, which were cross-haired on Caliban.

Caliban looked up, and his mouth moved.

His voice came out of a cabinet behind me.

"Very well done, my dear Lord Grandrith. I underestimated you. I made certain that you were halfway up the mountain before I took off after you. I didn't think you'd sneak all the way back down and attack my camp. But I was wrong!

"How well you've performed! But not well enough! Don't you know I have only to press a button on this transceiver, and all four vehicles will explode, along with the remaining missiles in your truck?"

I froze. Caliban had been listening in, perhaps even watching, and I did not think that he was lying.

I said, "If you blow me up, you also blow up Wilfred."

"Too bad!"

Behind me, Wilfred groaned. He rose unsteadily, one arm limp, his eyes as red as if his brain had burst. He said, "Not you, Doc! You were the only good man I ever knew. I trusted you, Doc, even if you were a honky. I loved you, Doc, like I never loved a man before!"

"You always did flap your big lips too much," Caliban said. "Well, my lord, are you leaving peacefully, without pressing that button, or do I have to end it all now and cheat both of us?"

"He means it! He'd kill us both!" Wilfred moaned. "Old Rivers and Simmons were right. Doc has turned evil! He's a regular Jekyll and Hyde!"

"Shut up, Wilfred," Caliban said emotionlessly.

"My lord, I have to blow up the trucks and jeeps in any event. One of my black colleagues, Ali Hamidu, has shinnied up a tree and scanned the scene with binoculars the power of which would astound even the scientists of this progressive century. He reports that the Albanian and his Arab mercenaries are sneaking up on you. They pulled the same trick you did, apparently. I think they spotted you when you came back down. Shame on you. Are you losing your touch? In any case, they see the light shining from the open roof of the camper."

I got out of the camper. Caliban's voice said, "Get back here! They've got the camp surrounded. You couldn't get two feet without being chopped down! I'm going to explode the two jeeps first, and then the supply truck! You stay in the camper until then, and take off under cover of the smoke! When you do, run like hell! The camper will be the biggest explosion by far!"

An automatic rifle began firing about fifty yards away. The bullets stitched the dirt and then ran across a jeep. Somebody shouted in Arabic; I thought it was a command to hold the fire. Probably, it was Noli shouting, because he wanted to take me alive.

I had no choice. I got back into the camper, the roof of which was closing up. Wilfred secured the door and the windows, and when the camper was tight, he said, "We're protected by double walls with fiber glass and steel wool insulation. It'd take a direct hit from a shell to get us."

He was watching the screen, which showed about thirty armed men slowly advancing through the bush. I said, "Didn't you see me when I was sneaking up on you?"

Wilfred curled back his lips and clenched his teeth. Then he said, "You were born under a lucky star, bwana honky. I was watching a leopard over the next hill and I didn't see you at all. When you got inside the camp, I couldn't use the beam to sight you then. You were too close. Otherwise . . ."

He paused, and then said, "I got orders not to kill you, anyway, unless it's absolutely necessary."

The first explosion rocked the camper, but the noise was muffled. The second came almost immediately after. And the third two seconds later. The last must have been the supply truck. The camper seemed to lift up and tilt at the same time, and the blast half-deafened us. If it had not been for the thick insulation, our eardrums would have been blown out.

Wilfred leaped up and opened the door and plunged out into the heavy smoke and the flames. He turned just before he disappeared and shouted at me. I could not hear him, but I could read his lips.

"Split, mother!"

16

I ran after Wilfred, but our courses diverged. My goal was to get down the slope of the hill as far as possible and to put as many trees behind me as possible. Wilfred had said there were ten missiles in the truck yet with a total explosive force equivalent to 400 pounds of TNT. There would not be much left of the hilltop after Caliban pressed the button.

I was about forty yards down the hill, out of the direct path of the blast, the greater energy of which would go upward. Then I felt the pressure; I did not hear it. I flew forward; a tree sprang up; I became unconscious.

When I regained my senses, I was still deaf. I could, however, hear the messages of pain in my eardrums, my head, and all my muscles.

The smoke was just beginning to clear away. The hilltop was gone. Most of the trees, branchless, splintered, uprooted, were halfway down the hill. One lay a foot from me. A little more force behind it would have dropped the trunk, heavy as a great boulder, on my head.

I rose slowly against the current of my pain. The moon was out behind the clouds now, and the sky seemed to be a particular shade of dark-blue. No doubt, I was furnishing the color, not the sky. The leaves of the trees were a sinister green, and the earth was a repulsive yellow-green. Everything was *stretched, elongated,* as if the world were a taut rubber band. The energy gathered in this band was waiting to be released when my hearing returned.

I was unarmed and naked except for the belt with its sheath and the knife.

Forty feet to my left, Wilfred lay face down. I turned him over. He had no visible wounds, but when I tore off his shirt, I saw on his lower back a bruise the size of a dinner plate. The bruise may have been caused by a truck wheel which lay about eight feet up the hill from him.

He opened his eyes and said something. I could not hear him, and it was too dark to read his lips. I found a match-folder in his pocket and struck a match. It may have been a foolish thing to do, but I did not think there would be any living men around for some time, and I wanted to know what he was trying to say.

The light was just enough for me to read his lips.

". . . not with a whimper but a bang, man . . . ain't life the shits . . . tell that bronze cat . . . no fucking good . . . God's a honky, you better believe it . . ." and then, "Mother!"

The last was not, I'm sure, a truncated pejorative. It was the final appeal to one who had answered his first appeal.

At that moment, I felt sad. If I had been able to know him under other circumstances, and if he could have abandoned all the masks, the mannerisms, the cliches which humans adopt for a group identity, then he and I might even have liked each other. But that was asking too much of most humans, and, moreover, I find that most humans have trouble being completely at ease when they're with me.

This, I suppose, is my fault.

I left him with mouth and eyes open. Before noon, the flies would be buzzing in and out of the mouth and the vultures would have plucked the eyes from the sockets.

The hilltop gave me nothing in the way of a weapon. I set off at a trot with the intention of going back up the mountain diagonally. I suspected that Caliban was even now racing down the mountain to check on my survival, unless he was able to see me through those super-binoculars. If I did lose him, I would do so only for a while. Eventually, he would be on my trail, for the simple reason that he was going where I was going. The two old men had told me that, although they probably did not know themselves. I doubted that Caliban would have said anything about the Nine to them, since it was forbidden. Also, he could take them only so far and then would have to go on alone. It was also forbidden to bring outsiders any closer than fifty miles to the caverns of the Nine.

I was thinking about this, and wishing that my deafness would clear up soon, when a piece of bark flew off a tree about a foot to my left. If I had not been looking in that direction, I would have been unaware of it, and the shooter might have been more accurate the second time.

So I thought at the moment. I dived to the ground and rolled beneath a bush in a slight hollow. When I peeked out, I saw a man, whose silhouette I recognized as the Albanian's, shooting a man with a burnoose, with a rifle. The man fell forward and did not get up. I jumped up to run away but by then Noli was only thirty feet away. I put my arms up in the air; the automatic could not have missed. I don't think he would have killed me, but he would have crippled me with bullets in the legs.

I did not know how he and the Arab had survived. They must have been further down the hill when the first jeep went up and they had managed to get away before the other explosions got to them. He said something to me. I shook my head and pointed at my ears. He pointed at his own, and I knew he was deaf, too. The Arab must have been deaf, and Noli had probably shouted at him that I was to be taken alive. Undoubtedly, the Arab had received orders to this effect more than once. But, shaken by the explosions, perhaps eager to revenge his fellows, he had fired at me. Noli was not close enough to knock him out with the rifle, so he had been forced to kill him.

He had to tie my hands and to do this required my cooperation, which I was not likely to give. He solved his problem by hitting me over the head with the barrel of the rifle. I ducked and so reduced some of the impact of the blow, but not enough.

When I awoke, my head ached as if it had sucked in every pain in the area for fifty miles around. My brain seemed to throb like a mangled and infected hand. My eyes hurt as if the optic nerves had been extruded into the eyeballs. My hands were connected behind me with what I later determined was a pair of handcuffs. A hangman's noose was around my neck, and the other end of the rope was tied to the handcuff's chain. My arms had been hauled up almost as far as they could behind me with the result that I pulled on the rope and choked myself unless I kept my arms up high. In this state, I could not test the strength of the handcuff's chain without strangling myself.

Later, Noli would remove the rope during the daytime, but at night he always replaced it.

Noli made signs which told me what he wanted. I would lead him to the source of the gold. And I would also tell him, when I was able, the secret of my juvenescence.

He was taking seriously what most people considered to be a tale of fantasy. He seemed to have done his research well, however, and was convinced that I had a hoard of gold somewhere in this area and that I really was 80 years old.

The facts about me—some, anyway—are available to certain people. The secret archives of many governments and some very powerful individuals contain pages of facts and of speculations about me. These exist in Washington, London, Peking, Moscow, Paris, Rome, and other places. I know about them because the Nine told me of them.

Noli was either an agent of the Communist government of his country or a private agent. Or he was the former and had been sent to find the gold and was looking for the elixir for himself. I doubt that his government really believed in the elixir.

I transmitted to him my willingness to lead him to the gold. He was elated at this, and, at the same time, suspicious. He seemed to think I should have undergone at least a modicum of torture before agreeing to his demands.

I tried to tell him I did not think the torture was worth it, but I failed. He gave me the signal to precede him, and we went on down the hillside and then began climbing the mountain. By dawn, we were near the top. Noli was puffing and panting. His mouth hung open, his chest rose and fell rapidly, sweat silvered his face and enormous moustachios, and sweat blackened his clothes. He was in good condition for a man of fifty-five, which I estimated his age to be. Even a young athlete would have been under a strain to keep up with my pace. Time and again, Noli jammed his rifle in my back and when I turned around, he gestured that he wanted to rest.

Twice, we ate and drank. He carried a canteen of water and had three cans of spam in his pocket. He gave me half a can while he ate one. I wondered what he intended to do after we ran out of food. He might be able to shoot some game, but he would dislike to do this, since it would advertise our presence.

Nightfall found us on the western side of the next mountain two hundred yards below the peak. My ankles were tied with a rope and my handcuffed hands were also tied to a rope the other end of which was around the trunk of a slim tree. The position was uncomfortable. My bowels had moved during the night, and I was able to get only a few inches from the mess, and I had to piss down my leg. Also, it got cold and wet. Mists and then chilling dew covered us. I have been used to worse much of my life. I did not intend to try to escape the first night, unless an irresistible opportunity came along. I would sleep and gather my strength while Noli slept uneasily and in much discomfort. He awoke frequently and sat up to inspect me or prowled around for a while before trying to seize a few more minutes of sleep. Or so he told me the next day. I slept very well.

Dawn was no more red-eyed than he, and it was much fresher.

He stood above me and pissed on me. Probably

as revenge for having rested while he suffered and also part of his psychological warfare. It did not bother me. The urine was warm and felt pleasant, and I have been pissed on by others, all now as dead and as cold as last night's urine.

He untied the ropes and let me get up. I had to piss then. He watched me with an enigmatic look. But his penis was still hanging out of his pants, and, as he watched me, it swelled and grew hard. He looked down and then up at me and smiled. He then forced it within his pants and gestured for me to lead. I knew what he was thinking. The Albanians have been heavily influenced by the Turks, although it is not necessary to enlist history to account for certain attitudes. There are enough Enver Nolis in West Europe, the Americas, Africa, and Asia, none originating from Turkish influences.

At noon, we were at the foot of the mountain. He ate another can of spam, and I got a fourth of another. My stomach was growling, and I could feel my strength evaporating. My hearing was by then almost completely returned, and I could hear his stomach when he was close. He was hungry, despite getting the lion's share of the food.

The next morning, he was in worse condition. Hunger was beginning to erode him. He needed more food than he was getting even if he had been resting, but the loss of energy in climbing the mountains and in loss of sleep was great. At midnoon, his hunger got the best of his desire for concealment. A mountain pangolin ran out from behind a bush as we were going across a small plateau which was so rocky it contained less vegetation than other areas. The beast rolled over and over at the impact of the .38. The shot came from behind me and was unexpected. I jumped and whirled. He smiled. He had food and he also had discovered that I was not as deaf as I had pretended.

He picked up the animal, and we traveled three miles before he thought it safe to halt. With his own knife, he cut the beast out of its armor, threw the entrails away, and then dug a hole. He managed to get a small, relatively smokeless, fire going. He curled the armor of pangolin into a bowl, filled it with water from a nearby cataract, put the bowl in the hole, and the hot stones into the water. He sliced the meat and threw it into the armor. He kept taking the stones out as they cooled and putting in hot ones.

The result was a lukewarm but meat-rich soup. There was enough for both of us and enough for another meal left over. He unlocked my hands from behind me, locked them again before me, and had me carry the armor-bowl with its soup contents. I had to give him credit for some ingenuity.

17

That evening, after tying me even more tightly, Enver ate most of the soup and then slept for several hours. When he awoke, he looked up at the mists and the distorted moon behind them. He crawled over to me and said, in English, "I am cold. And I am also hot, my lord. Hot with passion."

This was the sort of monologue that my biographer might have put in his romances but which more discriminating readers would reject as absurd. They forget that books are often imitated by people.

I said nothing. Noli put his arms around me, and, shivering, clung to me for a while. Then he startled me by running his tongue up and down my spine from the nape of my neck to the base. He then lowered his hand and put it around in front of me and began playing with my penis. He moved the foreskin back and forth very softly and slowly. The heat of his breath on my back and the heat of his hand on my penis, and the lesser heat of his clothed body on my back felt pleasant.

I had not been so handled by a male since I was a youth and living with The Folk. Sexual experimentation among The Folk is permitted the young from the time they feel like doing it until they pick a mate. The males of my age, from the time we could get a hard-on, stuck our penises in each other's anuses, and sucked on penises long before we could ejaculate. The females were right there with us, playing with each other and with the males.

The hairy playmates of my childhood, however, had small penises. When they attained adulthood, and stood six feet and weighed three hundred pounds, they still had penises only about two inches long when erect.

Before the hair grew on my pubes, my *kq*, as it is called in their speech, was the marvel of the tribe. When I became a man, it was the desire of the females and the envy of the males and caused me much trouble from both.

When I became able to ejaculate, I still played sexually with the male and female young, buggered and was buggered, sucked and was sucked. This was not continuous, of course. Most of our play was the sort found among all young primates (man included), racing, wrestling, playing the jungle version of king-of-the-hill, harassing the very old, hunting for rodents, insects, and bird eggs, and playing leopard-and-victim. And so on. But we also spent at least half an hour a day in exciting each other sexually. We did much of this in full view of the elders and with their permission.

Only when pubescence began did the elders repress the juveniles, sometimes quite savagely.

The result is that I grew up with almost no sexual inhibitions. I was inhibited about using violence to gain a sexual end, since this was the one thing the elders stopped at once if they saw it. And they punished us severely.

When I came of sexual age, I had already lost any desire for the males. Not that, under the proper, or perhaps I should say improper, circumstances, I might not have resorted to homosexuality. But I was not a compulsive homosexual, nor did I know any among The Folk. Compulsive, that is, neurotic, homosexuality seems to be the characteristic of civilization, although there is some among the so-called savages. Compulsive behavior of any kind is neurotic. Which is why I was so disturbed about my orgasmic reactions to my killings.

Noli played skillfully with me. His hand was big, but it was almost as gentle and knowledgeable as my wife's. He must have had much practice.

I failed to respond in the slightest.

If my aberration had been absent, I might have had an erection and an orgasm eventually. Friction alone can do much, and I was not frightened of him. I was angry, but I doubt that this would have inhibited an erection.

After a while, he quit with an exclamation of disgust. He began to move his hard penis against my anus. He breathed harder, and then his hands clamped my buttocks and he spread them open. The huge glans was, however, denied entrance. I have a very powerful sphincter, which I closed as far as I could. He shoved for a long time. Then he said, "Let me in, or I knock you out."

I didn't want another headache and possible brain damage, so I said, "Very well."

He spit on the end of his penis, I supposed, and, slowly but insistently, pushed the head in. The shaft slid through immediately thereafter.

I hurt, and I also felt as if I had to get rid of a huge turd. He began to slide the penis back and forth, and the pain increased. He grunted with each lunge, and I could feel the thick stiff hairs against the bare skin of my buttocks. His hands were around me again, one on my penis and one cupping my testicles. He began squeezing on these. I clamped my teeth and endured the pain. Stoic as a wild beast, as my biographer would have said, if he had known about this, although he would have shut such a scene out of his mind, because it would have destroyed his image of me. I could be tortured in his romances, but I could not, of course, be buggered.

Noli was falsely sentimental as most of his kind, that is, homo sapiens. After groaning loudly and jabbing rapidly in his orgasm, he lay quiet awhile except for his heavy breathing. Then he murmured something which sounded endearing, in Albanian, I suppose. He caressed my face with his hands (I resisted the temptation to bite off a finger) and kissed the back of my neck several times. I suppose he would have acted the same way with a prostitute, male or female. He did not care for me any more than he would have for a whore, but he had to carry out the ritual of love.

In about fifteen minutes, he repeated his assault. I endured it. He kissed me on the neck and then got around before me and kissed my penis and ran his fingers gently between my testicles and the hollows of my thighs. I did not respond except to spit at him. He struck me hard on the face, got up, made sure I was tied securely, and then lay down to snore. No doubt, he dreamed of former loves.

18

That day, we put the water-rich green mountains behind us. We were in ranges as dry as a camel fossil. These mountains are subject to a local freak of climate, which diverts the rains to the mountains on the north and south. It is in this area that the valley which once held the gold was located.

We went down one mountainside and up another and the following day started down the other side. We were hungry because we had eaten nothing but a hare which Noli had killed with a shot that destroyed half of it. He put the carcass on top of a flat stone, tied me up, and then went to look for firewood.

I reached out a foot and closed my toes around the hare's ear and pulled the body to me. After shoving it against a bush to hold it, I got on my side and put my face against it and began eating on the part left open by the outgoing bullet.

When Noli returned, I had devoured everything but the skin, the entrails, and a goodly amount of meat barred from me by the bones. There was enough left for a meal for him, but he was furious. I think he had intended to let me have a leg and to keep the rest for himself. He called me a dirty bloody animal and beat me with the stock of his rifle. He did, however, pull his punches. Even in his rage he kept enough control to remember that I was the guide to wealth and immortality. The blows hurt, especially the ones over the kidneys. But I kept silent and did not move my face muscles.

"You're nothing but a wild beast," he said. "Look at you, with blood all over your mouth. You disgust me!"

I did not reply. Cursing, he turned to making a fire and to cooking the remains. After he had eaten, he felt better. We continued our journey.

The valley where the gold had been lay between two high, steep, and barren mountains. The topography resembles that described by my biographer as the site of the lost city which contained a secret underground chamber full of gold and jewels. My biographer also described the lovely high priestess of the sun cult of the degraded locals and her unrequited love for me. The basis for this romance was an actual ruined city. Or, I should say, about four acres of tumbled stone under earth and some stones uncovered by wind now and then, part of a wall, and the six-foot-high stub of a tower. It resembled the ruins of Zimbabwe in South Rhodesia. About four dozen people lived among the ruins in wattle-and-mud huts. With their peppercorn hair, yellow-brown skin, epicanthic folds, and tendency to female steatopygia, they resembled Bushmen. They may have been descended from the builders of the original city. They called the ruins *remog,* meaning, *father-stones.* They spoke a language unrelated to any other, as far as I know.

In 1911, during one of my long wandering journeys across Africa, I found this valley and the ruins. I did some preliminary digging at random, and when I found a gold bracelet and a gold figurine not six inches below the surface, I named this place Ophir, after the Biblical city of treasures. I returned with some equipment a few months later and made some deep cuts. I found no more gold, although I did discover broken pottery, a few beads, some carved ivory, and some impressions of weapons which had left a bronze residue. I also found some primitive gold melting and refining equipment.

I explored the mountainside behind the ruins and found some caved-in mines. There was still gold ore worth extracting on the ground, and I was sure that richer deposits were in the mountain.

When I started to dig in the ancient burial ground near the ruins, the natives became angry and drove me off. I returned at night to dig some more. The moon was full, they saw me, and they called the entire adult male population, that is, nine men. These rushed me from downwind and surprised me. I fought with my shovel for a while and then when its edge remained wedged in the skull, I killed a man with a knife thrown into his solar plexus and, with his club, smashed in some skulls. Another club took me from behind, and I awoke with a headache and with my hands and feet tied. The shaman of the tribe was a young female whose face was not too unpleasant. She had enormous fat buttocks and full uptilting breasts. She also had a very large vagina and may have been disappointed in the ability of the males to fill her. She came to me that night and dismissed the guards. I was not very responsive, but she sucked on me and worked me up to a full erection. After this, she sat down on me and bobbed up and down like a balloon on a string until we both had come. This went on all night until just before dawn. I fell asleep for a while and awoke with a piss hard-on. A fly landed on my sensitive glans and precipitated another ejaculation.

It was caught in the first spurt and died. I have never forgotten that. It may be the only one in the history of flies to have died in this manner.

The Ophirians were worshippers of the sun and moon and a number of other natural bodies and forces. I never did find out just which deity I was intended to be sacrificed to, or, indeed, that I was being sacrificed to anything. It was apparent that they intended to kill me. First, though, the female shaman meant to get out of me all I had to give. She came to me for six nights straight. On the seventh day, she communicated to me, through signs, that I was to die at noon.

I had been straining against the leather ropes binding me whenever I got the chance. I finally managed to break those binding my wrists. I broke the shaman's neck and killed the guard carrying my uncle's knife and killed another guard with that and with the club I killed the rest of the males except for an old man who fled. The entire village followed him into the mountains. I never saw them again. I felt regret about this, because, at that time, I did not kill human beings unless they attacked me. I felt that if they had explained how strongly they felt about the burial ground, I would have abstained from digging.

Later, I dug in the cemetery again and found a number of gold bracelets, figurines, and symbols the meaning of which I did not know. These have remained in my private collection in my home in the Cumberland.

The gold that made me one of the wealthiest men in the world—in potentio—came out of the mountain. It came out with much hard labor on my part. I did everything alone, the digging, the melting, the refining, and the final packing out of the mountains. I packed out golden ingots on my back for a hundred miles on the mountain trails, an ingot at a time, each ingot weighing a hundred pounds. And, of course, I handled the initial negotiations with the underground market.

More than once, I escaped abduction and murder at the hands of those who wanted to track me to the source or torture the information out of me. My biographer had planned to use some of these episodes for his romances before he died. However, as he had done in some previous episodes, he would have altered the truth so the villains would be after the immense treasure of gold and jewels in the mighty ruins of the inconceivably ancient city peopled by the degraded descendants of a civilization which disappeared below the ocean 12,000 years ago. The male citizens would have been fantastically ugly and the women would have been fantastically beautiful. I am not ridiculing him. I can see why his readers would prefer his colorful imagination to the reality.

The gold gave out after I had amassed about twenty million pounds (in English currency), although I believe that there is more deeper in the mountain. I buried the ruins so that no one would suspect that anyone had ever lived in this desolate valley. First, I made extensive diggings, recordings, and photographs, just like a professional archeologist. I had a Master's in archaeology from Oxford by then.

(An aside, for the reader's benefit. I also have an M.D. from Johns Hopkins and a Ph.D. in African Linguistics from the University of Berlin. I have not been entirely idle in my almost eighty years.)

I had destroyed all evidences of mining, too. I thought that it would be a long time before anybody found anything. Even in these times, when Africa is relatively crowded and men are everywhere, few get to these rugged mountains. Moreover, the area has a reputation among the natives for being demon-haunted.

So I was surprised when we came over the mountain and looked down into the valley. At least a hundred men were digging on the site of the ruins or on the west side of the valley.

Noli swore. He tied me to a tree and studied the valley through his binoculars for a long time. I took the opportunity to strain against the handcuffs, as I did every time his eyes were not on me. The metal was made of very tough material, otherwise I would have parted the links a long time ago. I stopped when Noli turned to untie me, and we went down the mountain, but away from the floor of the valley. When we had reached the top of the next mountain he again studied the intruders, after tying me to another tree.

"There's a strip of land which looks level enough for a plane to land on," he said. "Although from here you can't be sure. Is there a place where a plane could land?"

"There is," I said. "But these men may have come in by foot. I think someone told them where the gold is. Otherwise, they would have captured me first to make me tell. They would not have tried to kill me before they found out what they needed to know."

He looked through the glasses again. He said, "How did you know they were Kenyans?"

"It seemed likely," I said.

"They've removed their insignia because they're in Uganda, but they're Kenyan."

He put the binoculars down and turned to me. He was red-faced and scowling. The tips of his moustachios quivered.

"You said the gold was in the valley beyond this one!"

I did not answer. He began to beat me again. I kicked out against his shin and knocked him down and then kicked him in the chest with the sole of my foot. He rolled away and fought to regain his wind. I spat at him.

He looked as if he would like to kill me. He would have, since he knew, or thought he knew, where the gold was. But there was the elixir. He said, "You will pay dearly for this."

"I have paid," I said. "That kick was for the beating. But I still owe you for much more. And I am one who pays his debts."

"Is the gold really down there?" he said.

"They will find none," I said. "Not unless they dig much deeper than I did. The only way you, or they, can get my gold is to demand a ransom. My fortune is secure in fifty banks throughout the world."

He grimaced. He could walk only by limping. I had kicked him harder than I had intended.

"Caliban is down there," I said, "and he is showing himself so that the soldiers will chase him. But they won't catch him. They will catch us instead, unless we travel far and fast, because he will lead them to us."

He looked at the northern end of the valley, where we had crossed. The tiny figure should have been unidentifiable to the naked eye. He had, however, shed all his clothes. The sun gleamed on that metal-cap-like hair and the bronze skin. He moved as if he were a cloud driven by the wind.

A number of Kenyans were running towards him and firing, though he was so far from them they had no chance of hitting him. Others on the slope were after him, too. He angled in towards them. They may have been puzzled about that, but they took advantage of it.

He came up the mountainside like a great bronze-colored rock baboon. I have never seen a man run up such a steepness and rockiness so swiftly or bound so from projection to projection.

"He is leading them up to us," I said.

Noli had been watching him through the binoculars. He said, "Why is he doing that?"

He did not comment on Caliban's prodigious climbing. His expression was strange, however.

I saw no reason to tell Noli that Caliban was putting me to the test again.

"Unlock the handcuffs," I said. "I can't get away from you as long as I'm within range of your gun."

He smiled briefly and said, "You know I won't shoot unless I have to. No. You stay cuffed."

"At least let my hands be in front of me."

"No."

"You can't run very fast," I said. "The only way to stop them will be to roll rocks down and hope to start an avalanche. The slope here is a steep and loose talus. You'll need help. I can't help with my hands behind me."

He waved his rifle. "Let's go. We can still outrun them."

I saw no reason to go along with Noli an inch more. We had come to the parting of the ways.

I strained against the handcuffs. I thought I would rip out the muscles of my arms and the veins of my temples with my effort. There was a snap, and my hands came free. He backed away, his skin white and his eyes wide. He swore in Albanian.

I turned away from him and looked over the edge of the rock. Caliban was slowed down. The Kenyans had quit firing at him. About fifty were strung out in a rough line about three hundred yards long. The rest were still on the valley floor. They had stopped firing because they realized they could precipitate an avalanche.

I picked up a boulder which must have weighed three hundred pounds and lifted it above my head. I shouted at Caliban. He had stopped now. He was about forty feet below me. His feet were on a ledge so narrow that I could almost not see it, and his hands were gripping some projections invisible to me. His head was thrown back, and he stared straight up at me. He looked like a statue carved out of the mountain itself.

I shouted, "Catch, Caliban!" and heaved the boulder outwards.

I don't think he expected us to be so close. He must have thought we would be at least a half-mile on and desperately striving to increase the distance.

The boulder fell for twenty feet, hit an outcropping, bounded out, struck ten feet above Caliban, broke off rock and dust and bumped past him. I could see him dimly through the cloud.

I picked up a smaller boulder and tossed it after the first. It missed all the outcrops the first had struck and, as nearly as I could determine through the dust, should have hit Caliban. Or the place where he had been. Still was, I hoped. Or did I? I

A FEAST UNKNOWN   113

felt some sense of disappointment that the relationship was so soon over and that he had been so easily disposed of.

That is, if he had been. I would not have stayed a second in the same spot, and I doubted that he would.

The first boulder had leaped on down like a great legless kangaroo. It had hit something, a loose pile, an unstable boulder or cluster of boulders. The avalanche started. The dust rose so thickly that I could not see what was happening. A noise as of two clashing thunderstorms arose, and soon the flat rock on which I stood began to tremble. We retreated. The edge of the mountain did not, however, fall off. It remained firm, although it, too, became hidden in dust.

When the rumbling had ceased and the cloud had thinned, I crawled out onto the edge and looked down. The face of the mountain was somewhat changed. There were some fresh wounds in it, naked rock exposed by the slipping away of the massive piles. At the foot of the mountain, out across half of the valley, was a mass of rocks. No Kenyans were to be seen. Only their possessions, tents, supplies, and material, had escaped.

Nor was anything to be seen of Caliban.

Noli was still pale, but he managed a smile and said, "*We* certainly wiped them out, heh, Lord Grandrith?"

He was holding the rifle with both hands, and he was watching my hands. I said, "I know you have another pair of handcuffs in the pocket of your jacket. I will allow you to put them on me only if my hands are in front of me. There will be some very difficult climbing ahead, and it will be impossible for me to climb with my hands behind me. In fact, it may be impossible with handcuffs."

I held out my arms. He took the key out of his pocket and threw it to me. "Unlock those cuffs."

While I was doing so, he took out the other pair of cuffs.

"You will put them on yourself," he said. "You didn't really think I would get close enough to you for you to grab me, did you?"

"I thought I would try," I said.

He threw the cuffs at me and I caught them with one hand, spun, and released them as I completed the circle. The cuffs flew at him; he jerked the rifle up to ward them off; I was in at him, throwing myself like an American football blocker. The rifle blast seared my back; I hit him in the hips; he went down and over.

By the time he had gotten to his feet, I had the rifle.

At my order, he presented his back to me. I knocked him out with the rifle butt and chained his hands behind him. I put the key in his jacket pocket and sat down. When he regained consciousness, he groaned and fluttered his eyelids. I slapped his face to bring him to more quickly.

I lifted him up and passed a noose from his rope around his arms and body a few inches below his shoulders. I shoved him ahead. He balked but nevertheless went screaming over the edge. I pulled up on the rope so that it tightened before he had gone more than a body's length down. He dangled, his back scraping the perpendicular face of the cliff. He tried to look up at me, but the weight of his body and the pressure of the rock behind his head prevented him.

I lowered him slowly and gently. I did not want the rope to loosen and so drop him down the cliff. Then I jerked the rope and managed to turn him so he faced the cliff. He saw the tiny ledge below his feet. After some effort, he got his feet firmly placed on the narrow cropping. The heels of his boots hung over the air.

I let more slack into the rope and succeeded in working it loose from his body and pulling it back up. He must have wanted greatly to look upward, but he did not dare. He could maintain his position on the ledge only by pressing face and body in against the rock.

I called, "Noli! You can't go more than a few inches to the right or left! Yet, if you can get your hands in front of you, and somehow get the key out of your front pocket, and then unlock the cuffs, you can climb back up here!"

I paused. He said nothing. I said, "I'm giving you a chance to live, to get free! I'm leaving your rifle and bandolier and knife here, so that you might be able to get back to civilization, if you get out of your first predicament!

"Perhaps I'm being stupid! Maybe I should have tossed you over the edge, instead of giving you a chance to live! A very small chance, true, but still a chance!"

He did not say anything or move. He was probably afraid that the slightest motion would lose him his footing. Later, he would have to make the effort, no matter what the consequences. If he just remained there in paralysis, he would weaken, his legs would bend, and out and down he would go.

I relished that thought. It was so delightful, it gave me a semi-erection. For a moment, I was tempted to go back and drop stones on him until he did fall, just to find out if the fall itself would give me an orgasm.

I left the rifle as I had promised. First, I plugged the muzzle with dirt. If he should have the great nerve and limberness and strength and very good luck to get out of this situation, he would count himself very fortunate. He would inspect the rifle, of course, unless he was so upset or elated that he forgot his usual suspicions. If he did, and he fired it, he would lose his face.

I always check out any firearms that have been out of my sight for even a short time. Once, an enemy did the very thing to me that I was now doing to Noli.

19

Before leaving, I surveyed the valley again. The dust had almost entirely settled. On the slope of the mountain on the other side, several figures appeared. I looked through the binoculars. I could not be sure at this distance, but it seemed that the party was the two old men and the blacks.

I wondered how far Caliban intended to let them come. He knew the consequences if he deliberately brought outsiders anywhere near the next mountain.

That was his concern. I hurried on across the top of the mountain and halfway down found a sort of cave beneath three huge boulders. I slept uneasily on the cold hard stone. More than once I awoke, thinking I heard the rattle of a displaced rock or the scrape of a knife against stone. Twice, I dreamed that a huge shadowy figure was sneaking through the darkness towards me. Once, the eyes glowed with a strange swirling golden-flecked bronze light.

I dream, of course, as every human dreams. A psychologist once checked me out on that because I was convinced that I had had only one dream in my entire life. He awoke me when the proper eye movements told him I was dreaming, and I remembered my dreams.

That I now was aware of this dream indicated how deeply Doctor Caliban had affected me.

In the morning, I continued down the mountain. I was hungry and thirsty, and I wished I had cut

Noli's liver and heart out instead of wasting him for the sake of revenge. I knocked over a rock hyrax with a stone and ate that. Later, I found some grubs under a pile of dirt and I scooped up several handfuls of ants. In the afternoon, I caught a gray lizard which looked much like an American horned toad.

I also came across some fresh goat droppings. I passed these up. I was not hungry enough for them yet. I have survived at various times by eating the spoor of animals. Antelope and elephant turds are not too distasteful. Zebra excrement is almost relishable. Lion shit and that of other meat eaters is very unpalatable and only as a last resort would I eat them. But I have. If I had not done so, I would not now be alive.

At the bottom of the next-to-last ascent was a number of scattered bones of men and women. Some were very old and might have been lying out under the African sun for fifty years or more. A few seemed to be recent. The vultures, jackals, and ants had quickly stripped the flesh after their owners died falling off the face of the mountain, and the animals and the winds had scattered their bones.

The mountain which had killed them was very steep and smooth. It required professional mountain-climbers' equipment, if you did not know where to look. The Nine forbade any artificial aids whatsoever. There were places where a climber unafraid of heights, or with great courage, and equipped with strong fingers and toes, could clamber up the face of the four-thousand-foot cliff. I do not know how old these digit-holds are, but I would not be surprised to find out that humans—and subhumans —have been using them for at least 30,000 years.

The Nine could tell but have not, and no one dares ask.

Dusk fell when I was only 500 feet up. I crawled onto a ledge with a partial overhang and tried to sleep. The cold of the night did not bother me too much. I seem to be able to endure extremes of temperature that would dehydrate or give pneumonia to other men. What made my sleep fitful was the bronze giant with the glowing golden-bronze eyes and the big knife. He seemed to be prowling all night through the jungle of my dreams.

At dawn, I resumed climbing. The really difficult part of the ascent was behind me, and I went up like a monkey on a stick. Just as the sun began its slide down from the zenith, I reached the top of this cliff. There was a level stretch of rock about thirty yards square here, and another thousand feet of climbing. First, I had to get rid of all weapons and clothing. No one approached the Nine unless he or she was naked and empty-handed.

A shoulder-high granite boulder at one corner of the plateau looked as if it had fallen from above. A stranger would have passed it by without a second glance. I placed my hand three times in rapid succession on an egg-shaped projection on the boulder, waited nine seconds, and pressed six times. A section of the boulder slid up. A shelf inside contained a depression from which water bubbled. I drank deeply of this and then I put my belt, sheath, and knife and rope on the shelf beside a number of other articles. These had been left by predecessors. Among them was a bronze-colored belt with pockets which contained a number of interesting and puzzling devices. It had been worn, of course, by Doc Caliban. I thought he had been naked when last I saw him, but he was so far off I had not detected the belt. Now this was discarded.

Beside the belt was a bronze-colored square of paper. I picked it up. The handwriting was bold but beautiful:

I rescued your Albanian friend and sent him on an errand for me. I also detected the dirt in his rifle. He seemed shaken and grateful. I expect him to get over both states quickly. But I told him I would track him down and torture him as only a medical doctor with vast scientific resources could do if he failed me. He seemed to believe me. Also, my errand will enable him to revenge himself more than satisfactorily on you and will profit him monetarily. He will contact my agents, who will expedite his entry into England and thence to Castle Grandrith, where your wife now is. He will hold her until I get there. Of course, he may betray me and take matters into his own hands.

There was no signature, or need for one.

I bellowed with frustration and rage. Since I could not get my hands on Caliban, I attacked his possessions. I threw the belt, sheath, and knife over the ledge. I ripped the note to pieces and scattered them out over the face of the cliff. After that, I climbed swiftly, too swiftly, up the last cliff. Three times I almost fell off because of my lack of caution. With an effort, I cooled myself down, though it was some time before my shaking ceased.

The man's speed was very impressive. He had come along behind me and taken Noli from the ledge and then he had passed me. Of course I was not racing him; I had taken it relatively easy.

I told myself that I should turn back and get to England as swiftly as possible. However, Caliban might be lying to me so that I would do just that. If I failed to appear before the Nine at the appointed time, I would get no second chance for immortality. And the time I would have to stay in the caverns was very short compared to the time it would take Noli to get back to civilization. Unless Noli had been instructed to report to Simmons and Rivers, who would radio for a plane.

I knew that my wife would have insisted that I go on and let her take care of herself. She was extremely capable. If she had not been, she would long ago have been killed. She would not want me to lose the elixir for any reason and especially because of this situation.

There was also another reason, the strongest, for not turning back at once. Caliban would be waiting for me somewhere between here and the entrance to the caverns.

I had to make a decision which would take many civilized men days to agonize over. This decision took me two minutes, and that was the longest, slowest time I have ever taken.

Late that afternoon, I reached the top of the second cliff and drank from a small spring. The exit from the plateau led through a series of canyons several hundred feet deep and so narrow that both sides brushed my shoulders quite frequently. An hour's journey brought me out of them, but not before I caught a small snake that was in the act of swallowing a rodent. I ate both of them and, feeling much stronger, pushed on.

The canyon abruptly widened onto an apron of rock about thirty feet wide and sixty long. At its end was a crevasse which fell for three thousand feet to a river. The river was always in shadow at this point. It was between sister peaks, not over eighty feet apart at this height.

A natural bridge of granite spanned the abyss. It was twenty feet wide along the bottom and sixty feet deep. The Nine had had its upper portion carved away for a depth of twenty feet, so that, like the razor's edge bridge between the Heaven and Earth of the Muslims, a blade of rock was the only passage across. The only way across had to be on a surface three inches wide and eighty feet long.

At the other end of the arch was a broad ledge and an overhang and a blank wall of rock at the end of the ledge.

There was a seemingly natural fissure in the back of the recess. Behind this window stood a sentinel, one of whose duties was to make sure that every traveler walked across. Those who lost their nerves and sat down to scoot across were killed and tossed down into the river.

I have never seen anybody fall off the narrow arch or been thrown off, but then I have never seen anyone try to walk over it. I have always been unaccompanied when I made my required visits. I think that the Nine arrange matters so that the pilgrims of eternity do not see each other while on the way.

However, when I got into the caverns, I usually saw the same people. My wife always went at a different time, and I had never seen Caliban there. I suspected that the Nine, for reasons of their own, which I might or might not learn, had arranged our visits to coincide.

It did not matter. What did matter was that Caliban was waiting for me, as I had expected.

Naked, his arms extended for balance, he stood in the center of the bridge with one foot behind the other. He grinned when he saw me; the teeth were peculiarly white in the metallic reddish-brown face.

20

That penis was like a dark-bronze python sliding out of a nest of brown-red leaves. It gave me a slight shock to see it, it was so enormous. It was soft, yet it must have been at least three inches wide and eight inches long. The testicles were correspondingly huge.

The genitals were the one disproportion of the magnificent body. Revealed, they made him a freak.

21

I stopped at the edge of the abyss and set one foot on the bridge. The rock was black granite, smooth and cold when felt by the hand. My soles did not feel the stone, since the calluses on them were as thick and as tough as rhinoceros hide.

He seemed to expect me to say something, perhaps to ask him why he was after me. I saw no reason to talk. It was too late for words. The sooner I got him out of the way, the sooner I would get my business over with and the sooner I could get to England.

I stepped out on the bridge and slowly approached him, one foot behind the other, my hands held out. The wind blowing up from the river was cold. I was sweating despite the height and the lack of sun and the wind.

My penis was rising like a drawbridge.

Caliban looked at it and then shouted, savagely, "I will tear your prick off, my friend, and keep it for a trophy! It was with that that you raped my cousin, my beautiful Trish!"

I said nothing. I continued to advance.

"You killed her!" he shouted. "You raped and murdered her and you threw her body to the hyenas!"

I did not know what he was talking about. It was evident that he thought I had committed some

125

crime upon someone he loved. I knew it was useless to reason with him, so I kept on walking toward him. And my penis was now rigid and at a 45-degree angle to my belly. It seemed ready to burst with blood. This bothered me, because I needed every bit of energy for the combat. Also, I must admit, I felt ridiculous and so was at a disadvantage. This feeling resulted in anger, and I did not want my judgment dissolved in its heat.

I was now close enough to see the color of those peculiar eyes. They were whirlpools of gold-flecked bronze, and they did not look quite human.

"You monster!" he shouted. "Don't you care? Doesn't it disturb you at all?"

It was no use telling him I was innocent, and I knew that he had put his weapons aside for the same reason that I would have. I was the only great challenge he had ever met among men.

I stopped, pulled in my arms from the side, and extended them before me. He stepped forward, halted, and put out his hands. I moved forward another step, and we gripped each other's hands. I exerted pressure to throw him off balance; he did the same to me.

This was not to be a long, drawn out battle. There would be no kicking, gouging, kneeing, hitting with the fists or the edge of the palm. Our positions were far too precarious for those. Moreover, both of us, I believe, wanted to demonstrate his superior strength in a simple and undeniable manner.

I had never met so powerful a man. He was not as strong as a gorilla, but then neither am I. He was not quite as powerful as the strongest of the males among The Folk. But then neither am I.

We strained to throw the other to one side and so send him through the space between the mountains to the river three thousand feet below. Our muscles cracked; our bones creaked. Sweat oozed like our departing strength from our skin, stung our eyes, and ran coldly down our ribs and our crotches.

We swayed back and forth in this footless dance. He glared down at me, and I up at him. I don't know what he saw in the gray of mine, but I suspect that it was the same lust to kill that was in his gold-spotted bronze. We came closer and closer. Our arms were forced outwards by the pressure we applied and forced backwards, and we neared each other until our chests and noses were almost touching. His breath was hot on my wet face.

Then we came together. Our chests rubbed. Our bellies touched. And I felt that elephant trunk of a penis against mine.

I think that he was upset then. At least, his face changed from snarling hatred to an unreadable expression.

He looked as if he wanted to look down to verify what his other senses told him. He did not dare to do so, of course. He, no more than I, dared to change his attitude. The least unbalancing or weakening in one direction, and the other would upset him.

Eventually, one would weaken, and the end would be swift then.

Until that clasping of hands a few minutes before, I would not have believed that any human could withstand me so long. Now I knew that it was possible that I had met my match. More than my match.

I knew it, but I did not really believe it. If I had, I think I might have weakened just a trifle with the doubt and the surprise. And that would have been enough for him.

I was hoping that a similar doubt would corrode his strength just enough for my purposes. But there was nothing in the expression on his savagely handsome face or in those peculiar eyes or in the gracefully massive muscles to indicate that doubt was turning his bronze into lead.

By then, our peters were crossed like swords.

And I was beginning to feel the slow upbuild of an orgasm.

My aberrant condition was going to betray me. Kill me.

No matter how I fought it, I would be subject to a certain amount of transport and involuntary contraction of muscle and loss of force.

Caliban did not know what was happening, but he knew that something was occurring in me. He smiled thinly and said, "I am stronger than you, you filthy ape!"

I could feel the slight tremors in his belly and a slight jerking in his penis.

His eyes widened, and he said, "What the hell!"

He was beginning to feel the same sensation as I!

It was a question of who would ejaculate first, and I thought that it would be me.

I was about to release him, if possible, and throw myself backwards and away. If I did it quickly enough, and he was seized in an orgasm, I might be able to keep away from him until we were both over the spurtings, and we could then resume the fight on equal terms.

He bit his lip and said, "God! What's going on?"

I tensed for my effort to break that metalled grip.

A voice bellowed in English, "Stop! In the name of the Nine!"

22

The granite slab covering the entrance to the caverns had slid into a recess. Nine people stood on the apron of rock near the other end of the bridge. Eight were of the Nine. The tall long-bearded old man with the black patch over one eye was missing. The ninth person was a tall Negro dressed in the blue Roman toga-like robes of the Speaker for the Nine. He held a wooden staff, nine feet high, on top of which was carved a crux ansata. A third of the length down was a carved representation of the symbol which the Finns call *hannunvaakuna*.

He shouted at us again so loudly that the mountain returned an echo. "No more fighting! Come to me, and I will give you the order of the day!"

Caliban backed away from me until I could not reach him. He would not turn away until I said, "It's over. For now."

His penis was beginning to shrink and to drop. Mine stayed erect for a much longer time. In fact, for a minute, I thought I was going to have the orgasm.

The eight of the Nine were dressed in differently colored robes with hoods. Their faces were hidden, and they turned away and were gone before I reached the ledge. This was the first time I had ever seen more than three at a time. During the many years I had served the Nine, I had seen all of them. But it had always been three one year, another trio the next year, a third trio the following year, and then, the fourth year, the cycle began anew.

I could not imagine why the old man whom we addressed as *XauXaz* was not present. I did not ask. The Nine discouraged questions.

The Negro in blue was the majordomo, the Speaker for the Nine. He would serve for three months of the year and then go. I had been Speaker several years ago and my wife two years after that.

He said, "Peace between you two until the Nine say war. Follow me."

We halted in the first cave, where he went through the ritual of getting us through the guards. These were five men and five women, naked as everybody except the Nine and the Speaker, but armed with automatic rifles. Behind them were heavy-caliber machine guns, flame-throwers, a whippet tank, and a Bofors cannon. They were serving their four-hour duty, as did everyone who came through this entrance.

A woman took a sample of blood from our thumbs and disappeared into a wooden booth. She came out a moment later and handed two small cards to the Speaker. From a pocket in his robe he took two cards and matched them with the others. Then he handed all four to her and said, "Follow me!"

The next cavern, unlike the first, was not lit with batteries of lamps on the walls and overhead fluorescent cylinders. It was dark, and we progressed through it by placing our hands on the shoulders of the man before us. Since I had been the Speaker, I knew that he was following a narrow beam of sound transmitted through a small device in one ear. If he strayed to one side or the other, the sound would die out. I did not doubt that all sorts of scanning devices were studying us.

In the next cavern, which was empty, and was really a trap for any invader who got this far—the ceiling would fall on them and then the floor would drop out—I studied the Speaker. He was a tall, well-built, handsome Negro with a light-brown skin. He looked as if he were thirty.

Suddenly, I knew why he seemed so familiar. He was a New Yorker, a millionaire who had recently disappeared after the explosion of his yacht in Long Island Sound. Several people had been brought in for questioning, but no one had been arrested. The newspaper articles said he was 60 years old but looked remarkably younger. He was supposed by the more superstitious in New York City to be using voodoo to prolong his youth. The black militants had accused him of being an Uncle Tom and of refusing to use any of his fortune to help his people. Furthermore, a million dollars was missing from his bank account.

It was easy to understand the explosion and the disappearance, now I had seen him here. He was getting to the age when questioning and astonishment about his youthful looks would increase geometrically in proportion with the passage of time. He could use makeup to seem older, but that had its annoyances and limitations. The Nine had ordered that he "die." He could start a new identity elsewhere after he had served his three months as the Speaker.

I wondered if the Nine were thinking of the same thing for me. I could not go on forever with my present identity. Only the fact that I spent so much of my time away from civilization, and my passion for obscurity, had prevented an order from the Nine. Even so, when I went to England or elsewhere, I whitened my black hair and wrinkled my face.

I suspected that Caliban was in my position. Rivers and Simmons had mentioned briefly that "Doc" had not been able to entirely hide his name and qualities from the world. A writer of pulps had somehow learned something of his strange rearing and training, his extraordinary, perhaps unique, qualities and abilities, and something of the hidden place where he rehabilitated criminals. The writer had used Caliban as the basis for a character, under another name, of course, in a series of wild science-fictional adventures, most of which were the result of his imagination. But there had been some fact in them. Apparently, the two old men had figured prominently in these adventures but also under different names.

23

The fourth cavern was enormous. It contained a village of prefabricated huts with bright lights on the end of tall stone pillars illuminating the lower part of the cave. The huts were provided with lighting, heaters, hot and cold running water, liquor, tobacco, and furniture.

Although I had learned much when I was the Speaker and had been in twenty caverns, I did not know where the supplies came from or where the water was pumped or the electrical generators were housed. Nor did I know what entrance the Nine used.

Caliban and I were marched into the central square of the village and dismissed. He went into the house marked with a card bearing his name: I went into the house prepared for me. Here I shaved, showered, and then ate a meal cooked by a famous Parisian chef. I wanted to gorge myself but I ate relatively little. I did not care to have a heavy bloated stomach when I went through the ceremony in the Council Cave of the Nine.

The woman who served me was a big titian-haired Dane with the greenest eyes and the softest thickest reddest pubic hairs I have ever seen. She was only an inch shorter than I and truly had the figure of a goddess. I knew her well, since she often came to the caves at the same time as I.

After I had eaten, I lay down on the bed. She lay down beside me and began to kiss me. I responded fervently and stroked and cupped her great breasts, and gently rubbed the huge nipples. We went through the usual preludes of uninhibited and experienced couples, but when my penis failed to respond in the slightest to her skilled sucking, she stopped. She looked puzzled and hurt.

She said, "You must have been through something terrible."

"Nothing to talk about," I said.

"Nothing to talk about! That means nothing to you?"

I was silent. She said, "I heard about you and Caliban on the bridge." She shuddered. And then, surprisingly, she laughed.

"Cocks crossed," she said. "What is the matter with you two?"

"I wish I knew what is the matter with me," I said. "Is there something wrong with Caliban, too?"

"Aside from you, he's the most beautiful man I've ever seen. But he has that horsecock. He can only get it into very large women, you know."

That did not seem likely to me. I was a doctor and I had also read much in medical pathology. I had never heard of a single authenticated case of a man with a penis so large that he could not get it into a normally sized woman, provided that there was lubrication and the woman was not frightened and endowed with a powerful sphincter. I told the Countess Clara Aakjaer so.

She said, "You may be right. I told him to try me once, I thought I could take him. I was eager to try, but he said no, he knew it was no use. He wanted me to suck him off instead. I refused. I love to suck cock but only if it leads up to getting fucked. I'm funny that way.

"Anyway, I know that he has had a long love affair with his cousin, Trish Wilde."

"She's one of us?"

"Yes. She's an extraordinarily beautiful girl. She has his bronze coloring and even looks like a female Doc Caliban. But they never came here together. I just happened to be here once when she was. I knew her name but I didn't connect her with Doc until I happened to run into her when I was visiting New York. She took me up to Doc's apartments in the Empire State Building, and we had dinner together. We couldn't talk about our common interest in the Nine, of course, because his other guests were outsiders. But afterwards we had a long talk. Trish, by the way, warned me to stay away from him. Outside the caves, he's hers, she says.

"But she was very frank. She said Doc could get into her but only with a lot of pain for her and she usually sucked him off. The worst of it is, Doc has great moral resistance to fellatio."

"What?" I said.

"He was given a peculiar training from the age of two on," she said. "It made him the greatest athlete and strongest man in the world—with the exception of yourself, of course. I don't suppose he would have gotten to that state if he hadn't the physical foundation for it, he's got the biggest bones of any man I ever saw—except you, of course.

"He also was educated in the physical sciences and he became not only the greatest surgeon—under a different name by the way—but an extraordinary chemist, physicist, anthropologist, linguist, you name it. The man is disgustingly knowledgeable.

"His father raised him to be a superman, the

primary purpose of which was to do good and combat evil."

"Sounds like a super Boy Scout," I said.

"In a way, you're right. His father hated evil with a passion you might call psychotic. His father was killed by criminals, you know."

"I didn't," I said.

"Yes. Anyway, Doc was given a rigid moral training, and for a while he was thinking of becoming a minister. Would you believe that he had no sexual experience with a woman until he was twenty-seven?"

"With a woman?" I said.

"I mean he didn't even masturbate. He suppressed his sexual feelings. He prides himself on his self-control above everything, you know. He never brags about it, of course, he never brags about anything. Not bragging is part of the self-control bit. But you can tell he's proud. I suppose that he may have been inhibited by the very size of his whang; it may have embarrassed him. This reinforced his moral reasons and ability to do without women. He told his colleagues, Rivers, Simmons, and the other three—I forget their names—that he was too busy to get involved with women. Besides, he didn't want to endanger them."

"They didn't accept all of that," I said.

"When Doc was twenty-seven, and was busting up a drug-smuggling ring in Los Angeles, he was captured. A woman, a member of the gang, the leader's moll in fact, slipped him a drug and he was tied up and carried off to a house up Topanga Canyon, I think Trish called it. Anyway, while the other gang members were gone, the woman—Big-Eyes Llewellyn, that was her name—raped Doc.

She not only fucked him a number of times, she sucked his balls off."

"There was one woman who could get that bazooka in," I said.

"Yes, but Doc told Trish that she was a freak. Anyway, Doc tried not to respond but he failed hopelessly, abysmally. He found out what he was missing. The discovery did not delight him, it enraged him. He broke his bonds and killed the woman and escaped."

"He had to kill her?" I said.

"No. That was what sent Doc into the first sickness of his life. He almost went insane after that; his conscience almost killed him. He had lost self-control, and committed two evil acts, for the first time and in rapid succession. First, the woman had made him lose his self-control by fucking him and then sucking him off. Second, his reaction to this resulted in another loss of self-control, and he had killed the woman as you would kill a chicken, by wringing the neck until the head came off. He confessed to Trish, a few years later when he met her, that he had an orgasm when the blood jetted out of her neck. It splashed all over him and the room.

"He became very depressed and even suicidal for a year. He told no one what had happened. As far as his buddies were concerned, he had retired from society for a year to meditate and experiment. He went up to the Arctic Circle, somewhere in Canada, where he has a hideaway and stayed there for a long time. Then he came back with the intention of throwing himself into the battle against evil with a terrible fury. He would try to make up for what he had done by ridding the world of more evil.

"It was then that he met his cousin. Apparently, their fathers had not seen each other since they were teenagers. Trish's father had migrated from England to Canada and lost contact with the family. Doc's father also came from England but much later. It was only by accident that they met and then found out they were related.

"Doc and Trish fell in love. Doc told her all. Despite his moral prohibitions, he went to bed with her. She could take him, but it hurt her. She's a big girl with a small cunt, or so she said. Then Doc did a strange thing . . ."

"I saw that little Oriental greet him when he went into his house," I said. "She was very little."

I had not paid too much attention to her last few sentences. I had been thinking about his cousin and his accusations that I had murdered her. No wonder he hated me. But why did he think I had killed her?

"That's Patani. I hate her! She's so exquisite, so tiny and dainty. Don't worry. She won't try to take him into her cunt. She's a compulsive cocksucker. That's why she and Doc always get together when they're here."

She played with my penis for a while and then sucked on it a while. Again, it failed to respond. She said, "Have you really become impotent? No, that can't be so. You were crossing cocks with Doc, like Robin Hood and Little John with their quarter-staffs on the bridge. Say! You haven't gone fairy, have you?"

I said, "No."

There was no use trying to explain something I

did not understand myself. If I told her I could get an enormous erection and jet all over her if I killed her, I would have frightened her. Or at least made her uneasy. Few of those admitted to the caves frighten without great cause.

She asked me if I would at least take the edge off of her, and I said I would. There were plenty of other men who would have done more for her, and so I felt complimented that she would prefer less with me than more with others. I used two fingers on her until she had a number of orgasms, and I also rammed her with my tongue until she had a dozen more orgasms. Aside from my wife, Clara had the sweetest vagina I've ever tasted.

I felt excited but it was a numb excitement.

Clara kissed me—she seemed to enjoy the taste of her own cunt—and left me.

24

I know that many of the aficionados of the romances about me will be shocked by what Clara and I did. Even outraged. My "biographer" has depicted me as a man of absolutely unyielding morality. According to him, I remained unswervingly chaste and faithful to my wife when being tempted by very beautiful and passionate young women after I'd gone through long periods of continence. Many aficionados of these romances firmly believe the accounts of my superhuman—or neurotic—moral behavior. Perhaps they like to believe in a man who has the strength they lack.

On the other hand, many readers scoff at this attitude. They deny that any well-sexed man could resist such beauty under such conditions. Even the Victorians were not that Victorian.

The strange thing about this is that my biographer did not exaggerate or lie. When I got married (I knew little as yet of human customs), I gave my word I would be faithful to my wife. She elaborated on this after the ceremony and made me swear again that I would bed no other woman as long as we lived.

We did not know then, of course, about the Nine or the elixir. I understood her attitude and what she required because The Folk have a similar attitude. However, among The Folk, a male can have more than one wife at a time. And divorce is easy for both male and female.

There have been long periods when I was roaming the jungle or off on some expedition or other or on some mission for the Nine, and I did not see my wife. At these times, I have masturbated. Or, for several years, in the jungle, I took along a pet, a beautiful female leopard. This was never written into his romances by my biographer. In fact, he never heard of it because I never told him. I liked him very much and did not want to offend him or to shatter his image of me any more than it had been by previous disclosures. He was one of the few really likeable humans I have known.

I fell in love with Kuta in an unconventional manner. Some day, I'll write about this peculiar man-feline relationship. The third year, she ran off with a male leopard, I suppose because I couldn't give her cubs. Or perhaps she could no longer endure her jealousy of my wife and was afraid that she would attack her. Up to the time that I first loved Kuta, in a glade on a mountainside shortly before dusk, she had been very fond of my wife.

I did not feel that I was breaking my vow by masturbating or by mounting Kuta. That vow only included human females. And certainly Clio would not be jealous of a leopardess. Or she shouldn't be. I did not, however, say anything about Kuta until after she deserted me. Clio and I were in our London house celebrating our 7th wedding anniversary and my birthday when I said something about it. It was November 21, 1920. We had been drinking champagne, and that was a mistake because I drink so seldom that a little alcohol quickly uninhibits me. I told her about Kuta and so had to endure several hours of tears and verbal abuse. I finally managed to convince her that I had not been really unfaithful or committed a terrible crime against Nature. As far as I was concerned, the only crime against Nature was against my nature, which suffers when I don't have a frequent discharge of sexual energy. In other words, if I don't come at least six times a week, I get nervous and mean.

She forgave me, or said she did, and she is very open and truthful, within limits. She forgave me because I had been raised by The Folk and so was not fully responsible for my "uncivilized" behavior. I said I took full responsibility, and my behavior could be justified far more by logic than hers could be. She ignored this and said that I must promise not to do any such thing again. Not only were humans off-limits, so were animals, no matter how beautiful and cooperative.

I asked her if that included "jacking off." She was startled and, also, red-faced. I told her about my masturbations. I was so "natural" about it, I suppose, that she overcame her inhibitions about it. After a few more glasses of bubbly, she confessed that she masturbated, too, when I had been away for a long time. It took much courage for her to tell me this. She came from an upper middle-class Southern family with a puritanical Protestant background. In addition, her black "mammy," who had raised her since she was six, was a very strict Southern Baptist. Despite which, Clio managed to grow into a passionate not-particularly-prudish young woman with a tendency for what humans call "sexual experimentation." And she was able to free herself of those crippling conditioned reflexes that humans call racial prejudices. At least, as much as any North American white is able.

(I digress. But I tell my story as I wish. Moreover, the reader won't understand me or those I love if he doesn't see us three-dimensionally.)

Clio and I freely discussed our masturbations and the accompanying fantasies. She even made a joke about the size of the banana she needed to satisfy herself with after having had me for 7 years.

This vow of fidelity did not hold during a part of the year. It was suspended for whoever was attending the ceremonies in the caverns of the Nine. When we accepted the elixir of prolonged youth, we also had to accept certain conditions laid down by the Nine. We spoke once about it and after that ignored the subject. We had agreed that the elixir could not be purchased without a very high price. Nothing comes free. The price was worth it, or so we thought at the time. I had my doubts now and then, but they were not powerful.

Clara interrupted my thoughts by returning. She said, "I just ran into the little Thai. She was very upset. She said she felt repulsed by Doc. He looked so absolutely *evil* to her. Something has happened to him. He is not the same Doc she has known for so many years. So she just walked out on him."

I said, "Did he have a hard-on?"

"No, he never does unless you suck on him a while."

I thought of our meeting on the bridge.

Clara looked hard at me for a moment and then said, "I had an uneasy feeling when we started to make love, John. Or I should say when *I* started to make love. You had changed, too. It wasn't just the soft-on. Do you know, you're *evil,* too!"

This was a peculiar thing for her to say. I wanted to ask her more about her feelings but she left quickly.

The silence had to be filled with my thoughts. They buzzed like flies in a dead mouth.

It seemed to me that anybody who accepted the gift of the Nine, and so accepted their terms, was, in some measure, evil. It was true that the Nine had never required me to do anything which I thought of as evil. As yet. They had the power, by the terms, to ask me to do anything they wished.

I thought of the inevitable parallel, the story of Faust and the devil. Faust, however, made a sorry bargain, a short-termed one, and regretted it. We, however, if we were lucky, would live for at least 30,000 years, and, once dead, that was the end of it. Also, some of us would probably become members of the Nine, because even they died now and then. The last one had died 2000 years ago, and one of the servants of the Nine had taken his place. The next vacancy might not be for another 2000 years or it might be today.

I would say that to be offered a multimilleniaed youth is to be tempted irresistibly. I can picture a mentally sick person, a depressed person, or a very old person, rejecting the offer. But not anyone who loves life.

Why should the Nine share this prolonged life with others? I suppose because the elixir is far more binding than money. And also because the Nine believe in tradition, in the continuity of their secret body of people, the oldest by far of any bodies.

The intercom buzzed nine times, and the Speaker's voice began to call our names. Mine was fifth. Caliban's was eighth. By this alone, I knew something unusual was happening. In the 48 years I had been attending, no more than one pilgrim at a time went into the ceremony cave.

25

The entrance was carved out of rock, delta-shaped, and only large enough to admit one at a time. It was a tight squeeze for me.

The cave was well-lit only in the center. Elsewhere, it was dim dusk for the space of a few yards and then blackness. The rough granite floor sloped downwards from all sides to the center. At the bottom was a tiny lake of black water, and in its center was a truncated cone of large rough-hewn oaken blocks and beams. On top of the island, which was about twelve feet high, was a circular oaken table, a ring. Inside the ring were nine high-backed intricately carved oak and ash chairs. The Nine entered through a trapdoor in the middle of the wooden cone.

The ceiling was covered with darkness except in the center, where nine massive crystalline stalactites hung down, like glowing hanged men, from the night of the ceiling. The light came from nine giant torches of wood and pitch projecting from moveable stone pillars set around the edges of the platform top.

We lesser beings stood on the slope—there were no chairs for us—throughout the ceremony. There was silence except for the inevitable coughing, occasioned by nervousness, not colds, since those who drink the elixir have no physical diseases. We were not allowed to speak except in reply to the Nine.

After a long time, the Speaker came up through the hole in the island and stood to one side of the chairs, leaning his staff with its ankh and *hannun-vaakuna* outwards from him.

Slowly, one by one, the Nine appeared from the hole and took their assigned chairs. The last to appear was the most important, the old woman Anana.

Only eight of the Nine were here. The chair just to the right of Anana's was empty. It belonged to the giant white-bearded old man who wore a double-headed raven headpiece and a black patch over a good eye. We knew him only as XauXaz.

The eight were dressed in their monkish robes, but the hoods were hanging behind their necks, and they wore their headpieces. Anana's was the head of a wild sow, and the others wore the heads of a bear, a wolf, a hyena, a ram, a jaguar, a badger, and an elk.

The woman Anana looked us over for a long time. I have been close to her many times, so I knew that she looked as if she were 125 and kept Death away only by scaring him. I had reason to believe that she was 30,000 years.

Finally, she gestured at the Speaker. He walked to the empty chair beside her and lifted from its seat what the shadows had hidden. It was the two-headed raven headpiece of XauXaz. He placed it on the table before the chair and stamped the end of his staff against the oaken floor so that it boomed nine times.

He cried out in English in a loud voice that echoed back from the murkiness, "XauXaz has gone to his ancestors, as all must, even the Nine!"

The others picked up small stone cups and drank

from them and set them down. There was another silence. Apparently, this was to be all that would be said about XauXaz, who had sat in that chair, or one like it elsewhere, for at least 5000 years and perhaps for three times that long. The Nine may have had a previous ceremony during which they genuinely mourned him. I do not know. But when with us, they acted as if they believed in ceremony, but in a short one, only.

Anana seemed to shrink within herself, physically, though the force of her personality did not diminish. I was not joking when I said she was holding Death off by scaring him. I do not frighten easily, but I am very uneasy when in her presence.

After another painfully long pause, she stirred. She looked to her right at Ing, the old man who wore a bear's head, and to her left at Iwaldi, the gnomish old man who wore a badger's head. These two, with XauXaz, were, I believe, the oldest after Anana. I do not know what their age is, but I have been close enough more than once to hear the language which the three men spoke only among themselves. And I know enough of Indo-European linguistics to recognize several of the words. I have read them, in their hypothetical and reconstructed forms, though I had not, of course, heard them spoken by a native speaker. Until then, that is.

One word was "weraz," and the other was "taknwaz." I believe that these meant, respectively, "man" and "precious object." Ing, Iwaldi, and XauXaz were speaking a dialect of Primitive Germanic. This is the tongue from which is descended the modern Norse, English, High and Low German languages, and, earlier, Old English, Old Norse, Frankish, Gothic, Old Saxon, and so on.

The others ranged from seeming octogenarians to those who looked no more than 50. I knew something of each, since I had had contact daily for several weeks when I had been Speaker. One was a Hebrew born shortly before 1 A.D. Two were Mongolian but spoke a language between themselves I could not identify. One was a very old, very huge Negro, and he sometimes talked to himself in a language that I am sure is the ancestor of all the Bantu tongues of modern Africa. The seventh looked as if he were a North American Indian. He also looked so Mongolian, however, that he could be an Olmec of ancient Mexico. Ing looked Nordic. Iwaldi was a dark-skinned dwarf with very broad shoulders, a huge head, slight epicanthic folds, long thick gnarled arms, great hands like the roots of an oak tree, and very short thick bowed legs. His white hair fell to his buttocks, and his white beard to his knees. He looked as if he belonged to a very different stock of Caucasian. Yet he spoke Primitive Germanic with Ing and XauXaz and seemed very close to them, as if they had known each other for a long time and had unusually common interests.

Anana said, "The mourning is over for us. And the chair is still empty. Who shall sit in the High's seat?"

The torches flickered on the naked men and women standing on the downslope. The light was dim, yet I could see that skin of the woman near me was goose-pimpled. It may have been the cold dampness of the cavern or the anticipation—apprehensive—of the ceremony, or it may have been the suddenly increased tension from Anana's words. We knew, without having been told, that one of us was going to be nominated for a seat with the Nine.

I had counted 49 people, including myself. There were, I knew, many more than that in the organization. These people must be those whom the Nine considered their best candidates. Doctor Caliban stood on my left about 20 feet away. There was nothing between us to block the view. I studied him during the silence. He was indeed a magnificent man. By the peculiar light of the torches, he looked more than ever like a bronze statue. He was not, however, Hellenic. No Athenian sculptor would have created a male figure so divinely proportioned except for the genitals. They were gargantuan, and, for some reason, the penis was half-erect. It was of a far darker bronze than the surrounding skin, being engorged with blood.

At that moment, the statue came to life. Caliban shifted his weight to his left leg, and a second later he turned his head slightly and looked out of the corners of his eyes at me. His gaze was downward; a slight smile—not amused—made fluid the corners of the lips and the eyes seemed to light up from an inner explosion. This was, of course, an illusion of the flickering torchlight.

I looked down. Not until that moment had I realized that my hatred and my desire to kill him had erected my penis. I also realized that my own skin was almost as bronzish as Caliban's, even to the darker bronze of the penis.

The Danish countess, Clara, was staring at my erection. She was undoubtedly wondering why she had failed and what there was in this situation to arouse me.

The Speaker thumped his staff on the oaken floor again. It was as if a stalactite had fallen. Almost everybody jumped. I did; I react swiftly to stimuli unless I have some reason to control myself. Caliban did not jump. He merely smiled on seeing my response, and he looked utterly savage as he did so, and then he turned his head to look back at the Nine.

The Speaker told us, briefly, what we would do. Because of the death of XauXaz, we would go through the ceremony in the presence of the other servants. All except two would experience the same ceremony as before. These two were the final candidates, chosen from the group in this cavern. If the two candidates did not meet the requirements of the Nine, if both failed, then other candidates would be chosen from the rest of the group. That, however, would be at a later time, since the test would occupy the two for a while.

Silence fell again like a piece of darkness from the ceiling. The Nine seemed to be thinking of other things. Perhaps they were remembering the last time a new man had taken a seat.

The cry of the Speaker cracked the darkness.

"Lord Grandrith! Doctor Caliban! Approach! Wade through the waters! Climb the Tree to the Table of the Gods!"

We walked down the slope and into the lake. The waters were cold. The blood in my legs jelled, quivered, and was dead. This deadness went up my legs, up my thighs, and then the waters covered my testicles and my penis, which had lost its swelling as soon as it hit the water. The testicles tried to retreat into the cavity of my belly, and then they froze. My bowels became ice. The lower part of my spine was a tree with roots exposed to the Arctic sea.

Climbing up the oak logs to the top of the structure did not thaw me much. The ascent was not

easy because of the partial paralysis and because
the logs were slimy. I don't know what was the
ultimate fate of anyone who slipped back into the
water and then could not make the climb.

Caliban and I got to the top at the same time.
At the low-voiced direction of the Speaker, we stood
side by side and faced Anana across the table. She
looked even more wrinkled than I remembered her,
as if Time had folded up her face like a bag and
then, changing his mind, had unfolded it to give her
a chance to live longer. The dark blue eyes in that
face like a fist were bright, however. And deep. The
many thousands of years had drilled far into the
region behind the eyes. There was something
ineffably sphinx-like about her, and, at the same
time, something unidentifiable. That nameless quality was frightening. She, and three others of the
Nine, are the only human beings that ever made me
feel touched with fear. These four may not be human. When a man lives past a thousand years, he
may become more—or less—than human.

Anana's voice was a whisper. She spoke in English with echoes of a tongue that perished long
before bronze was invented.

"What is your quarrel with him, Grandrith?"

I believed that she knew very well what my quarrel was. She probably knew far more than I, since
she would also have the facts about Caliban. Also,
I was beginning to wonder if she was not, in part at
least, responsible for the state in which Caliban and
I were enmeshed.

The Speaker bellowed out her question. The
words flew back from the distant walls like invisible
bats.

I said, "Caliban attacked me without provocation."

Out of the corner of my eye, I saw the bronze figure shudder a little.

"Did you, Caliban?"

The Speaker shouted her words.

"No. He lies."

The Speaker repeated in a voice like a bull's, "No. He lies!"

I was beginning to get irritated by the thunderish repetitions and the bat-like echoes, which seemed to jeer. Ordinarily, such things do not bother me. The unusualness of the ceremony, its unknown and possibly sinister development, the irrational motives for Caliban's hatred, my desire to kill him and get him out of the way, and my nervousness to get to England to protect Clio combined to make me abnormally sensitive.

Anana said, "Why did you attack Grandrith?"

"He raped and murdered my cousin, Trish Wilde."

"You know this to be a fact?"

"She was with a botanical expedition near the Uganda-Kenya border. A naked man ran into the camp at night, knocked Trish out, and carried her off. Some of the natives identified the man as Grandrith. They tried to follow but lost the trail. They did run across two natives who had seen Grandrith raping my cousin."

He paused, and a sound like a suppressed sob came from him.

"They interrupted him; he took off with Trish over his shoulder, running like an antelope. She's a big woman, weighs 150 pounds. Who else could carry her off like that? And then Trish's colleagues found her two days later . . . what was left . . . the hyenas and the vultures . . ."

He drew in a deep breath, but his face was expressionless.

"There must have been enough to identify her."

"Only bones. Her skull was missing. But the bones were those of a Caucasian female of her age, that is, twenty-five, in appearance. Actually, she's sixty."

"The skull was never found?"

"No. It's presumed a hyena or perhaps a leopard carried it off."

"Do you know anything of Grandrith?" Anana said.

"Until 1948, I had thought he was a writer's creation, a character in a series of fantastic novels," Caliban said. "Not until then did I find out, by accident, that there was a factual basis to the fictions. I was curious and did some investigating through agents. I learned some things about him, not much, but enough to make me suspect that he was one of us. I did not follow up the investigation because I became occupied with other matters."

"Your brain transplant experiments," Anana whispered. She smiled a terrible smile, and she extended two fingers of her left hand. This was a sign to the Speaker not to repeat her words.

"We have learned a number of things about you recently. We suspect that you have also been researching with the idea of independently producing the elixir. So far, you have not succeeded. And we have good reason to think that you will never succeed. But this does not displease us. We have not forbidden our servants to try to make their own elixir. And if you had not tried, you would not have come up to our expectations of you.

"However, that is not my main point. I point out to you that your investigation showed that Grandrith was, in many respects, like you. You are undoubtedly the two greatest athletes that the world has produced for several thousand years. Which is the greatest remains to be tested. You two even resemble each other facially, though your different coloring tends to conceal it."

This was a long speech in public for one of the Nine. I wondered what she was getting at—or to—but I did not say anything, of course.

She leaned forward and stretched out her skinny arms with the great veins like asphyxiated snakes. She said, "Come closer."

We, knowing what was expected, moved until our thighs pressed against the table edge and our testicles rested on the surface. My flesh had warmed up, but when Anana's hand cupped my testicles, they felt cold indeed. It seemed to me that anyone whose blood flowed that slowly could not have long to live.

I did not flinch. I had never flinched when she had done this, even though I knew what she would soon be doing.

Then I saw that this procedure might be different. Certainly, she could not use a sharp flint knife on me with the other hand since it was holding Caliban's testicles.

She lifted the sacs as if she were estimating the weight and worth of meat in grocery bags. She said, "They are noble indeed. And warm with life. How many . . . ?"

Her voice trailed off. She looked up and smiled.

Her teeth were black. Not from rottenness but from something she chewed. It was not betel; its odor was unidentifiable. I suspect that once all her people chewed this plant and that the plant had become extinct except in some garden in some very private well-guarded house somewhere.

"Today," she said, "you will not have to give up part of your flesh to the knife. You will eat with us in preparation for your contest. The next time we meet here to eat, only one of you will be at this table. Or at any table."

Apparently, there was to be no more discussion of our grievances or any arbitration of our case. They did not care who was wrong or wronged. They probably did not even acknowledge that wrong existed except in human minds. I say human because I do not think that they thought of themselves as human. Though they could die, they must have considered themselves as gods. No human could live that long and have such power and not think himself divine.

Would I, if I became one of the Nine, come to think as they?

Severed though I am from most human attitudes, or I should say, loosely connected, I still fully share some. The infrahuman has not entirely eaten out the human in me. I feel a certain—or uncertain— amount of sympathy and empathy for humans, for some humans. I would not wish to become even more alienated. I knew how it felt to see those with whom I most identified die away. As far as I knew, The Folk, never numerous, had become nothing.

"It has been two thousand years since this pre-seating ceremony was held," she said.

She gestured at the lean, dark-bearded, scimitar-nosed man with the ram's head. I had heard him speak of Caesar Augustus, Tiberius, and Herod Antipas when I was Speaker.

"At that time, Grandrith, your ancestral island was inhabited by the tattooed British and Picts and your English ancestors still lived in what was to be later called Denmark. And as for America, Doctor Caliban, no one knew of it—except the Nine and their servants. We kept the Phoenicians and the Romans and the Saracens from following up their discovery of the Americas, and we aborted the Norse colonization. We were thinking for a while about establishing an Iroquois-Cherokee empire. The first Europeans would have found a united people armed with fire arms and riding horses. But the final decision was to let things happen as they would.

"The point is that when the last vacancy occurred, when Thrithjaz died . . ."

That would be Primitive Germanic for third, I thought.

". . . neither the English nor the Americans existed as such. But times change, even for us, and we have seen many nations and tongues born and die."

She lifted a finger at the Speaker. He directed me to stand at the far right, by the wrinkled, squat Negro with the hyena headpiece and Caliban at the far left, by the man with the ram headpiece. The Speaker then thudded the butt of the staff and began calling out names.

The ceremony was like those I had attended at one of the "eaten" and directed when I was Speaker. There were differences, however. Before, Anana had always fed first. Now, Caliban and I were treated as guests of honor. Anana took the testicles of a big moustachioed man with her left hand and cut the scrotum on one side with a long-bladed flint knife. The man looked down and did not look away even when the pinkish egg-shaped gland rolled out on the table. His dark skin did become pale and then gray; sweat rolled down his body; he gripped the table edge as if he were trying to leave his fingerprints in the wood.

As the Speaker, I had seen him go through this before and did not expect him to faint and fall off the structure into the cold black waters. I have seen some men faint. No one helps them. Usually, the water shocks them back into consciousness and most climb back up, however painful the ascent. Several could not, or would not, climb again. The guards took these away, and I never saw them again.

The ceremony must have been originated in the Old Stone Age, perhaps 300,000 years ago or more. It was probably old when Anana was born.

Anana picked up the testicle and placed it on the table before her after smelling it. The Speaker had stepped over the table; he now came around and smeared ointment from a jar onto the wound. While he did this, he chanted a few lines in an unknown language. The bleeding, which was not great, stopped altogether. Anana handed her stone cup to the Speaker, who gave the man a mouthful of the liquid. This tastes like mead to me, but I do not think it is. The pain would be gone within five minutes. Inside a month, provided the man got the proper food and rest, the testicles would be regrown. Not only did the elixir provide a prolonged youth and freedom from disease, it gave regenerative powers.

Anana sliced the gland into twelve more or less

equal slices. She sent one to me via the Speaker and one to Caliban. One piece was thrown into the water and one was placed before the empty chair. Each of the Nine took a slice and ate it raw. I chewed and swallowed mine with gusto, because the testicle is one of the few pieces of human meat worth eating.

The moustachioed man, dismissed by the Speaker, climbed down slowly and painfully. The second person called was on top of the structure before the first had waded out through the waters.

26

I had only to turn my head to see Caliban because the table was curved and we sat, as it were, at the ends of opposite horns of a crescent moon. His face was expressionless; it did not show the repulsion I would have expected from a civilized man. Either he was in strong control of his emotions, which would agree with what his two colleagues said, or he was genuinely indifferent to, or perhaps even enjoying, the meat.

I was disappointed. I would have liked to have seen him disgrace himself by vomiting.

The next person summoned was a beautiful mulatto. Her hair was black and kinky, *au naturel,* and her skin was as dark as a wild hare's eye. The eyes were a startling light blue. She was the wife of the Speaker and had disappeared with him when the explosion blew up the yacht. I recognized her because she had attended ceremonies when I did. I had bedded her not infrequently and had, of course, toungued her all over.

I think Anana knew this. She seemed to know everything about us as if she were God and we were Her sparrows. Thus she knew I would have no objections to performing the ceremony with her. Caliban, however, was a white American born in 1903 and so more than probably had the usual conditioned reflexes of his "class." This may be why Anana designated Myra to go to him. If he did have any objections, he did not reveal them by expression.

He extended a hand to help her get up on the table, picked her up as if she were a hollow dummy and placed her on her back. She put her legs over his shoulders, and he spent some time with his face buried against the thick stiff hairs I knew so well and the slit dripping with honey-thick lubricating fluid.

Myra made an attempt to respond. She writhed and moaned a little, but I doubted that she was doing anything except acting. She must have been too tense to relax. The only woman whom I thought could in reality let loose and have an orgasm during this ceremony was the Danish giantess. I'm sure that the final act hurt her just as much as any of the women, but she could live for the moment as few can.

Finally, Caliban bit down. The woman stiffened, her fists driving the nails into the skin. (I saw the blood on the tips and palms when she got up.) Her feet bent and turned inward and her toes clenched. Her jaw clamped shut to keep the scream inside, although the Nine had not forbidden screaming.

Caliban lifted her up. He had some blood on his juice-smeared lips and chin, and he was chewing the clitoris. The Speaker, his face set, smeared some ointment on her wound. Myra, gray beneath the brown skin, walked across the table unsteadily and climbed painfully off the table and down the logs of the structure.

This was the first time that I had seen a husband and wife in the caverns at the same time. I thought that it must be rather hard on him to watch her with Caliban; I do not think that I could control my jealousy if Clio were doing this in front of me with him. I would have tried to kill him—perhaps. I knew that Clio was doing what the other women were doing. A man or a woman cannot keep their youth and vitality forever without wanting some variety, and I did not expect her to be a saint. But I also did not want to know what she was doing, even hear about it, let alone see it.

It may be that the Nine were punishing him for some reason. Or perhaps they were testing him.

I was given the honor of eating the next woman, a beauty from the Punjab. My experience in biting off clitorises was nil, but I succeeded quickly. The clitoris, aside from the delicious scent and taste of the moisture and fluid of a healthy woman's vagina, tasted like the man's testicle.

After her, a man was called up. His testicle was cut out and sliced and the pieces passed around. This time, each of us took only a small bite and then threw the remainder on the floor behind us. It was evident that we could not eat all the flesh of 47 people. The Nine had pets in their private chambers who would eat what we could not.

The third person called was Clara, and Anana licked at her until she came and then bit off the clitoris.

After that, the ceremony went swiftly with no foreplay for the women. There were too many to spend time dawdling.

At the end, the 47 men and women were sitting or standing on the slope across the waters. A few groaned. Several had passed out after—making it back, but all regained consciousness and walked out, unaided, when the Speaker dismissed them.

They were free to leave. Most would not hear from the Nine until the summons came for the yearly payment of flesh or their turn to be the Speaker.

Aside from these normal duties, I had heard from the Nine only seven times in 48 years. I was required to carry out assignments in Thailand, Rhodesia, Brazil, Czechoslovakia, the States, Jerusalem, and Berlin. One occupied me a year, during which I did not see my beloved Clio. I performed all missions to the full satisfaction of the Nine, although I came close to being killed several dozen times. Each assignment would have made a splendid book for my biographer. He never heard of them, of course, and he would have been forced to heavily censor them if he had. And he would have been horrified at the manner in which I did some things.

After the cavern was cleared of all but those on the oaken island, there was silence. The only sound was the sputtering of torches and an occasional licking of blood from lips and chins. The odor of blood and saliva and sweat and clitorises and testicles was strong. Caliban was gazing malignantly at me. I stared at him for a moment and then looked away, since I did not want to indulge in a childish I-can-outstare-you contest.

Finally, Anana rustled her robes and said, "You two have experienced some very disturbing, highly abnormal reactions lately, haven't you?"

Simultaneously, we said, "Yes."

"Caliban," she said. "*Doctor* Caliban. What is your explanation?"

His slight smile showed that he had caught the sarcasm. He said, "I have no answer, except . . ."

"Continue."

"The elixir may have something to do with it."

He pointed at the stone cups and the stone pitcher with which the Speaker refilled the cups. That gesture meant that he believed that the elixir was in the mead-tasting liquid. He did not know that it was. None of the servants knew. We supposed that it was because we were given nothing else special to drink. The Nine referred to the elixir without telling us when we were getting it.

"I can't believe that any psychobiological mechanism could suddenly start operating after all these years unless it were released by the long-term action of the elixir. Of course, the mechanism must have been deeply buried in me, although I had not the slightest inkling that it existed. Grandrith also seems to be suffering from a similar aberration. Since he has been taking the elixir, too, it offers the only element common to us.

"I admit that I don't understand what this mechanism is or why he should have one also. I use the term mechanism, but I could just as well say trauma or engram."

That beautiful voice was so hypnotic that I almost nodded into sleep. For a moment, it lulled my hatred of him. When Anana spoke, she startled me.

"Grandrith. *Doctor* Grandrith. What is your explanation?"

Caliban's eyes opened just a trifle. I don't think he had known that I was an M.D.

"Unlike Caliban, I am not the greatest doctor in the world, or even in Kenya. But I can think, and that's doing more than most doctors I have known. I agree with Caliban that the elixir must be responsible for bringing an already-existing aberration to the surface. I seem to be incapable of getting an erection while loving a woman, unless I am inflicting pain on her. Perhaps you noticed that I had a slight erection while I was biting off that woman's clitoris. It was the idea of the pain she was having, which I was giving, not the sexual aspect that excited me. If I had thought I was going to kill her, I would have had a big hard-on.

"I am very disturbed. I have, however, been so busy keeping alive that I haven't had much time to think about it.

"If you know the answer, please tell me."

My petition indicated my desperation. Nobody asked the Nine, especially Anana, for anything without placing himself in peril.

She did not reply. I said, "It is possible that the elixir may have nothing to do with it. My aberration came with a shock, the explosions of the shells. Caliban may have suffered a shock, too. But it is strange that we suffer from much the same thing."

I was thinking of the news of his cousin's rape and death.

"The beautiful Patricia Wilde," Anana said. "So I will see her no more. Like flowers they . . . never mind. It's an old old story. We are not concerned with what our servants do to each other, as long as they are not disobeying us or interfering with our plans. But at the moment, Caliban, you have sent off a man to kidnap Grandrith's wife, in revenge for what you think he did to your cousin. This is not at all like you, who have combatted evil all your life and traveled the world over doing good."

The sarcasm was so light in tone that I almost missed it.

"It seems the only right thing to do," Caliban said. "Grandrith must pay for the hideous evil he's done."

"Through more evil?"

"I don't consider it to be evil!" he said with the most heat in his voice I had yet heard.

"You admitted you have a psychic aberration."

"The aberration," Caliban said, "consists of this. And nothing else. I can't get an erection unless I inflict pain or death or am thinking about it."

He was one up on me. If I could just work up a hard-on while loving by thinking about murdering someone . . . but what kind of loving would that be? Responsive on the surface and inside totally removed from my Clio. Imagine forth terror and pain and death, while she thought I was melting into her with love.

Anana said nothing for a while. The others sat as if they were sleeping. The torches were beginning to burn out, and the blackness from the ceiling was sinking towards us. The blackness was gaining substance and, hence, weight. The air even seemed to be compressed beneath it. Instead of getting warmer, the denser air became colder.

Anana cleared her throat and said, "Grandrith, you had two uncles. One died in Africa, as you well know. The other went at an early age to America because he had assaulted and nearly killed one of his teachers. Your family never heard of him again. He took the name of Wilde and became a doctor."

Caliban could be startled. He jerked his head around to stare at Anana, and his eyes had become large.

"You know who your father was, Grandrith," Anana said. "Your uncle did not know what had happened to him; he left your father hiding somewhere in Whitechapel. The world knew of your father but it never knew his real name nor what became of him after the murders ceased. We knew, however, because he was one of us. He went to the States, too, and there he became a doctor. This was after the madness passed from him. He became a doctor, like his younger brother, and, indeed, some years afterwards accidentally found him. The youngest brother had a daughter, and your father had a son in America."

She paused. My heart was clenching with the excitement and the anticipation. I also felt a little sick, because I knew what she was going to say.

"All were exceedingly strong men with tendencies to madnesses. All were doctors, too, as if the knife were your totem, your desire, your bliss. All lovers of violence."

She stopped speaking again. The silence was like that between the beats of a dying heart.

Then, from Caliban, softly, a weird rising-falling whistle, and, even more softly, "Incredible!"

"You two have the same father."

27

In less than a minute after Anana had made that statement, we two were blindfolded and led out through the trapdoor in the platform. A hypodermic knocked me out, and I regained consciousness in a single-motored plane. A short time later, the plane landed, and I was led out and the blindfold removed. The landing strip was at the bottom of a deep valley. The green-shielded mountains were everywhere around.

The pilot gave me brief instructions and flew away, leaving me naked and armed only with my hunting knife, which was still bent.

Caliban, I was told, had been taken to a place near the valley of Ophir and released. His instructions were the same as mine. One of us was to return within a month with the other's head and genitals. The victor would then take the seat left empty by XauXaz.

I knew my appropriate location. If I stopped only to hunt when absolutely necessary and got only three hours of sleep at night, I could get through the mountains in five days to a strip used by a Ugandan mining company. A plane might not be available for some time, however.

I had wondered at first why the Nine had placed us so far apart. The area was so vast, we could have looked for a year for each other without success. The Nine, of course, did not expect us to do this. I was not going to waste time searching for

169

Caliban while Clio was in danger in England. Caliban would know that, too. He was probably heading for the nearest air strip now, or had got into touch with his two old colleagues and had them radio for a plane. If this happened, he would outstrip me in the race by four or five days.

I set off. It was a half hour past dawn. A brightly feathered kingfisher swooped down and ahead of me and then soared back up. The native blacks and The Folk would have taken this as a good omen, but I had long ago given up the idea of a higher being who was interested in me. Nevertheless, on seeing the kingfisher, I felt heartened. Perhaps, down there, where the childhood treasures are, I still believed.

I knew this area well. Some years ago, I had built a tree house here not too dissimilar to that shown in those bad and lying movies made about me. In fact, I got the idea from the movies. It was as comfortable as a house can be in the thin-air water-heavy atmosphere of the high mountain rain forest. Clio lived there with me for a while. The absence of a number of people to talk to, the silence, the cold, and the wet got to her nerves. After two months, she insisted that I take her back to the Kenyan plantation. Of the sixty days, three had been idyllic.

That day and part of the night, I climbed two mountains. The next day, I was only half a mile from my old tree house. I could not afford the time, but I detoured to see it anyway. I always have a nostalgia for any place in which I have lived any time at all, except for the town house in London, which is surrounded by too many people, too much noise, and too many unpleasant odors.

In the thickness, the air was not moving. When I smelled the dead body of a human adult male who had not been dead more than an hour, I knew he had to be close. A few steps this way and that showed me the direction to go.

My biographer has stated many times that I have nostrils as sensitive as an animal's. He described this as due to my upbringing in the jungle. This was nonsense, and he knew it. No amount of practice will increase the sensitivity of the human nose. My nose is, however, not normal. I am a mutant, as I have said in previous volumes, and I have described my several mutations in detail in Volume IV. My sense of smell is equivalent to a bloodhound's. This has its advantages. It also has its disadvantages. You humans have no idea of what the odor of gasoline fumes does to me.

Inside a minute, I came across broken bushes, plants stepped upon and just rising, squashed insects, and other evidences of a struggle. A leopard-skin loincloth was under a bush. Beyond it, the body of a male Caucasian lay on its side. He was about six feet six inches in height and must have weighed 300 pounds. He was very muscular but also fat and big-paunched. He was clean-shaven. His black hair was cut in bangs just above the eyes, and it grew shoulder-length behind. A leopard-skin band went around his head. The left side of his skull was bloody and caved in. His eyes were dark gray. His right arm, which had been torn off his body, was not in sight. Neither were his penis and testicles, which had been ripped off.

A trail of blood led from his body. I followed it and came across a big knife, much like my uncle's knife before long usage had worn it stiletto-thin. I deduced that the killer had knocked this out of the man's hand with the club which I found ten feet further on. Its end bore much blood.

When I came across two sets of tracks in some soft earth, my heart beat faster. I felt choked with a sense of homecoming and of love. They were the prints of two Folk, a female and male adult.

I hurried to catch up with them. Tears ran down my cheeks. I had thought that all The Folk were dead, their kind gone forever.

The trail led to the tree house so directly that I was sure the two were deliberately heading for it. Other tracks showed that the dead man had come from its direction less than 60 minutes ago.

When I was just outside the small clearing, in the center of which was the great tree with my house, I stopped. I looked through a break in the green wall and saw the female sitting with her back against a tree. She was holding an infant not quite a year old. I was close enough to smell them, and the infant was sweating the scent of near-death. Its eyes were closed, it was breathing shallowly and rapidly, and its lungs bubbled. Its body was wet.

The mother was stinking of grief and hopelessness. Her dull gaze was fixed on the male and the female under him by the big tree.

I was surprised when I saw what he was doing. In the first place, ferocious as a male of The Folk can be under some circumstances, he is shy when humans are in the area. If not cornered, he will run. But it was evident that this male had killed the man and at once gone to the tree house with his present activity in mind. I don't know what made this male behave so unusually. Perhaps, as I later speculated, his abnormal behavior was caused by a combination of long isolation from his tribe (all dead), the sickness of the infant and the female's concern for it and refusal to mate with him, and the lust aroused by observing the man's rapings of his woman prisoner.

Also, there was the sudden madness which sometimes grips the older adult males of The Folk. This results in their running amok, however. I have never seen the temporary insanity cause any kind of sexual behavior; it always causes a desire to kill all within reach. And this male was not trying to kill the woman unless it was with his cock.

If that was his intent, it was a failure. The woman was paralyzed with terror, but otherwise she was not being hurt. The largest erect penis I've ever seen among The Folk was two inches long and 3/8ths of an inch thick (estimated). If she had been a virgin, she would probably have remained one (technically so) no matter how many times he banged her.

He was on top of her and giving a short subdued scream and his body was shaking. A moment later, he renewed his thrustings.

The Folk have buttocks, which no true apes have, and hips constructed more like those of homo sapiens than of the gorilla, just as their feet are more hominoid than simian. (Like a Neanderthal's, I should say.)

The woman's arms were behind and under her, by which I deduced that they were tied. Her ankles had been tied together. Someone had untied them, although one end of the rope was around an ankle and the other end tied to a bush. Her legs had been forced open and up over the shoulders of the male.

The Folk normally use this position, unlike the apes, who usually favor the rear approach.

The skin of the woman had the peculiar beautiful bronze hue of Doctor Caliban, and the long hair spread out on the ground behind her was his dark metallic red-bronze. Her face was not visible.

I moved around the edge of the clearing until I could see that the male was kissing her. (This way of showing affection or sexual desire is customary among The Folk.)

This probably horrified her far more than the relatively innocuous rape. That great half-apish face had been thrust against hers, and those chimpanzee-thin lips had slobbered all over her face.

It was this that made me think he must be half-mad with sexual frustration. To one of The Folk, a human is a very ugly and repulsive creature. Only a perverted Folk would want to kiss a human.

I scouted around carefully, making sure that no one else was in the area. Then I stepped out of the bushes, seeing at the same time the arm of the dead man under a bush where the male had thrown it. The genitals had probably been eaten.

I gave a soft cry, *"Krhgh!"*

The male stiffened and came up off the woman so violently that her legs were thrown forward and she was momentarily jack-knifed. He whirled to face me.

28

He was one of the largest I'd ever seen. He was at least six feet two inches tall and weighed about three hundred and fifty pounds. He did not look as nearly gorilloid as my biographer has described The Folk. (As I have fully explained in Volume I, my biographer wrote his first story about me before he knew me. He got all his facts—and misinformation—from records and from a man who had known one of the persons who found me when I was eighteen. Using mainly his imagination, he described The Folk as much more apish than they are. By the time he knew the truth, he could not describe them correctly and maintain consistency in his novels.)

His arms, almost as thick with muscles as a gorilla's, were as short in proportion to his trunk as a man's. The legs were shorter, however, and bowed. The body was covered with thick straight rusty-red hair which formed a covering not as thick as a chimpanzee's. The skin was as black as a bush Negro's. The bones were approximately 2½ times as thick as a man's, thus giving a broad attachment for the massive muscles.

(My own bones are almost twice as thick as a modern man's. I could pass for a Cro-Magnon.)

The head was large and long and had a sagital crest, like a gorilla's, for the attachment of the massive jaw muscles. The jaws were quite prognathous, and the canine teeth were as large as a gorilla's.

The teeth had a "simian gap" for the accommodation of the tips of the lower canines. The Folk are primarily vegetarians, though they eat small animals when they get a chance. The chin was absent. The supra-orbital ridges were massive, and the forehead was very low. (The average adult male cranium capacity is 800 cubic centimeters, an estimate based on my study of four skulls.)

The eyes were deep sunk and a russet red, although most of The Folk have dark or light brown eyes.

Under the lower jaw was a sac which swelled out when the male challenged another, or a predator, or just wanted to howl at the moon.

The male was sweating, although not as heavily as he would have if he had been a man. The Folk have always been forest dwellers and share a paucity of sweat glands with most forest animals.

All in all, he looked like a giant variety of Zinjanthropus, and he may have been a descendant of this supposedly extinct australopithecine.

The clearing seemed to crackle and to spark, like a cat's fur rubbed the wrong way. His hairs bristled; his eyes became even redder; his open mouth showed the thick yellow teeth and sharp canines and incisors, a red tongue, and the black pit of a throat. The sac on his neck swelled out.

The back of my neck felt as if my hairs were also bristling. I automatically adopted the stiff-legged sidewise walk of belligerency as I circled him. As soon as I became aware of it, I broke the stance, bent my knees, and opened my left hand. My right hand was empty, because I did not want to threaten him with the knife I had found in the grass. He might be talked into cooperation if I did not scare him with the bright human weapon.

The male growled and then said, "*Yh shth-tb.*" That is, "I am Leopard-Breaker."

I replied in the same whispering speech of The Folk, "*Yh tlhs.*" That is, "I am Worm."

The speech of The Folk does contain some voiced consonants, mostly back-of-the-throat sounds, but the majority of words consist of unvoiced consonants. They have only one vowel, similar to the sound of *u* in the English *cut* or of *o* in *done,* and this vowel is not often used.

Worm is the literal translation of my name. My biographer used a euphemistic translation, one which reflected his pigmentation orientation. The Folk, however, considered degrees of hairiness to be more important than color. I also had other names: Bird Nose, Big Cock, Smart Ass, Bright Eyes, Fat Mouth, and Monkey Shit. But I was generally known as *tlhs* or Worm. This name is not as derogatory as humans might think; The Folk consider the worm to be a beautiful creature and very tasty and nutritious. I could have taken a more dignified and impressive name after I came of age and killed the chief of our tribe, but I preferred Worm. To me, it meant the worm that turned.

He howled at me, "I am Leopard-Breaker!"

"I am Worm!" I shouted. "Leave the female alone. Or I will kill you."

"What? A worm would kill a breaker of leopards?"

"I have killed many many leopards," I said, flashing my fingers to indicate an immense number. "I have killed many of the great fighters of The Folk. I have killed many lions."

He looked puzzled, and I knew that he did not know the word which the west coast Folk use. He had probably never seen or heard of a lion.

"I will kill you!" he screamed.

I decided to brandish my knife. When he saw it, he looked around for another stick to knock the knife out of my hand as he had done to the first owner.

I said, "Let us be friends, Leopard-Breaker."

He screamed with all the air in his throat-sac, "Kill!"

And he charged.

I threw the knife. It should have gone in to the hilt in his paunch. He lowered his head, however, so swiftly that it protected his belly, though he did not do it on purpose, I'm sure. The knife struck the top of that thick-boned head, cut the scalp, and flew off. His head rammed into my belly, and his arms snapped together.

Not until I had thrown the knife had I become aware that my penis was bristling as much as my hair. Moreover, just as the knife left my hand, I became aware of an approaching orgasm. This disconcerted me and unbalanced my timing and coordination and slowed me. Otherwise, I would have sidestepped his arms.

He carried me up and backwards, as he ran swiftly forward with the intention of crashing me into a tree trunk. My arms were free, so I interlocked my fingers and brought the edges of both palms down close to my belly and on top of that crest. Though he grunted, he drove on. Again, I came down with my hands but in a slanting blow on the back of that muscle-slabbed, heavy-vertabraed neck. He grunted and slowed down, and I slammed him again on the neck. If he had been a human, he would have had a broken, or at least fractured, neck.

He dropped me and then fell on top of me. I shoved him off and twisted away, seeing at the same time, a foot away, the tree against which he had meant to break my back.

He regained his senses very quickly and kicked out behind him. My feet went from under me, and my right leg between the knee and ankle felt numbed as if a zebra had kicked it. He rolled over and bounded to his feet. Instead of leaping at me, which he should have done with my leg half-paralyzed, he ran off to get a thick heavy piece of thornwood, which was close to the woman.

She lifted her legs as he bent over to pick up the club, and she kicked. Her heels caught him on the side of his jaw. If it had been a man's jaw, it would have shattered. He dropped on his face without a sound.

Limping, I ran towards *shth-tb,* but he rose unsteadily and turned towards me. The woman, who had pulled herself along on her back with her heels —another indication of the strength in those long and beautifully shaped legs—kicked him in the ankle. This was done at the expense of a rope burn, because the rope around one ankle slid up her leg. It hurt her; her face twisted.

The male went down again. Roaring, though not as loudly as he had been, he again struggled to his feet. She smote him on the side of his jaw once more with her two feet, and then, after he had fallen, she rammed a heel into his nose.

I had picked up the knife. I rolled him over on his back. Blood ran from his nose, and his eyes were crossed. His jaw hung askew as if it were broken.

"*Kghd?*" I said.

He did not reply verbally. His big wrinkled hairy hand shot out and gripped the woman's ankle. She gasped and tried to kick loose but could not break the grip. He sat up and dragged her towards him, breaking the rope. He kept his crossed eyes on—or towards—me. He had acted so swiftly that he had caught me unaware; I had broken my own rule for just a few seconds and now must pay. Rather, she must pay for my lack of caution in approaching him.

He could break her neck before I could get to her, and if I raised the knife to throw it, he would crack it.

Despite this, I threw the knife. I could do nothing else. He was going to kill her no matter what I did.

My hurling the knife made him loose his grip for a moment, because he had thought he had me buffaloed. She bent her neck down instead of trying to jerk away and bit his penis. He screamed with surprise and agony and threw his hands up in the air. My knife went into his solar plexus with a sound as of an axe hitting soft wood. His eyes uncrossed, rolled up, the lids closed, and he fell on his back. His hands clenched, unclenched, clenched, and then were still.

I had lost control then. I was on my knees, holding myself up with both hands, and jerking with the spasms of the orgasm. The grass was puddled with the gravy fluid. Of all my kills since this had started, this was the most intense ecstasy. It was as exquisite—and almost as tender and one-making —as when Clio and I loved.

I think it was because I had killed a great male of The Folk. I have always loved The Folk, but at the same time I have hated, deep down, the adult male. Too many of them caused me too much pain and terror when I was young. To me, killing one of them was a far greater feat than killing any number of human males. And there was the additional thrill (later, it was a deep sadness) of killing what was probably the last male of The Folk. I had paid them back fully and finally for the bullyings and horrors of my childhood.

29

The woman stared as if she could not believe what she had seen. I rose, pulled the knife from the belly, and wiped it on his hairy skin. The female still squatted at the other end of the clearing with her infant. Ignoring the woman's requests to cut the rope loose from her wrists, I walked to the female. She looked up with eyes black as the bottom of an open grave at night. The infant looked dead.

"I won't harm you," I said. "You may stay here and share my food, if you wish. I had to kill *shth-tb*. He forced me to."

She said nothing. Slowly, painfully, she got to her feet, looked once at the corpse of her mate, turned, and was gone into the jungle. I did not go after her. There was nothing I could do for her. Moreover, I did not have time to spare.

I cut the woman's ropes and helped her to her feet, since her arms and hands were in pain after the blood started circulating. She was at least six feet tall and very well formed. She had a fine haunch that curved out like an apple and looked almost as hard when she tensed her gluteus maximum on feeling my hand. I withdrew it and stepped back. She rubbed her wrists, said, "It hurts," and looked speculatively at me. The bronze hair was below her shoulders, wavy, and looked remarkably unmussed-up. She had no makeup but managed to look beautiful without it. Her pubic hairs were unusually thick and two shades darker than the metallic head hair.

She saw me looking at her and smiled slightly. I did not know what the smile was supposed to mean.

"If you're going to try to rape me," she said, "I hope you're not as inept as the last two. And let me rest first and eat something. I'm tired, sore, hungry, and shaken up. I've been abducted and mauled and chewed on and repeatedly splashed on the belly with the premature ejaculations of that demented creature. Or do you know whom I'm talking about?"

"He's dead," I said. "The ape killed him."

She said, "Oh!" and then, "That's no ape. It's a subhuman if ever I saw one, and I haven't, except in anthropology books. I didn't know that these things really existed, I'd always thought they were native myths. But it certainly isn't built for raping a female homo sapien. Not that it tickled me so I felt like laughing."

I had to admire her. Most women would have been hysterical, nor would I have blamed them.

"That monster—the human one—thought he was you, you know. So did I. You are he, aren't you? Could we eat? There's plenty of food in the tree house. Canned," she added with another smile. "That wild man had a year's supply of everything."

I said, "Be at ease. I have no intention of raping you. I couldn't if I wanted to."

"Every male I run into is ejaculating all over the place," she said.

Then she said something that startled me. "It's almost as big as Doc's. And just about as useless, I'll bet."

She was very cool and very strange, though I suppose she must have thought me rather weird, too. I let her precede me to the house. She was a woman, but she had shown herself to be uncommonly dangerous. I did not want her behind me until I knew I could trust her.

The tree house was about fifty feet up and situated on a platform which ran entirely around the trunk and was supported by four huge branches radiating towards the cardinal points of the compass. It was built of bamboo and thatched with elephant's ear leaves and grasses. It had three rooms. The ascent to it had to be made by stainless steel rungs which I had hammered into the trunk. Wooden rungs would have rotted in a year or two.

Trish Wilde (she had not introduced herself yet) got a fire going in the stone fireplace and wrapped herself in a blanket before it.

The house was a mess. The floors were littered with open cans, scraps of food covered by insects, and even a pile of excrement in one corner. If the crazy man had been imitating me, he must have thought I had the sanitary habits of a slum dweller. One of the bamboo and grass couches looked as if it had been taking punishment. One leg was broken off and the bottom was sagging.

The woman said, "Oh, by the way, I'm Trish Wilde, and I was assistant botanist to Doctor Everfields, a world-famous botanist, and we were searching for exotic plants when I was carried off. If the crazy man hadn't surprised me so, I would have kicked his kneecap loose and then smashed his balls and that would have been that.

"Once he got me up here, he hammered at me

until he broke the couch. He never did get his thing into me. He kept coming on my belly. But he almost bit my nipples off."

"I can see that," I said.

"He stank, and he had a big belly, and he slobbered all over me. I think he wanted to stick his cock in my mouth, but he knew I'd bite it off if he did."

She was well educated but she talked like a wharf-dock whore. Certainly, she must moderate her talk in other situations. I did not know why she felt she could speak so uninhibitedly with me. Perhaps it was because she thought, and quite rightly, that my infrahuman rearing had left me without emotional reactions to the so-called "tabu" words.

"How tired are you?" I said.

"I have some energy left. Why?"

It was necessary to tell her part of my story if I were to get her to come with me voluntarily. I knew she was a member of the Nine's organization, so I would not be revealing secrets. I told her what had happened since the dawn the Kenyans' attacked, but I left out all reference to her cousin. I also made it appear that Noli had escaped from me but had sworn to go to England and take revenge on Clio.

"Have you had this year's elixir?" I said.

"No," she said. "I'm not due for the caverns until next month."

Clio was also scheduled to go then. I did not tell her that. She would know that as soon as she saw Clio, who, presumably, had made the pilgrimage with her many times.

"I am leaving within the hour," I said. "I'll be

traveling as swiftly as I can and sleeping little. If you want to come with me, you're welcome. It is easy for a stranger to get lost in these mountains, and I would not like to see you try to go it alone. Nevertheless, if you can't keep up with me, I will leave you behind."

"I could use a good night's sleep," she said. "But I don't want to wander around these mountains until I die or get picked up by some horny natives. I'll go with you."

I was glad that she said that, because I had made up my mind that she was coming with me no matter what she said. She could be a tradeoff if Caliban succeeded in getting hold of Clio.

We ate and drank and then made up a bundle for each. This consisted of a rainhat, poncho, blanket, a breakdown .22 rifle and cartridges, matches, and cans of food. Immediately after, we set off.

Despite our pace, which was rapid for the thick heavy growth of the rain forest, she had breath enough to chatter on and on. She told me of her childhood, her high school and college days, of meeting Doc, of the mysterious deaths of her father and her uncle. She had gone off with Doc and his five colleagues on several adventures. She owned a nation-wide chain of clothing shops and much property. She had a master's degree in psychology but had returned to school, after many years, and gotten a Ph.D. in botany.

I strongly suspected that this was at Doc's request. He was undoubtedly attempting to find the elixir, and he would have wanted her to help him.

The ingredients for the elixir might be in plants unknown or little known.

She said, "I might still be tied up in the tree house if I hadn't talked him into letting me come down so I could walk around. After he let me lope around the clearing, like a dog on a leash, he tied me to the bush and tried to rape me again. Then he just happened to see the subhumans through a break in the vegetation; they'd been watching us all the while. He chased them, calling the male 'Brother!' and demanding that he stop and talk to him. Apparently, he winded the ape-man, or else the female couldn't go any more. So the big male must have turned and fought and killed him, and then he returned to the clearing. He saw that crazy man trying to fuck me, and it must have put ideas in his head.

"That weirdo really thought he was you. And that he was king of the jungle and all that."

"He wasn't the first," I said.

A number of questions directed my attention from her monologue. Even if the man were one of those poor devils who had brooded so long about me they had become me in their minds, how had he found my tree house? And what about the body of the young Caucasian female which the others in the expedition had thought was Trish's? What about the story of the natives who said they had witnessed the naked man's raping and carrying off of Trish? And why had I been let loose by the Nine so near the house?

For the first time in this business, I began to consider seriously that I was being manipulated —or steered, at least—by the Nine.

Also, this sudden and compelling equation of killing with sexual intercourse could be a side effect of the elixir, and one expected by the Nine. Caliban had something similar and our father had been affected but in a different manner.

30

"Are we really trying to make fifty miles a day?" she said hours later. "In this dark and in this tangle? When do we start swinging through the trees?"

"When we weigh no more than a monkey," I said. "I know we can make that mileage. I've done it. Fifty miles in 16 hours."

She sighed wearily and said, "Doc could do it, too. But I don't know about me."

She was strong, and she was game, but the time came when I was half-carrying her. There were times also when she was sleeping while walking. Finally, I let her slump under a tree, wrapped her up in her poncho and blanket, and then lay down near her. I awoke with a start, as vibrating as a suddenly awakened animal, and had my knife ready to stab the intruder. I realized then that she was crawling under my blanket.

"I'm cold and lonely," she murmured. "I want to snuggle against a warm body, nice male flesh. Don't get any wrong ideas, you big ape. Besides, I'm too tired."

She fell asleep and began snoring softly. I don't see how she expected me not to respond, since my penis was jammed between her buttocks and, after a while, when she turned, against the hairy slit. But she was safe. Although her softness and roundness and warmth and woman odor were very pleasant, they did not have the normal effect upon me. I drifted off to sleep, thinking of Trish and of Clio, but dreamed of my foster mother, *kl,* the female of The Folk who had raised me as her own and as more than her own and whom I had loved as the only being worth loving.

I slept longer than I had intended. The sun was slipping through the arms of the great trees over us. I had to urinate, and, as so often happens in the morning on awakening, my penis was rigid.

Trish, awakening when I rolled away, looked down and saw it. Her eyes widened, and she said, "Doc!" and then, "Oh!"

What happened after this was not predictable. If I'd been asked what I expected would happen, I would have replied that I would rise and step behind the tree to avoid offending her, and would have urinated. And the piss hard-on would have been gone.

At this point I am tempted to discuss what is, to me, the impossibility of a "state"—such as a "piss hard-on"—appearing or disappearing. But I resist. Besides, my psychological difficulties with the English language, with all human languages, with the self-contradictory *Weltanschauung* of English, is described fully in Volume II of my memoirs.

I repeat. The expected—almost logical—course of events did not take place.

It was to be taken for granted that Trish Wilde would not be attracted by the sight of my erection. She was no nymphomaniac, as far as I knew. She had been through many days of extremely trying, even distressing, and exhausting experiences. She had been exerting herself on the first day of our journey to such an extent that she might well have preferred to die rather than get up out of bed.

Neither of us had bathed; we reeked of sweat, blood, and jism. I was a stranger who, though he had rescued her and offered her no threat, was still a mysterious and possibly sinister person. She had been in love with her cousin for many years. She had recently been the object of attempted rapes by a crazed man and a—to her—monstrous half-human. Hence, she could be expected to regard copulation with less than eagerness.

Moreover, she was hungry, her mouth must have been dry, and she undoubtedly had to piss.

And there had been no time for any warmth or tenderness to develop between us.

I could go on. I have made my point.

On the other hand, I did remind her of Doc (she was to tell me later). And the long love affair had resulted in much frustration for her. She had not suffered absolute sexual deprivation with Caliban. Although he could only get his giant penis into her somewhat small vagina by causing her pain, she was still able to have an orgasm. However, she usually substituted fellatio for coitus. This was to his great satisfaction, because he did not really like coitus. In the beginning, she had been excited by the act but had been left feeling unsatisfied. Then Doc had conditioned her, with much practice, verbal tricks, and some hypnotism, to have orgasms when she sucked on him. In fact, through his conditioning, she was able to have orgasms by manipulations of her nipples.

These climaxes were not, in some indefinable manner, as "satisfactory," even though they were often intense. She felt a craving for his penis in her womb. The other acts did not bring the "closeness" she felt when he was between her legs.

The other element making for a still unsatisfactory intercourse with Doc was that his own orgasms seemed to be too dull. He never "went out of his mind" or out of control.

Only now and then, when she "sucked him off, blew the fuse on his cock," as she so inelegantly phrased it, was he able to lose control enough to feel the exquisiteness he should feel. Afterwards, he seemed ashamed of the feeling.

All this I learned later, of course.

At the moment, she was aware of my erection, and yet she had been told I would get none as response to a woman. She thought her mere proximity had done for me what the active labor of the Countess Clara had not been able to do. She felt flattered.

And she may have felt that she was giving me something in payment for having rescued her.

Whatever the reasons, they impelled her to kiss me on the mouth and at the same time to run her fingers down my chest to the pubic hairs and then to close them gently on my penis.

It may be that she had been denied sexual satisfaction so long that she would have taken on any man whom she could respect. She was a very passionate woman, and she had not been entirely faithful to Caliban. In the beginning she was, but during the past twelve years, she had bedded a dozen men. This was one of the almost inevitable results of prolonged youth.

I thought of Clio, of the time I was wasting in getting to her, and of my unfaithfulness. I was out of the cavern now, and so our normal relationship was, theoretically, in force.

But my desire to find out if my normal sexual

responses were restored was too strong. I had to
know that I was not permanently crippled.

I turned to her and kissed her lips. Then I kissed
her eyes and her nose and the tips of her ears and
stuck my tongue into her ear and kissed the side of
her neck and so on down to her large, firm, great-
nippled breasts, where I stayed for some time while
I inserted a finger into her vagina and gently slid it
back and forth until she lubricated fully and
moaned and then had a number of shuddering orgasms. I then kissed her belly and tongued her
clitoris and the insides of her labia.

After that, she sucked on my dong, running her
tongue over its head. I hoped that the erection
was now due to her, not to retention of urine.
Certainly, I felt as if she were responsible.

Getting into her was not easy. I had to push,
withdraw, push again, get up and apply some medical vaseline from our medicine box, and get down
and push again. Slowly, the lips opened, and the
head went halfway in, and then all the way in. The
shaft followed easily after that. She kept her eyes
closed and several times groaned and clenched her
teeth. Truly, she seemed to have an organ the size
of a small ten-year-old girl's. (I knew this from my
internship while getting my M.D.)

I came several minutes after entry. Instead of
withdrawing, I remained on top of her and left the
semi-hard cock in her. She began to squeeze on it
with her sphincter, which was powerful and, seemingly, tireless. It was like a weak but loving fist
sending telegraphic messages. My peter swelled up
again, and I began going back and forth with her
legs over my shoulders and my hands around her
hips and under her thighs so that the tips of my

fingers caressed the edges of her labia. The second orgasm did not arrive until quite a few minutes later. I almost passed out from the intensity; I saw great red jungle flowers shooting up from green stalks, exploding in scarlet, and collapsing.

Tears came to her eyes. She had had a "flaming" orgasm, as she put it.

I said I was happy, and I kissed her. She responded warmly. Actually, I was feeling guilty. It was not being unfaithful that caused this. I have never—deep down—seen much sense in this oath of fidelity when a man and his woman are separated for long periods of time, but I had kept my word because it was my word. And would have kept it for always if I had aged as other men do.

I was feeling guilty because I had spent time in my own pleasure instead of traveling as swiftly as possible for England, where Clio *might* be in danger.

31

The rains started that night. We were miserable. Despite this, we slept well under the rain-proof ponchos and blankets. Trish was as worn out as an old knife by the grinding of the 16 hours of battle to get through the cold wet tangle of the rain forest. She ate a few bites and dropped off, snuggling against me. And in the morning, after we had eaten and rolled up our supplies, we set off. There was no more loving beyond an abortive attempt by Trish one afternoon when we had rested a while and the sun had come out. It was a failure.

In three days, as I had projected, we were out of the mountains and at the mining company airstrip. This was used to shuttle executives to the capital and back.

The executives and the pilot of the twin-engined Cessna knew me, but they refused to let me go on the next scheduled trip. I would have to wait. And one commented that I was open to arrest for being in Uganda without a passport.

I took the plane anyway. After knocking the pilot out and yanking the three executives from the plane, with Trish's capable help, I piloted the craft downwind, towards the north. A few bullet holes appeared in the fuselage behind us as we left the ground, and the radio bleated in Buganda and English, warning us we would be shot down by military planes.

I swung west. And 20 hours later, I was approaching the southern shore of England (Land's End) about ten feet above the sea. We were fully dressed and armed and I was flying another plane, a 2-motored turboprop craft. My connections and my good credit and name had secured the plane, gas, and supplies on the way. We were now entering England unnoticed (we hoped) and without passports.

Trish had demanded that we try to get into contact with Caliban while our plane was being refueled at an airport near Rabat, Morocco. I did not object. Caliban should know that she was with me. He would no longer have any reason to attack me or Clio. Or I should say Clio, since the Nine had decreed that one of us must kill the other. On thinking this over, I decided that the news that she was now alive would not reassure him. I had her, and he would not know what I planned to do with her. He thought I was mad, and he might think I meant to harm her.

I did if he killed Clio.

Or did I? I felt like it. Had felt like it, rather. But I now was very fond of her, respected her, and knew her as a human being. Moreover, I could not harbor the idea of revenge on Caliban through hurting her. He was the one I wanted to kill.

No, I could not harm her. But I could make Caliban think I would if he did not lay off of Clio.

So I made every effort to contact Caliban. I sent radio messages to London and Paris and I sent other messages via several underground organizations I had worked with during the war and during a mission for the Nine.

They reported back that no one had managed to find him.

This did not upset Trish. She had full confidence that he would get the message. He might have it now but had not replied, because he was often strangely reticent. He acted instead of talking. In fact, he might even now be on his way to Castle Grandrith to help me against Noli.

I smiled but said nothing.

As we passed Land's End on our right, she asked me a number of questions about our destination and its history. She had never been to the Lake District and knew little about it except that it was supposed to be England's "pocket Switzerland" and Wordsworth and Coleridge and Southey had lived there.

I told her that Cumberland County was in the extreme northwestern corner of England. The mountains (I would call them foothills) are remains of a massive dome-shaped earth movement which took place about 40 million years ago. The mountains were deeply cut by lake-filled valleys. The Cumberland County was one of the most densely wooded regions of England even long after the Norman conquest. The oak, ash, and birch were the principal indigenous trees, and sycamore and larch were common.

The earliest evidence of man there could be dated to the New Stone Age, about 2500 B.C. There were a number of "druid" circles of stone in the Lake District. There was a circle, in fact, on the estate of Grandrith. Looking west from the windows of Catstarn Hall, you could see the massive upright stone slabs on a hilltop beyond the castle. Looking north, you could see on top of a hill that huge and queerly shaped slab of granite which was called, for some reason, the High Chair.

There was a local legend connected with it. The people of the village of Cloamby say that when the two ravens come back, the old man will sit. No one seems to know what this means.

My ancestors included the aboriginals, of course, the short dark people who might have been related to the Picts of Scotland, which is close by, and to the Firbolg of Ireland. The Celts invaded the island and exterminated or absorbed them. Later, Romans conquered much of Cumbria, but their investment was mainly military. This area, until the 19th-century, was a back country somewhat aloof from the mainstream but not entirely. After the Romans left, the English Northumbrians held the country. The Vikings came in 875 A.D. and the majority of place names in Cumberland are of Norse origin.

An Eirik Randgrith, a Norwegian sea-king turned farmer, established a log-and-stone fort on the present site of the castle. This was near the small village of Graefwulf, which was destroyed 50 years later. The present village of Cloamby replaced it about thirty years afterwards. These events took place between 900 and 980 A.D.

Randgrith means Shield-Destroyer. Randgrith was supposed to have been a huge man, very strong, and given to fits of melancholy and violence. His grandson was presumably converted to Christianity, but the Randgriths were suspected of heresy for a long time. At least 20 of them over a period of 600 years were burned or hung for witchcraft. Despite this, the family managed to retain their lands and even add to them at times.

Cumberland was held alternately by the Scotch and Normans for a long time. In the 17th-century

Civil War, the Cumbrians were generally loyal to the Stewarts.

Sometime in the 13th century, Randgrith became Grandrith by a metathesis probably influenced by the Norman "grand." The name is now pronounced Grunith.

The family was always distinguished by a large size, great strength, and a tendency to mental instability and eccentricity. It has usually been content to keep to its own part of the country or to go far abroad. It has been conservative, if not reactionary. It had clung to the old religions fiercely, although often secretly. The evidence is that the family privately worshipped the old Germanic gods long after Cumberland was ostensibly Catholic, and that it remained Catholic long after Cumberland was ostensibly Protestant.

I told Trish that the Grandriths were related to the Howards and the Russells and the royal family, not that that meant anything to me. I told her the story that William II, or Rufus, the Conqueror's son, had raped a Lady Ulrica Randgrith, who gave birth to his son. It is recorded in the family chronicle (but a hundred years after the event) that Rufus was responsible for the gray eyes of the family. (This is, of course, genetic nonsense.) It is also recorded that Rufus was killed in the New Forest, not by Walter Tirel or Ralph of Aix, but by the brother of the raped woman.

While I talked, the sun set behind the Atlantic to the left. England became a dark bulk with a few scattered lights, which were actually large towns. Then I swung out towards the middle of the sea, still only about ten feet above the moon-sparkling waters.

I thought of my ancestors and their country. When I first came there as lord of Grandrith Castle, Catstarn Hall, and Cloamby Village, I had not known my family history. Or even the history of England. Later, after much reading and travel, I understood much more. Yet I have never been entirely at ease on my estate or in England. I feel as if I were born of African earth and have no ancestors. The past was dissolved when I gave voice to my first cry on the seashore by the equatorial jungle.

32

My agent, stationed in the forest near the castle, responded to my call. Trish listened in.

I said, "Any news of Lady Grandrith yet?"

"Nothing, sir," the man said. "All we still know is that she left London to come here. She should have been here hours ago and may be. There were lights in the castle for about an hour, sir, but I couldn't get close enough to see who was using them. The drapes in the hall windows are closed tight, sir. I can't see any activity there, but I get the impression that there's much going on."

"Have you heard from the other man?" I said, referring to his companion.

"No, sir. The situation is the same as when I last reported. He went to investigate the castle and the hall; he said he might knock on the door and pretend to be a lost traveler; I never heard from him again."

"Have you found out anything about the two strangers who were buying such large supplies of food and liquor in Greystoke?" I said.

"Nothing, sir. They left before I heard about them so I couldn't put a tail on them. If Noli's men have moved in, as we suspect, then they may have been his."

"Ask him if he's heard anything from Doc or anything about him," Trish said eagerly.

The agent said he had heard nothing, but then

he'd been out of contact with the London men for about 6 hours.

"Have you been able to look in the garage or the barns?" I said.

"No, sir. They're both still tightly locked and the windows are curtained. If there are an unusual number of cars in there, I can't find out without trying to break in. And as you said . . ."

"That's right," I said. "I don't want to let them know that anybody's on to their game."

His voice had not sounded quite right, but there was much static due to the storm approaching from Ireland. I said, "We'll be landing on the strip in approximately one hour. You be ready to cover us, because if Noli is in the hall or the castle, he and his men will come swarming out. We'll run into the woods and then plan our strategy from there. Signals as arranged. Four blinks by me, six by you."

"Right, sir. Four and six."

I shut off the transceiver. The man had not quite sounded like my agent, but perhaps it was he, and he was taking this opportunity to warn me. The signals had been three blinks by me and five by him.

I told Trish what I suspected. She said, "If they've got him alive, they'll get everything out of him. And they'll kill him when they realize he's tricked them."

"They'll kill him, anyway. And he's probably already dead. They must have gotten everything from him. That voice was close to the real agent's, but not quite close enough."

I did not, of course, tell her that the man holding Catstarn Hall and Castle Grandrith might be Caliban, although I doubted it. Noli had a head start on him. If Noli was there, then Caliban might be in as much danger as I. Noli would try to double-cross Caliban, and Caliban must know that. Perhaps Caliban was amused by this, and stimulated, since it made the odds greater against him.

I turned the radio back on. We were approaching a black wall, the storm from Ireland. The weather reports said that its front was now over Keswick and moving east. The rain was heavy with winds at 40 miles per hour. The plane bored into the blackness and began bucking. At the same time, I pulled her up, because I did not want to run into a vessel. At three thousand feet, I was picked up by the coastal radar, and the challenges started coming. I gave them a false identity, said I was an Irish flier blown off course. The identity lasted about six minutes. On receiving information from Ireland, the station challenged me again and told me to land or I would be shot down. I did not know how they were going to manage that, since I doubted they would send a missile against a small plane and no military plane would find me while the storm was progressing.

However, I pretended engine trouble, made a last-minute appeal, and dived the plane. The lights enabled me to pick up the sea surface just in time; even so we must have been licked on the under-fuselage by the waves. Surface vessels or no, I clung to a twenty-foot ceiling and did not pull her up until I saw lights. This should be Whitehaven, and from here on I had to maintain at least a five-thousand-foot ceiling. If the weather had been clear, I would have hedgehopped in. It was not, so there was nothing else to do. I could not help Clio—if she was not past helping already—if we smashed up against the Skiddaw or some other mountain.

"There's a small airport at Penrith," I said. "That's about 5 miles from Grandrith. The port doesn't have radar instruments to guide us in; we'll have to make a visual landing."

"And there's no visibility except when the lightning flashes," she said, peering through the rain at a massive upthrust revealed by a streak of whiteness. Thunder bellowed; the plane rocked.

She said, "Penrith. Is that name related to Grandrith?"

"No. Penrith is Celtic, one of the few Welsh place names in the Lake District. Grandrith, if you'll remember, comes from the Norse Randgrith."

She was trying to make small talk to cover up her nervousness. I went along with her to help her.

"Once we land," I said, "we have to move fast. There's no use in trying to convince the port authorities of a false identity. We'll just get out and into the closest available car and leave. If somebody recognizes me, I'll have to explain later."

She checked our automatics, my .38, her .32, the breakdown .22, six hand grenades, and a small crossbow. I wore a knife in a sheath back of my neck. She was similarly armed. In addition, she had a two-barreled derringer.

She put screwdrivers, pliers, and a jumper cable in the pocket of my raincoat.

"We could parachute down," Trish said. "The country is unpopulated back of your estate, you said. There'd be no danger of the plane crashing into a house."

"There are too many trees around there," I said. "Moreover, Noli will be looking for us to do just that, you can bet. And if I were able to make a landing on the road near Cloamby in this rain, you can bet that Noli would know it before we landed. He's listening in to the radar reports on us. He must have short-wave equipment. He'd have a car down on the road with his thugs and be ready for us."

"Then he'll have men waiting at Penrith for us."

"He won't know I'm going there until the last minute, if I have anything to say about it. He'll be able to send men then, but they'll be too late then, I hope."

"He may have figured out that that's the only place you *can* land," she said. "In which case, his men will be on the way now."

"That's possible. We'll see."

The radio reported that visibility was still zero but that the winds had dropped to 20 miles per hour. The airports in the entire county were closed except for emergency landings.

The military might be thinking like Noli and also have men waiting at Penrith. I did not tell Trish that; she was nervous enough.

I went by Keswick city somewhere in the blackness below and over the lower edge of the great Skiddaw Forest and probably over Burnt Horse and then Mungrisdale Common. The Bowscale Fell (peak height of 2306 feet) was beneath us, if I reckoned correctly and if my own radar was functioning correctly. Then I was over my own estates but could see nothing, of course. I had taken this route instead of going directly to Penrith because I wanted to throw both Noli and the military off.

I cut in again to the frequency on which my presumed agent had been operating. I said, "Start signaling."

He sounded nervous. He said, "Surely, m'lord,

you're not going to land here! It's impossible! You'll get killed!"

Noli and Caliban would say the same thing. Noli would want me alive for the elixir (unless Caliban had told him that the elixir could only be gotten from the Nine, and he was not likely to do that). Caliban would not want his cousin killed (if he knew that she was with me). Nor would he want me killed, since he intended to do that with his bare hands.

I wondered what the Nine would think if one of us died an accidental death? Would the survivor then have to fight the next candidate? Or did the Nine want one of us dead for some unknown reason?

I replied to the man whom, by now, I was convinced was pretending to be the agent.

I said, "What do you advise?"

"The airport at Penrith is by far your best chance," he replied eagerly.

"I think I'll land on the road into Mungrisdale," I said. "I'll get a car there."

"You can't do that, m'lord!" he said. "It'd be suicide! At least Penrith has landing lights!"

"Mungrisdale it is, anyway," I said.

However, I agreed with him. My plan had been to lure Noli or Caliban into sending men down the road from Cloamby to Mungrisdale and detouring them from Penrith until it was too late. If Noli was intelligent, however, he would send men to Penrith anyway, if he had not done so already.

I realized then that I was convinced that it was Noli down there. Caliban might be close, but he was only on his way to, not in, Grandrith. The time element made this seem likely.

I put the plane into a steep dive from five thousand feet and did not begin to level out until the radar showed that I was 500 feet above ground level. Actually, we were probably much closer. There was just enough visibility for me to see several hundred feet ahead. Since the topography varied much within a short time, our progress resembled that of a very irregular sine wave. Trish gasped once and then closed her eyes. A moment later, she said, "I'm all right now. I just put my fate in the hands of the great god Old Crow."

I did not have much time to indulge in conversation. Nevertheless, I said, "Old Crow?"

"Yes. When I was very little, I heard my father say, more than once, that the greatest thing in the world was Old Crow. In my child's mind, I thought that Old Crow must be a great Indian chief, like Sitting Bull or Hiawatha. Then I thought that it must be the Great Spirit of the Indians and that my father had a place reserved for him in the Happy Hunting Grounds. So I started to pray to Old Crow. Later, when I found out that it wasn't an Indian god but a whiskey, I refused to admit my mistake. A god was created in my mind, and it has stayed there since. And I am especially honored above all humankind, because only I have been admitted to the worship of the great god Old Crow."

By the time she had quit talking, we were close to Penrith. The radio was getting hysterical. Apparently the military had picked me up, and both frequencies, the port's and the military's, were screaming warnings, threats, and pleas at me.

I thought for a moment of crashing the plane on the Penrith golf course, which is a fairly large one, and parachuting in. I abandoned the idea at once, because I did not want to take a chance on killing someone. No, it would have to be the airport.

I dropped down fast, banked, and came in at the port as if I intended to strafe it. The lights suddenly became visible; I was coming in at the correct location and angle, though too swiftly. The lights along the strip were blurs, and the big lights on top of the control tower were diffused stars. I dropped the plane in from too great a height, not caring if I drove the wheels up through the wings. We struck hard but the wheels and gear held, and the tires did not blow. On the second bounce, I straightened her out and cut the engine speed and feathered the props more. The end of the runway still came up too swiftly, and I went past it, across the grass, and was able to stop it only just short of the parking lot fence.

There was no time to sit and gasp in air and take time to unjangle our nerves. We scrambled out with our bundles in our arms, opened them, put on the raincoats, stuck the automatics in our pockets, and ran towards the gate with the rest of the weapons in our arms.

The doors to the control tower and the passenger buildings were open; figures were running through them towards us, wildly waving their arms. The parking lot held six cars, none of them military or police. Perhaps they did not really think we would try to land there after all the foofaraw, or perhaps they had been delayed for some reason.

Trish used her pencil flashlight to light our path as we ran. We got to the cars well ahead of the people from the buildings. Moreover, these at first ran towards the plane; they did not know we were in the parking lot until a few minutes later. The six cars were a Hillman Minx, two Volkswagens, an MG, a Facel-Vega, and an Aston-Martin DB4. All were locked and none had keys in the ignition locks.

I smashed in the window of the Aston-Martin and reached in and unlocked the door. Then I raised the hood and, while Trish held the flashlight, went to work with screwdriver and pliers. It took only a minute to jump the wires, but by then we could hear voices, muffled by the wind and the rain. I completed the connections, put the hood down gently, and we scrambled into the car. At that moment, a pair of headlights swung around the corner of a building at the far end of the street which ended at the gates of the airport.

A man yelled, "Here! I say! What do you think you're doing there?"

Five men ran towards us. I put the car into gear and took off with a squealing of tires. Wet as the pavement was, the rubber burned. There was a pinging sound as we went through the open gates. A hole appeared in the windshield between us. I shifted to second. A second car had appeared behind the first down the street. In my rear view mirror I could see a pair of headlights come on in the parking lot.

Trish was busy taking the automatic from my pocket and laying it on the seat beside me, breaking open the .22, and assembling it.

Flames spurted from alongside the first auto heading for us. I began swerving but had little room to maneuver because the hundred-yard gap between us was narrowing swiftly. I was doing 60 mph by then, and the oncoming cars were probably doing

40 mph. It swerved away when I did. The driver had acted defensively; he must have thought I intended to crash him or was playing "chicken" and he did not want a head-on crash with an impact of 100 mph.

In any event, we both skidded. I compensated properly but the Aston-Martin continued to turn, moving forward also and spinning around its vertical axis. The other also turned. Like two waltzers, or ice-skaters, we passed each other, our fronts missing by an inch or so. As we did so, Trish fired her automatic three times.

She said, "I think I got one! A hand flew up and dropped a gun out the window!"

Our car ended its whirl pointed in the right direction, so I just kept on going.

33

The second car must have put on its brakes. It was skidding but the driver apparently got off the brakes in time to regain control. Jets of fire leaped from its side as it went by. And then we were past each other.

Trish, looking through the rear window, said, "The first car has stopped; it's headed away from us. So's the other one. They'll have to turn around. But the one that was in the lot—it's coming. Watch out!"

The warning was not for me but for the third car. Its driver had tried to stop it when he saw the roadway blocked by the two vehicles. He skidded and slammed into one of the cars, their two sides, right and left, colliding, according to Trish. The lights of one went out.

I took the corner with a minor skid, straightened out, and was on my way for a straight shot for six blocks. I had to go through the "Square." I was on A66, my immediate destination was A594, leading westward out of town. The six blocks were traversed with no sign of pursuit. Since I slowed down before taking the corner, I did not skid much. Several cars honked angrily as I flew by. I was splashing water on both sides as if I were a motorboat trying for a speed record. Pedestrians, hearing me at a distance, raced for the sides of buildings, against which they flattened themselves. Their efforts to avoid getting hit were successful but they could not dodge the spray. I could imagine the fists and the curses. They were lucky they did not get run over. And, for all I knew, the pursuing cars would hit some.

Just before I turned the next corner for a shot at the central part of town, two cars came in sight behind us. One had only a single headlamp working.

A policeman stepped out of a pub and blew his whistle hysterically. I kept on, and he jumped back into the doorway as a blanket of water rose to cover him. I almost lost control again rounding another corner and then I was two blocks away from Market "Square." Trish, leaning out of the window, emptied a clip at the pursuers. The lead car swerved, and she exclaimed that she must have shot the driver. But it straightened out and flames jetted in reply from both sides of the car. As far as I knew, no bullets struck our vehicle.

Then I was roaring into the "Square" but double-clutching to gear down. At the end of the "Square" a large white board sign with the word ARNISONS shone in my beams. I swung left and, again, could not keep from skidding. Fifty miles an hour was too much for wet pavement and such an abrupt movement. As the car's rear end described its arc, my headlights passed across the black letters on the white plate. A594 KESWICK. This sign was on a black and white pole on a triangle of cement between three roads. A watchtower stood on the triangle behind the signpost.

The beams swung past that and illumined the front of the Midland Bank, and the car's rear went over the curbing of the triangle and struck the road sign. The pole bent with a crash; the car slid off it and continued on down A594, past the bank and headed westerly.

I was lucky not to blow a tire or overturn. The pole must have damaged the side of the car, and I had been thrown against my seat and shoulder belt towards the right. She had been pressed against the door.

The first car to follow us was not as lucky. It was about 40 feet behind us and going, I estimated, at 60 mph. I don't think the driver was familiar with this town, otherwise, he would have been more cautious. It skidded, too, and went up over the curb of the island, completely bent the pole under it, and smashed broadside into the tower. Its lights went out, and I did not see it again.

The car behind it did not try to turn. It put on its brakes and skidded on down the street past the tower and out of sight behind the bank. However, it must have turned around swiftly, because a minute later I saw its lights a half-mile behind me.

The third car, which I presumed was driven by some of the airport personnel, did not appear again.

A594 bent slightly southwest out of Penrith and then, near the Greystoke Pillar, a monument, turned northwesterly. Between Penrith and the village of Greystoke was a stretch of five miles with only farmhouses on either side of the road and not many of them. The road was excellent, a Minister of Transport motorway. Despite the driving rain and wind, I was going at 80 mph and occasionally at 90. I traveled this fast only because I knew the road well. I was hoping that my pursuers had no local men among them.

Although I kept most of my mind on the driving,

I could spare some for thinking about the situation. Those men had fired at me with intent to kill, not just to warn. It did not seem likely that Caliban's men would shoot at me if he knew his cousin was with me. Moreover, Caliban wanted to handle me personally.

Noli knew where the gold was, or where it had been. He wanted the elixir, however, and he needed me alive to tell him how to get it. Or did he? If he had Clio—I felt cold then—he could get the secret out of her. And so there was no reason for him to keep me alive except for personal vengeance. But he knew how dangerous I was and may have decided to let the torture go for an assurance that I was no longer a threat to him.

If I was right about Noli, then he was double-crossing Caliban. Noli was not only trying to frustrate Caliban's plans for me, he was trying to kill Trish.

I began to think that Noli was not so intelligent after all. Didn't he realize that Caliban was extremely dangerous? Noli's actions were those of a man who lets two tigers out of a cage, both of whom want to do nothing but kill him.

I topped a hill then and looked across the dip to the top of the next hill. I saw, fuzzily through the rain, lights on or near the top of the hill. And, at that moment, the rain ceased. The wipers cleared the windshield, and I saw that there must be more than one car on the other side of that hill. Two sets of beams turned sidewise, briefly shone out past the hill, and were turned off. If it hadn't been for the rain suddenly quitting, I might not have known that two cars were turned broadside to block the motorway.

The car behind me speeded up. Either the men in it felt more confident now that they could see better or they were in radio contact with those ahead. I suspected that both were true.

I did not increase my speed more than 5 mph going down the hill. The pursuer drew up behind me, doing approximately 95 mph. When about 30 feet away, its occupants fired six shots, one of which put a hole in the window behind me and in the windshield. I jerked because the bullet burned the top of my shoulder. I asked Trish to feel under my shirt, and she said that I was welted but there seemed to be no blood.

After that, the car dropped away. This convinced me that they were in radio contact. By the time I was almost to the crest of the hill the car was only halfway up and still slowing down.

I took my foot off the gas pedal as I came over the hilltop. The hill ran at a 45-degree angle at this point. Bright in the glow of my lamps were the two barricading cars, only 180 feet ahead. They were in tandem with the rear of one off the road and the nose of the other sticking over the edge of the pavement. A hundred yards down, a third car was parked half on the road, facing us.

Nine men stood by the two broadside cars. Three were on the left beyond the ditch and holding submachine guns. Six were by the ditch to the right and holding pistols and rifles.

They began firing immediately. Trish crouched down but fired with her automatic at the men on the right. The hand grenades lay on the floor at her feet, ready for use.

Events happened so swiftly there was time only to react. I took the left side because there was more room on the wet clayey ground between the car and the ditch. Also, because there were only three weapons on that side, even if they were rapid-firing.

Gearing down, I ran at the left-hand car with my left wheels on the mire and my right on the pavement. I was crouched down as far as I could get and still see.

At this close range, we should have been riddled. But in the excitement and uncertainty, as almost always happens, the firing was anything but accurate. And the men must have been concerned about my crashing into them. Holes did appear in the plastic just above my head. Bullets whistled by. Something burning hit my neck. It was, I think, a deflected bullet that just touched the skin with its hot metal and then dropped onto my shoulder.

The three men with the submachine guns scattered because I could easily have slid across the mud and into them. They realized, too late, that I was not going to stop and let them shoot me and that I might be intent on running over them even if I got killed in the process. It was well for us that they broke, because if they had stood their ground they could have blasted us at point-blank range. I swung off the road onto the shoulder, there was a slight bump as my skidding rear struck the nose of the blocking car, and we were in the mud.

Just before that, Trish, with a coolness and precision that I had no time to admire then, tossed a grenade. She did not see where it struck, of course, but it must have been stopped by the wheels or some part of the car.

Our vehicle shot through the mud, towards the ditch. I geared down to first and we straightened out and slid close enough to the road for my right-side wheels to get back upon the pavement. I got back onto the road completely just as the grenade blew up. Trish said it exploded under the right-hand car, not the left-hand one, under which she had thrown it. It did not matter. Both cars went up in flames and smoke as their gas tanks exploded. Three of the men on the right side had run across the ditch to fire at us. They were caught by the outgush and set afire.

The third car, parked down the road on the right side, protected three men firing at us. Two men were on the other side of the hood, shooting rifles. A third was stationed behind the car and firing with a tommy. This, unlike the others, had tracer bullets.

We should have been skewered. But the explosions of the two cars must have shaken them up, even if they were hardened professionals. I further unnerved them by angling across the road, accelerating swiftly, as I aimed directly at them. The tracers hit the pavement to my right and behind us and then swung up towards us. I turned the front of the car away at the last moment, skidding again, while Trish continued firing with my .38. Just before the headlamps swung away from them, I saw one man behind the hood throw up his hands and fall backwards. The man with the tommy, thinking I was going to ram the car, which I almost did anyway, ran to the left, and my rear, skidding around, knocked him into the air and against his car.

Then we were gone with the fires lighting our rear for many miles.

Trish began to shake. She held on to me and cried a little. I felt a little shakiness, too, but it was caused by my exultation.

I rejoiced too soon. Somehow, the car that had chased me from Penrith got by the burning cars. And the car down the road was manned by the survivors. I had not gone more than two miles before I saw the lights of two cars behind me. They were overtaking me swiftly. These were not the sort of men to be easily discouraged.

So far, my gas tank was three-quarters full and the oil pressure and engine temperature were normal. No tires had been struck, even if, surely, the tires had been shot at.

I passed Bunkers Hill, a farm with a three-quarters castellated house. This farm, with another, Fort Putnam, further down the road, were the works of the Duke of Greystoke in 1780. The then duke was pro-American and a militant Whig, and he built the two places to celebrate the Yankee victories after which they were named. The sight of them made me consider, for a moment, asking the resident of Greystoke Castle for help. He was my very good friend, and I can count those on my fingers. Then I remembered that he was in Alaska. Moreover, I could not, no matter how desperate the situation, bring this sort of trouble on him. For other reasons, I had not contacted the authorities to help me. I was certain that Clio would be killed if the constabulary or other slow-moving and cautious authorities showed up at Grandrith. Delivering her had to be done with a sudden attack.

Another reason for not bringing in the authorities was the Nine. This was a private, or internal, affair, and there should be as little publicity and as much obfuscation as possible. Of course, if it would have helped Clio, I would have defied the Nine. I was becoming half-convinced that neither of us would be in any trouble if the Nine had not shaped events for their own dark purposes.

Now, what with the business at the airport, the crash in Penrith, and the burning cars on the motorway, the authorities would be busy soon enough and on our trails.

A half-mile past Fort Putnam, the two cars began to overtake me. I could not get the Aston-Martin past eighty now, which convinced me that the car had been damaged by bullets. Moreover, the two pursuers were doing 100 at least. They would gain more on me when I approached Greystoke, because I did not intend to enter it above 50.

A quarter-mile outside the small village of Greystoke the engine temperature began to climb. Steam was pouring out from under the hood now. The radiator had been pierced, and I could not go much further before the engine locked. I told Trish to be ready to abandon the car and to start running.

There was no one on the streets and no lights visible when we drove into Greystoke. The pursuers were out of sight, down in a dip. For several seconds I thought of cutting north, quitting the Aston-Martin, and stealing another vehicle. The road north, which runs on the eastern side of Greystoke Forest, is not even a second-class motorway. It is crossed north of the forest by a similar road which goes westerly to another road which would take me southerly on the west side of Greystoke Forest to the road that leads eventually to my estate. This road is narrow and winding but tar-surfaced. The route would be much longer than the other way, but it had the advantage that my pursuers would not expect me to take it.

However, they would just go on to Grandrith

and wait there for me, as they should have done in the first place. It was best to take the shortest route. I might be able to make my pursuers suffer more losses. The more opposition that was dead before I got to my destination, the better.

I would leave A594 in Greystoke and take the short-cut metalled road which paralleled an old Roman road and went by way of Barffs Wood. My pursuers could radio ahead and have a roadblock waiting for me at the junction of two roads, but they could do this no matter what way I went.

The road I would take out of the village met another running north from A594. This would take me past Berrier, Murrah, and Murrah Hall to a road which, in turn, would take me to my estate between the River Caldew and the Raven Crags.

As I sped into the middle of town, several things happened at once. The engine temperature indicator shot up. A door in a house by the road swung open and two men, dressed in cyclist's clothes, stepped out. I had been in the middle of the road but I swung to the right to avoid them if they were going to cross the road. I saw a huge object, perhaps 20 feet high and eight broad. It was draped with a tarpaulin.

Just as I steered right, my front right tire blew.

34

The tire may have been weakened by a bullet or when it struck the curb at Penrith. I did not apply brakes, of course, but wrenched the wheel to direct us away from the tarpaulin-hidden object in the middle of the square. The car skidded and shuddered at the same time and slid nose-first into the base of the object. We were thrown forward but restrained by our seat and shoulder belts. The car hissed as the last of the water poured out of her smashed radiator.

We could see nothing because the tarpaulin had fallen over us. We got out of our belts, stuck the guns and ammo boxes in the pockets of our coats, and also took the bundle containing the crossbow, the bolts, and grenades. I shoved the .22 under the car.

The cyclists, laughing and cursing at the same time, their North country accents even more thickened with liquor, were trying to pull the tarpaulin off us. Then they shouted with alarm and told each other to jump out of the way. Something gave a tremendous crash immediately before our car.

We got out from under. Our first concern was that our pursuers had not caught up with us. There were no lights as yet from their cars, but lights were going on in shops and houses by the road.

The thing under the tarpaulin had toppled over away from us, fortunately. For a few seconds I could not see what it was, and then when the lights came on and Trish's flashlight illuminated it, I did not understand what I was seeing. Then it became a configuration I recognized.

Several years before, a rich American aficionado of the author Edgar Rice Burroughs had proposed to set up in the center of Greystoke a giant bronze statue of Tarzan battling a gorilla. As any reader of Burroughs knows, Tarzan was supposed to be an English viscount, "Lord" Greystoke. The American had decided that a statue of the ape-man should be put up in Greystoke to commemorate his ancestral town.

Many natives of Greystoke objected for various reasons. Some pointed out that Greystoke was not the real title of Tarzan. The first book in the series admitted that it was a name chosen to hide Tarzan's true identity. Thus, the real Greystoke had nothing to do with Tarzan. The pro-statue people admitted this but said it made no difference. The statue would bring the town much publicity, since everybody knew about Tarzan, even if many did not know that Burroughs was the author who had created him or that Tarzan was a titled Englishman. The tourists would flock in and the village would prosper.

The "Lord" of Greystoke was consulted for his opinion. Laughing, he said he did not object. He was not Tarzan, but this statue was all in good spirits and intent and it would bring in money, if that was what the villagers desired.

The last that I had heard, the issue had not been settled. But here was the statue, now on the ground and broken in several places. Though bronze and large, it did not weigh much. It was hollow and thin.

One of the cyclists seeing us emerge cried, "Now you've done it! It was to be unveiled tomorrow noon, rain or no!"

The other said, "And bloody good riddance, too! I say the monster's a traffic hazard, right? Here's this poor couple running into it, and it not even properly blessed by the city fathers, God bless their drunken souls!"

"Don't talk that way, Arnie!" the other said, laughing.

I laughed; even though our car was wrecked, our pursuers might be on us any moment, and my stomach had a belt burn. If I survived, I would have another laugh in private with the owner of Grey-stoke.

The first of the chasers lit the end of narrow street. As yet, it was not on the straightaway.

I took out a number of bills, American money, and said, "You chaps. Here's over a thousand pounds. Will you rent me your cycles, immediately, no questions asked? Give me your names; I'll return the cycles later."

"No, why should we?" one said.

The other said, "This is very fishy, Tommy. Who're you running from?"

They weaved a little and stank of Guinness. I said to Trish, "No time to argue or bargain. And here come more people. Knock them out; get their keys."

We laid them out with chops of the palm edge on the neck. I did not like doing it, but we had to. I stuffed the money in the jacket of one, took his goggles off, took out his keys, and ran to the house outside of which the two cycles were parked.

It was not necessary to ask Trish if she could operate a cycle, because she had told me about her passion for them. The vehicles were BSA Lightnings, powerful brutes capable of 100 mph. We kicked over the motors, made sure that the bundle was secured tightly to the rack, thrummed the motors, and then tore out of the other end of the square as the first of the pursuers roared into the square. A quick backward look showed me that they would have to stop. There were too many people gathered around the statue, car, and unconscious cyclists. A policeman's whistle shrilled above the roar of our motors, and then it was gone.

35

Before we had gotten opposite Barffs Wood, the lights of Noli's men were a mile behind. Trish, who had been behind me about twenty yards, drew even and gestured at her fuel gauge. Then she held up a thumb and finger in an O. She was close to being out of gas.

She could transfer to my cycle, but the weight would slow us down too much. I looked behind, estimated how quickly the two cars would get to us, and indicated to Trish that we would stop just as soon as we got over the crest of a hill. As we dipped on the downslope, I cut my light and she followed suit. When we had stopped, I said, "We'll put the bikes on the road, both lanes!"

It was a variation of the roadblock that they had set up for us. The bikes were let fall on their sides, and while Trish undid the bundle in response to my quick orders, I punched the gas tank of my bike with my screwdriver. Then I dragged the bike ten feet this way and that and back to its original spot. Trish, meanwhile, had gotten out the crossbow, a small type with a handle like the butt of a pistol. It could be fired with one hand and had no great range but could bury the full length of its bolt in a man within sixty feet.

Trish ran to take her station on the right-hand side of the road in a grove of trees. Behind her, hidden by the trees, were the ruins of the old Roman road. The lights of the first car came up swiftly.

It was doing at least 90 mph. The second was about 8 car lengths behind.

As the first came over the crest, I loosed a bolt at the left front tire. The driver saw the cycles in the road before him; brakes screeched; the car began to skid; it struck the left-hand machine; and it rolled over and over. My bolt had apparently missed, but it did not matter. Its inclusion was a case of overkill, anyway.

I had dropped the crossbow, snatched out my automatic, and fired into the gas tank of my cycle. The tank exploded, and the fire spread out over the road. The second car was screeching as the driver pumped his brakes and swerved to the right side of the road to avoid the burning cycle. He struck the other cycle and was considerably slowed down. The cycle was sent spinning to one side, and the car kept on going. It stopped behind the upside down car. There was a silence and a motionlessness for a few seconds as the five men inside it stared at the wrecked vehicle, the two bodies thrown out of the road, and the four within the car.

I ran down the left side of the road along the ditch. Trish's automatic flamed twice from the trees. The car abruptly backed, its tires burning rubber and screaming. Then it shot along the left side of the road to pass the wreck, its right wheels on the pavement, its left in the mire.

The men in it were firing wildly in the general direction of Trish, whom they could not see. Despite this, she stepped out then from behind the big oak and tossed a grenade. It struck on the pavement in the path of the car. The explosion caused another screeching of brakes and a swerving from the road. Suddenly, the car was in the mire but still moving forward. It slid to one side, straightened as the driver fought it and then was back on the pavement. In the meantime, I had been firing at it and so had Trish. But it went on.

I bit my lip. We had lost all our transportation now the gamble had not paid off. I was hoping to get that car without wrecking it.

The lights of the car receded, then slowed, and suddenly they were no longer moving. I shouted to Trish to be careful, it might be a trick, and ran towards it. When I got closer, I could see those within silhouetted against the beams from the headlamps. The door by the driver's seat was open, and two men were pulling him out. He had been hit.

One man dropped the body and whirled. I fired, and Trish's shot came out of the darkness. He fell backwards over the driver's body. The other man was firing into the darkness with no idea of where we were. I shifted the crossbow to my right hand, aimed, and saw him throw the automatic up into the air and then double over, clutching his leg. When Trish and I moved in, we found that the bolt had gone through his thigh and several inches were sticking out in back.

I had intended to question him, but he died a moment later. A previous wound in the ribs, plus the shock of the bolt and more loss of blood, had put him out of our reach.

A voice speaking what I thought was Albanian was issuing from the car radio. It was questioning and, when no answer came, was threaded with rage and then with hysteria. There was no point in letting Noli know what had happened, so I repressed the temptation to crow over him. I turned it off and started to haul the other bodies out. Afterwards, we collected all the arms and ammunition from the other car and put them in ours. Two men in the wrecked vehicle were unconscious but moaning. I put them out of their misery with a slash across the jugular vein.

The truck of both cars contained flares, which I put on the floor of the rear of the big American car. They might have a use. We drove off at 11 p.m. The skies were still cloudy, and it was lightning and thundering again in the distant west, this side of Blencathra mountain.

36

Without incident, we drove all the way to the road at the foot of Raven Crags at the highest speed which the road conditions permitted. We kept a watch out for a copter. If Noli had one, he might send it off to find out why his men were not reporting in.

When we neared the fork of the road which led to the left of the village of Cloamby and straight ahead up the fell to Grandrith, we slowed down. I turned off the lights and poked along, because I suspected that Noli might have stationed men at the fork. A half a mile before the crossroads, I stopped at the bottom of a hill, and Trish and I proceeded on foot. This would delay us, but I was so sure that an ambush would be waiting for us I had to take extreme caution.

We circled through the heavy brush on higher ground. After intent observation, occupying ten minutes of quietly listening and peering, we found two men. They were on the north side of the road and a few yards below the fork. They were smoking, and, although they kept the flames cupped in their palms, I saw them. I also smelled the smoke. Reasonably certain that no others were around, I carefully approached them. They were on a slight eminence, screened by brush. Besides their tommies, they were armed with a bazooka. One had a walkie-talkie.

The road was only forty feet away; they could

scarcely have missed us if we had driven by. I crawled back to Trish and told her what I had seen and what we should do. Before proceeding, I subjected the woods to another intent scrutiny by eye, ear, and nose. It was well that I did. A third man was, fifteen feet up on the broad limb of a giant oak thirty feet behind the others. He had been stationed there, I presume, in case I was wily enough to do just what I was doing. He was facing away from them and had not seen or heard me because I am not one to make any noise in the woods. I found him because he sighed softly once and once moved his weapon against the bark.

It took some time to get Trish quietly into a position where she could get a good shot at him with the crossbow. I left her and crawled back to the tree. They were talking softly in English. One was born within the sound of Bow Bells and one must have been born in Germany near the Dutch border.

I said, "Freeze! Don't make a sound!"

At my orders they turned around slowly, hands on their necks. I got behind them, and they advanced towards the man in the tree. One of them, at my softly spoken command, told him to throw his rifle down and then climb down. When the sniper hesitated, I told him he was covered on both sides. I did not add that I would kill his colleagues if he disobeyed. I doubted that he would care about them.

They were tough men but also, by *their* definition of reality, realists. They gave me information quickly enough. I told them I would kill a man for each unanswered question or unsatisfactory answer and torture the last one. They believed me. Perhaps they had been informed of the failures of the others to kill me.

Noli had recruited them through.an agent, and they had been flown up here with ten men and landed on the meadow north of Catstarn. Others had come by car and on another flight of the big helicopter. There were probably thirty-five to forty men in Catstarn Hall and Castle Grandrith. Noli might not believe in God, but he certainly believed in overkill. Of course, he had Caliban to worry about, too.

Those of his men not Albanian—about half— had been paid $5000 apiece and promised another $5000 after the job was completed. That is, after I was killed.

Noli had told them they might have to deal with another enemy, a Doctor Caliban. But not if I was killed soon and they got away.

Where was my wife?

When I asked this, my heart was squeezing, and I was shaking a little. I expected the worst.

Their spokesman replied that she was holed up in the castle. When the copter had descended and the cars had come in in a two-pronged attack, she had fled to the castle with a rifle. She had wounded two men during her flight.

The castle was across the tarn from the hall. It had been in ruins since the time of Oliver Cromwell, but I had rebuilt part of it. The keep was massively constructed and built as a refuge for atom bomb attacks or an emergency like this. The great stone doors had been closed behind her, and she could not, as yet, be pried loose. Bazookas had launched missiles against it without success. Clio sat inside with an untouchable source of oxygen and plenty of supplies. She could be blasted out if enough powder and time were used, but Noli had quit trying. He was afraid of attracting the villagers. The five domestics were still alive but locked up in a storeroom.

This had happened two days ago at dawn.

The three men had been diverging, as if they were corners of a very slowly growing triangle, while I was questioning them. Perhaps they hoped that, since it was so dark and they were moving so slowly, I would not notice. Even if I had been blind, I could have told that they were moving away, since their body odors were getting slightly weaker.

I don't think that they would have tried anything if they had believed that I was going to let them go. But they must have decided that I would not dare to release them, since they could get to a phone in the nearby village of Cloamby or at a farmhouse on the secondary road and call Noli. It was possible that Noli had cut the telephone lines, but I could not trust them to tell me the truth about that.

One of them barked, "Take them!" and dived off to the left. The other two jumped for the right, one diving at my feet. There was a twang as Trish's crossbow cut loose. I fired four times. The top of the head of the man coming at me must have been blown off, because, as I later found out, my pants were wet with blood and brains. His head almost struck my leg as he fell. The fellow nearest me had his pistol out (I had suspected that they were carrying weapons under their coats but did not want to frisk them in the dark.) My second bullet hit him in the shoulder; his pistol flamed to one side;

he was hit two more times before he struck ground. The third, of course, had been pierced at point blank range with the crossbow bolt.

I made sure all three were dead by using my knife. Then we stood above the bodies, listening. There were no sounds, nothing to indicate that our shots had alarmed anybody.

I said, "Let's get back to the car."

We walked back, and then drove it up to where the men lay, loaded in the weapons and the walkie-talkie, and were on our way. The road was steep and narrow here and wound up and back and forth on the face of the mountain. At the top, it began to run through heavy woods, winding back and forth for a mile and then coming out on a fairly level stretch of 500 acres.

The tarn was a rough question mark-shaped lake about a half-mile long and two hundred yards wide. The castle was on the west side of the lower end of the tarn and the rather large chateau of Catstarn Hall was opposite the castle. The garages, servants quarters, and stables were north of the Hall. To the west, on a high hill, was the huge granite rock roughly shaped like a chair. This is the High Chair which I referred to before and which is connected with the enigmatic local saying. The original Randgrith is supposed to be buried by its base.

The walkie-talkie squawked as we drove into the woods, and a man said, in English, "Murray! What the hell's the matter with you? Report!"

Trish was driving. I imitated Murray's voice as best I could (I am an excellent mimic) and said, "Murray here. No sign of Grandrith yet."

There was silence. Then the man said, "Have you forgotten something, Murray?"

It was evident I had. I had forgotten to question Murray about passwords over the walkie-talkie. He had told me the code used for identification in getting into the Hall and the castle, but I had blundered in this respect.

So now they would be even more on their guard.

In the distance was a faint whirring noise. It sounded like a helicopter rising, and it was probably coming to investigate.

We abandoned the car after maneuvering it on the narrow road to face the other way. I left the keys under a bush near it. If we had to, we might be able to race away in it.

As I got out of the car, I heard another sound. It was quickly overridden by the chopping of the approaching helicopter, but not before I knew that a plane with propellors was nearby. Then we were in the woods, and the copter was hovering about 50 feet above the car, its searchlight poking around the woods. We made our way westwards. Through breaks in the vegetation, I looked for the plane. I could see nothing, not even a darkness flitting across the sky. I suspected that the plane was Caliban's.

Another storm was advancing towards us. The thunder and lightning were nearer, and the wind had increased.

The copter continued to fly back and forth, its beam probing. It did not have much chance of spotting us in the very heavy undergrowth. I have always encouraged the opposite of park woods in my forests.

We got to the edge of the clearing. A hundred yards across the lawn was the back of Catstarn Hall. Its three-story rambling Tudor structure was splotched with white in the blackness. It looked unlit until someone briefly opened a door. Light jumped out like a lion from a cage.

At that moment, a distant flash of lightning revealed a 2-motored amphibian descending from the south. It was landing broadside to the wind but had to do so because the tarn runs longest from south to north. It was crabbing to keep from drifting and also slipping in at a very steep angle. Its lights were not on. Apparently the pilot was depending on the lightning flashes for his illumination, and also on his radar for the altitude detection.

There were more lightning flashes. The copter abruptly turned from the hunt and headed towards the tarn. Four men ran out of the house towards another copter, a smaller craft guyed down on the meadow between the Hall and the stables. Murray had not told me about this copter.

The amphibian's motors roared as it straightened out and flew up from the tarn, only thirty feet below it. Two more lightning flashes showed two small objects streaking from the plane. One struck near the copter on the ground. The other hit the big copter in the air. The machine on the ground was knocked over on its side by the explosion, which ripped the guy wires apart. The big copter became a great flaming globe and fell on the roof of the Hall.

By the light of the fire, the amphibian returned and landed on the tarn.

Trish and I took advantage of the confusion to run across the meadow south of the Hall. We went about 60 feet from the house, which was emptying itself of men as if it were vomiting them. The entire roof and the middle section of the Hall were burning brightly.

I carried two knives, an automatic, the bazooka, two grenades, and two bazooka missiles. Trish carried a knife, an automatic, the crossbow and six bolts, and another missile. Our destination was the castle.

By the time we got past the house, the amphibian had waddled out of the water and was proceeding swiftly on its wheels. It raced away from the south end of the lake, turned, and sped towards the men by the burning house. Submachine guns from the men and a heavy machine gun from the castle battlements pulsed flame at it. A rush of flame and a loud explosion came from the battlements where the machine gun had been. Briefly, by the firelight, I had seen the missile as a dark streak.

But forty feet away from the first explosion, a red jet shot out, something black whizzed towards the plane, and the nose was enveloped in smoke and it jumped a little. Smoke covered the amphibian, and when it was whisked away by the wind, a big hole in the belly, near the nose, was revealed. One of its wheels was gone, and the craft was listing.

The crew must have scrambled out on the other side and started running towards the castle. Red flame winked again on the battlements, and the amphibian, taking a direct hit, blew up with a roar and a white fifty-foot high gush. Ammunition inside it continued to explode. Trish and I were knocked off our feet and half-deafened and, for a minute, enveloped by smoke.

We got up, and I shouted for her to follow me. Something whooshed by us and ripped apart the air and shook the earth from fifty yards behind us (or so I estimated). We continued on around the plane. Noli's men must have seen us by the light of the burning, exploding plane, but intermittently, because we were veiled by puffs of smoke. A glance showed me that a number were running after us. They had to give the plane a wide skirting, however.

Ahead, three figures raced for the main entrance of the castle. The portcullis was up, and the draw-bridge was down. The castle was surrounded by a moat which I had deepened and supplied by the tarn through an underground pipe.

The giant in the lead was undoubtedly Doctor Caliban. The two behind him were the old men, Rivers and Simmons. Each carried a small sub-machine gun and wore dark coveralls and black coal-scuttle helmets.

I did not know why Caliban brought the old men along. Perhaps he did so because they were deeply attached to Trish and wanted to be in on her rescue. Perhaps they wished to die with their boots on, fighting to attain some sort of Valhalla. Perhaps Caliban had had so little warning that these two were the only ones available and their aid was better than none. Probably, they came along be-cause of a combination of all the reasons I have suggested. I will say one thing for them. For men of 80, they were remarkably agile and swift.

The third bazooka missile from the battlements, coming at a steep angle, blew up the end of the drawbridge behind them and hurled them forward and onto the floor of the bridge. They picked themselves up and ran through the great arch below the portcullis.

I did not like to use my bazooka yet, but I had to do so. We were now the targets of the men on the battlements, and we had much more ground to cross than Caliban and crew before we reached cover. After loading the bazooka, I put it on my shoulder and Trish aimed and fired it. The explosion was ten feet below the spot where I had seen the rocket's jet. We ran forward with the hope that the nearness of the hit would upset and delay them. But their missile exploded on the ground about forty feet behind us.

I halted again, and loaded, and Trish fired. This time the missile hit about ten feet to the right of their estimated location and approximately a foot below the crenellations. The crenellations disappeared, and so did the bazooka men.

Meanwhile, our pursuers had rounded the plane, which had ceased to explode but not to burn. They began shooting at us. I turned with the bazooka loaded with our last missile and fired at the group. They threw themselves on the ground, and the missile went over their heads and blew up a tree on the edge of the meadows. However, they all jumped up and ran away behind the protection of the plane. I knew they would be back in a minute, so I threw the tube down, and we ran to the drawbridge.

We had to jump a gap of eight feet, which was easy for Trish even with her burden of weapons. A submachine gun in the battlements began firing at us. We got into the courtyard before he could bring his spray of lead around to catch us. The mob behind us, and the men above, were not all of Noli's forces. Explosions inside the castle told us that Caliban was meeting resistance from others.

I tried to raise the drawbridge, but the chains had been sawed apart. A head, silhouetted against the glare, appeared above us, and the short snout of a tommy poked out. Trish aimed carefully. The bullet screamed off the stone, and the head with-drew.

"Where's Doc?" Trish cried. "I want Doc!"

So far she had been as much aid as the best of men. But the time was to come when I would have to watch her because she might turn against me. That would not be, however, unless she got a chance to talk to him.

"We'll find him," I said.

We went through the closest of the nine entrances in the courtyard. This led up a narrow winding stair-case for four stories, at which point an iron-bound oaken door blocked us. Noli's men had used the other two routes to the battlement walls. They had not found the key to unlock this and had refrained from blowing it open. I turned the huge dragon-headed knob six times to the right, pushed in on it, and turned it three times to the left. It opened slowly with a slight squeaking despite all my stealth.

There were three bodies on the stones and three men standing. One was on my right and looking down into the yard, presumably for us. The other two were looking towards the flames. They were manning a .50-caliber machine gun.

We stepped out. I shot the man with the tommy in the back with my crossbow. The other two did not hear or see us. I reloaded and aimed just as one man turned towards us. My bolt caught him in the belly, and Trish's two shots carried the other backwards and against the stone wall.

I looked down at the bridge. The last of the men from the Hall was just entering the courtyard. I pulled the pins of two grenades in rapid succession and tossed them down on the bridge near the end of the gap. When the smoke cleared, a fifteen-foot gap existed between the bridge end and the lip of the moat.

Trish and I poked the dead men's tommies over the embrasure within the yard and fired blindly down. A storm of bullets chipped stone off and one knocked Trish's weapon from her hand. It fell down into the yard. I think they must have emptied the clips in their automatics and rifles and reloaded and emptied them again. They shot as if they had an inexhaustible supply of ammunition.

37

Somebody suddenly realized that they were short of bullets. He shouted an order. I peeked over the edge and saw several men running into the castle. One body was sprawled on the stones. I leaned my tommy out and began firing but had to withdraw because they were not entirely out of bullets.

The next half-hour was one of siege. Noli's men came up the two stairways open to them. I kept an eye on the one through which we had entered, too, because it could be blasted open with a grenade. We used very short bursts to keep them from coming up the two ways; they replied with torrents of long bursts. It was amazing how so many bullets were expended with, as far as I knew, no casualties.

There was also shooting in the other part of the castle, way off. Then, silence.

After a while, we were silent, too, because we had used up the tommy's ammunition and all but five bullets apiece in our automatic pistols. I carried the machine gun and its tripod to the top of one of the stairways and waited.

The time came when I wondered if everybody was either out of ammunition or almost so. Noli and his men had been forced to run out of the Hall so swiftly that they could only scoop up the ammunition handy. Caliban and the two old men had been forced to run from the plane with little chance to get much ammunition. The men stationed in the castle had supplies, too, but these were probably limited.

I had seen no evidence of anything except tommies, rifles, and pistols. I had the only grenade in the place, as far as I knew. Of course, everybody must have a knife. And there were the maces, bludgeons, spears, and battleaxes on the walls of various rooms.

I fired several rounds from the heavy machine gun down the stairs. When the gun ceased, seven reports came from below. Stone chips stung my back and bullets shrilled. Trish, at my orders, fired once down her stairway and got eight in reply.

"They're out of ammunition, Trish!" I yelled. "I'm charging them!"

I threw an empty tommy down the stairs. Three shots were fired.

Trish did the same thing and got two bullets. They probably had at least a few more rounds.

Someone shouted, "Noli wants us! He's got Caliban cornered! Caliban's out of ammo! So are we! But we got the numbers!"

It was a trick. Otherwise, why let me know that they were withdrawing?

Possibly, most of them were out, and the few who still had some rounds would be left on guard.

I crept down the steps, going slowly, with the .50-caliber held in both arms. Faintly, the shuffling of many feet sounded. Then, silence. Most of those below had departed, though it might be just to the next room.

I went back up the stairs and did what I could have done before if I had had a good reason. I told Trish to patrol back and forth between the two staircases while I was gone. With my automatic in its holster and a grenade in my pocket, and my knives, I climbed down the wall on the outside above the moat. I used the half-brick projections, a provision of some ancestor who had wanted as many escape routes as possible.

At the first window I came to, an embrasure so narrow I would have scraped off my skin if I had gone through, I looked in. The room had been emptied except for two men. Each was stationed on the side of the entrance to the staircase, and each held an automatic. I fired twice through the window. One did not die immediately, and he looked very surprised.

I had one bullet left.

After the silence of a minute was the sound of running shoes. The men stationed below Trish's staircase were coming to investigate. Some of them, anyway. Evidently they thought the two shots were from their colleagues, who probably had orders to fire only if they actually saw me.

They ran into the room and stopped short. They were bewildered. It was incredible, I suppose, that I could have come down the stairs, killed the two ambushers, and gotten out without the others seeing me.

My last bullet took one in the chest. The other two fired blindly at the window as they ran from the room. I went through, scraping skin off beneath my clothes and for a second not sure that I wouldn't be stuck. I ran to the dead men, and ejected their clips. Their guns were all .45's, so the ammunition would not fit my .38. From the three, I got six bullets for one clip and inserted it in a .45.

I called back up to warn Trish and then went up. She took the automatic and the crossbow, while I carried the big machine gun. I descended one staircase. Trish took the other. The two men were standing out in the hall between the two rooms and discussing what they should do. I fired at the stone walls at an angle to ricochet bullets at them without exposing myself. They ran away and Trish killed them with three shots. That left four rounds in her automatic and three bolts for the crossbow. I had twenty rounds in the belt of the .50-caliber.

It was inevitable that some of those who had left would return on hearing the firing. I emptied my machine gun down the steps and blew three apart. When a man stuck his head out through the door below, I threw the machine gun at him. He dodged back in time to avoid being hit.

"There must be more than one outside that door," I said. "We could go around them; there are at least five other staircases to the next story. But I don't like to have them behind us. I think I'll use the grenade."

I went down the stairs while Trish, from above, kept her .45 pointed at the door. She had insisted that she was an expert in using the big powerful weapon, but I have no faith in its accuracy, especially if handled by a woman who, though strong, is still not a strong man. I did not want to be shot by the .45 while she was trying to hit our enemies.

I listened a while and determined that at least three men were talking out there. I could not detect the odor of more than three, but the gunpowder was so strong I was handicapped.

"Jesus Christ!" a man said. "He can't have much

ammo left, even if he did get all the stuff from the blokes upstairs. I say we ought to rush him."

"Don't be a dumbshit," another said.

"Well, hell, if we stay here, he can go down another flight of steps and come up behind us. Or just leave us sitting here."

"Fine," said a third. "Let Noli and his bunch handle him."

"Hell, they ain't got any ammo left! What'll they handle him with?"

"We got all that's left," the first man said, "and that ain't much. Six rounds between us three. Don't waste no more."

"If they got more than we think they got, our goose is cooked," the second said.

"We could take off," said one who sounded like a Yankee. "Shit, this ain't panning out like it was supposed to. This was supposed to be a breeze, a pushover. I ain't seen anything like this since I was in the Congo."

"We took Noli's money, and so we're staying," said another. "Besides, if we run out now, we'll lose the other five thousand and maybe a hell of a lot more. There's that gold he promised us."

"How you gonna spend all that money if you're six feet under?"

I pulled the pin on the grenade, counted to three, and tossed it. It struck with a metallic sound. There was a silence, then a series of yells and scuffle of feet. I flattened against the wall, turned my head away, and jammed my fingers in my ears. Even so, the roar half-deafened me, and the smoke billowing through the arch set me to coughing.

When the smoke was cleared, I looked in. All

three were dead against the walls, their clothes and parts of their bodies blown off. Unfortunately, the explosion had ruined two guns, bending their barrels slightly and set off the ammunition in the third and blowing it apart.

38

The crossbow bolts and the remaining bullets were disposed of inside the next two minutes. We were on the ground floor and crossing the great entry room, lit by a number of bulbs in artificial torches in sconces, when a shadow fell across us from above. I jumped and whirled; Trish screamed. A suit of armor that belonged to my 15th-century ancestor, John Loamges de Clizieux William Cloamby, Baron of Grandrith, struck the floor beside Trish. She fired up at the dark gallery, and a shadowy figure ran along the hall of the gallery, hugging the wall as it crouched. The .45 was emptied, but a ricochet must have hit the man, because he staggered over and fell across the railing.

A man appeared at the far end of the entry room with a pistol in his hand and fired. My bolt took him in the shoulder and he whirled with the impact and fell. I loaded the crossbow again, while another man ran out from the hallway and dived to get the fallen automatic. He fired and missed, too, and I did not. That was his only chance, because the gun was now empty.

The wounded man was gray with shock. I said, "How many more ambushers?"

He stared at me with big pain-glazed eyes and said, "None. Everybody else is down there with Caliban and his men."

"Any guns among them?" I said.

"No. Noli let us have what was left because you

were still armed. He's got enough men to run over three Calibans and then some."

"Don't be too sure of that," I said, and I cut his throat.

Trish became even paler and swayed. "Do you have to do that?" she whispered.

"I don't want live enemies at my back," I said.

We went through three rooms and down a hall towards the rear of the castle and then down a tightly corkscrewing case of stone steps. This led to the dungeon, which was a huge room with a number of cells with iron bars, some old torture machines, and, in one wall, the stone door to the atom bomb shelter. The room was well lit by a number of electric torches in sconces and several batteries of lamps overhead. It was a dead end room. The stone door to the shelter was pitted and gouged with Noli's efforts to blast it open.

The room was a babel of shouts and screams and a chaos of struggling men. I paused a few seconds. The chaos became a pattern, fluid, but still a pattern.

At the far end of the room was Caliban. He was not totally visible because he was immersed in bodies. About 14 men were trying to get at him. Some were trying to get away, however, I quickly saw. They held knives, the butts of pistols, brass knuckles, and one had a mace taken from the wall upstairs. Some were armed only with their fists or were trying to use their feet or their hands, karate style.

The goal of their weapons seemed to be a whirlwind. He could not be halted long enough for anybody to get in a crippling blow or thrust. The flesh around him was a bag trying to contain one man, and when the man pushed, the bag swelled out on one side and collapsed on the other. His hands were a blur; they chopped, poked, and his elbows rammed, and his feet kicked frontwards and backwards. He did not seem to be holding a knife, but blood was spurting from stabs of his fingers. Shrieks of agony rose as he snapped wrist bones and fractured shinbones, crushed insteps, punctured an eye, tore an ear off, slammed a man so hard against three others that they all fell.

I have never seen a man move so swiftly or powerfully or skillfully. He seemed to be more of a natural force than a mere man. Yet, he was doomed. In a matter of seconds, a knife would go through a soft part or the butt of a gun slam into his skull and momentarily make him open to other weapons. Most of his clothes had been torn off, and he was splashed with blood everywhere.

There were unconscious or dead men on the floor around him. Eight at least. And six sitting up on the floor, too hurt to get up.

The two old men were halfway down the room, their backs against the wall. They were clubbing at the five men against them. Four men lay on the floor.

Simmons and Rivers went down even as I took stock of the situation. The slender Rivers succumbed to brass knuckles against his temple. The apish Simmons, bellowing as if he were enjoying the fight, fell several seconds later. A huge, black-haired, blue-jawed man stepped in just as Simmons brought the barrel of his weapon down on the head of a bandy-legged red-haired man. The huge man slammed Simmons on the side of the neck with the butt of a pistol. Simmons dropped his gun, and another man thrust a knife into the white-haired gorilla chest.

The old men were covered with blood, and their clothes were half-torn off. But they had given a battle of which young men would have been proud.

There was blood on the walls, on the floor, and on almost everybody in the room. Only Noli seemed untouched. He stood in the center of the room, his back to me, waving a long knife and bellowing orders, unheard, at those around Caliban. The men who had downed Simmons and Rivers joined the others. Nobody saw us standing at the foot of the stairs.

Trish, behind me, said, "Doc!"

"You stay here," I said.

I handed her the crossbow.

"One bolt only left."

I did not tell her not to waste it. It would have been an insult and a stupid thing to say.

I roared out like a male of The Folk challenging a leopard or defying a male of a strange band. I lacked the throat sac, but I have very powerful lungs.

That froze everybody except Caliban, who took advantage of the paralysis to twist a man's head until the neck snapped.

Nobody paid him any attention. Noli turned slowly as his bald head and face lost much of its redness.

I roared again and charged. Noli crouched with his knife up.

I don't really know what happened next. I did a bad thing, that is, a nonsurvival thing. I succumbed to my rage, to my desire to kill the man who had assaulted me and had endangered my wife.

I saw through a red shot with black. And I recovered my senses only at the end.

Why his men did not interfere, I do not know. Perhaps things went too swiftly. Perhaps they, who had suffered so much from Caliban and his men while Noli stood aside, wanted to see how he would handle himself.

They saw.

I had taken his knife away from him. I had ripped his clothes off. He was entirely naked. Somehow, whether with the knife or with my fingers, I had cut around his anus, and severed it from the surrounding connecting tissues. And then, while he screamed, I raised him with one arm by a buttock, while holding the end of his bloody anus with the other. And I shot him away with my arm, giving him a half-spin so until then that I had ejaculated.

Screaming, he soared. Every bit of adrenalin possible to my body must have surged through me, I threw him so far.

His intestines, approximately 24 feet long, trailed out behind him and then tore loose from his body.

He landed on his face and sprawled with arms out. He was still living, though gray with shock. His intestines were strung out on the floor behind him.

He jerked once and died.

I dropped the bloody end.

I had shocked even myself. I was not aware until then that I had ejaculated.

Since I had copulated with Trish, I had not had an orgasm. The several killings in between her and Noli had not, as before, resulted in ejaculations. I had been aware of semi-erections during them but had grown so accustomed that I had ignored them.

If I thought about them at all, I hoped that the aberration was weakening.

I knew now that my unconscious forces had been summoning up a store, and conserving it, for just this.

The ecstasy had been missing or I had been so overcome with rage that I was unconscious of it.

39

Nobody moved. They could not accept what they had seen. And, when their senses thawed, they began to realize what they faced.

They were eighteen effectives. Behind them was Doc Caliban and before them was someone who, at that moment, must have seemed even more terrible.

Caliban, during the scene with Noli, had been as stone-struck as the others. He regained his volition first and struck twice, once with a kick in the base of a spine and immediately after with a chop on the side of a neck. The eighteen had become sixteen.

Nine turned towards him. I charged the remaining seven with a knife, and the room became a melee again. My knife went into a belly, but I took a gash from another across my shoulder. A throat got the first two inches of my knife, and a pair of brass knuckles banged and bloodied my cheek. The third man to get my knife took it in the solar plexus, and then it was knocked out of my hand by a blow from the butt of a rifle. The hand was paralyzed for a minute despite which I grabbed a wrist with my left hand while kicking a man's kneecap loose with my foot, jerked, and tore the man's arm loose from his socket. I whirled him around and into the bodies of two rushing me. All three went down. I leaped past a mace—but not without being gashed—kicked one of the men getting up off the floor and broke his neck, whirled, and leaped at the man with the mace.

He swung mightily; I dodged back and then in, felt the mace crack along one shoulder, rammed into him, and carried him backwards against the wall where his skull was cracked. The mace was close enough for me to leap at it like a cat after a mouse and pick it up before the survivor could get it. He had a knife, but he backed away, and then flipped it up and caught it, adjusted it, and threw it. My mace was on its way; it hit the knife and both went off course. The man was enabled to duck the mace, and immediately thereafter he decided he had had more than enough. He tried to run away, but I caught him by the back of the neck and squeezed. His face turned purple, and he dangled at arm's length while I rammed him twice with my fists in the kidneys. When he was released, he sprawled motionless on the floor.

I whirled. Three of the nine were down. A man was stepping back, preparing to throw a knife at Caliban. Now that there were fewer to crowd around, the danger for Caliban was, paradoxically, greater. There was room to throw knives and wield rifles as clubs.

The man threw his arm back, and then he stiffened. The knife fell from his hand, and he was on the floor. I had heard the twang of the string and the zzzt! of the bolt. Trish had not wasted her one shot.

I was glad that it was gone, because I did not want her to have it when the end would come.

I charged in, ripped the ears off a man, and, as he turned screaming, chopped his ribs with the side of my palm. He fell forward, and I drove his chin up with my knee and cracked his neck.

Caliban had seized the wrist of a man stabbing at him with a knife, run ahead, turning the man, twisting the wrist so the knife dropped, and then stopped and pulled him over his back. The man cartwheeled through the air and slammed up against a wall.

Three were left. One charged me although I think he was more interested in getting by me than at me. I might have let them go but I did not think there should be anybody left who could testify about the events here. The man charging me was short but enormous of girth, weighing an estimated 340 pounds and with the short arms and legs of a champion weight-lifter. His nose had been smashed and he was bleeding from his chest. I ran towards him and kicked him in the belly. He went oof! as his air left him. Before he could recover, I broke three of his fingers and then chopped him again across the nose. Blood spurted from his nose and mouth. My knuckle drove his eye back into the socket, and my knee knocked him unconscious. I picked up a knife and split open the huge belly.

The other two had been caught by Caliban, who had smashed their heads together. They dangled at the end of each hand, while he held them by the necks and squeezed. When their life was gone, he dropped them.

Only then did I realize that he was wearing a metallic, razor-edged, sharp-pointed device on the middle finger of both hands. It was this that made so much blood spurt when he seemed to have barely touched them.

The only sound in the huge room was the labored breathing of Caliban and myself. Both of us were naked except for our shoes, bloodied all over, and bleeding from a dozen deep or minor gashes. The stench of sweat, blood, piss, and shit was strong, exceeded only by the not-yet-gone odor of terror from the now dead men.

40

Trish started towards Caliban. He gestured, indicating she should stay away, and said, "No matter what happens, Trish, you are not to interfere! Do you understand? You are not to interfere in any way until it's over!"

She shrank back, her bloody hand covering her bloody mouth. Her eyes were wide and fixed.

I backed away because I wanted a little time to try to bring him to his senses. He followed me, stalking like a huge bronze-skinned tiger.

"Caliban," I said, "*there* is your cousin. *Our* cousin. Alive and safe. She will tell you I had nothing whatsoever to do with her abduction. Or her rape. On the contrary, I saved her. Ask her! She will tell you what a terrible mistake you have made."

I did not care that the Nine had decreed that one must bring back the head and genitals of the other. In that moment, I had made the decision that I was no longer a servant of the Nine. I was their enemy, even if it meant losing immortality. I could no longer pay the price. Faust, you might say, wanted his soul back.

He said nothing but moved closer. Then he stopped and removed the finger-ring-knives and his shoes and socks. He wanted us to meet, naked and bare-handed, fighting as two males of The Folk fought for the chieftainship.

"Caliban," I said, "do not misunderstand me. I would never plead for myself. But I do not want us to be the tools and playthings of the Nine. I believe that the Nine have done us great evil for their own cryptic reasons. They arranged for Trish to be abducted by the man pretending to be me. They arranged for the body of a woman to be found, and they probably had her killed just for that reason. The Nine probably had something to do with the Kenyans' attempt to obliterate me. You know what enormous, if invisible, power they have.

"Listen! I am convinced that my own birth, in its very extraordinary circumstances, was due to the Nine's machinations. There are some very puzzling things in my uncle's diary. I think he was the victim of the Nine, and that I am the result of an experiment by the Nine. I think that they arranged that I should be adopted by a female of The Folk and raised as a wild boy in the jungle among the sub-humans.

"I am convinced that their designs have been even deeper. I think they had something to do with the madness of our father."

Trish gasped and said, "Your *father? Your* father?"

I moved a step backwards. Caliban advanced by one step. His great hands, seemingly muscled with bridge cables beneath the glistening red-brown skin, were out and half-clenched. He was saying, as he had said on the natural bridge over the chasm, "No judo or karate or tricks. Power and speed only. We shall see who is the strongest and swiftest."

I wondered if he had heard anything I had said. I refused to back any more. I waited.

I said, "Caliban, you haven't read the Grandrith family records. Your family's record. You don't know of the mystery surrounding our paternal grandfather, do you? He shot himself at the age of 55. He looked as if he were thirty. He had three sons, but his wife, when she was very sick and thought she was dying, told an aunt that her husband had been sterile. The aunt wrote this in a diary in a code, which I cracked easily. The aunt said that she suspected a very tall, very powerful, very handsome but elderly gentleman from Norway who visited them quite frequently. The aunt wrote that she would think her suspicions insane, because the old gentleman looked as if he were over 90. But he had a very strong personality, a strange, compelling, and sometimes repelling, radiation. Radiation is the word she used, I suppose, to communicate an outpouring of psychic strength. And she knew that he had seduced one of the maids in the wine cellar. The maid testified to that.

"The old gentleman, a Mister Bileyg, had a white beard that reached to his navel, and a patch over his right eye. And he was the biggest boned man she had ever seen."

Caliban frowned and said, "What are you talking about, Grandrith?"

"That man was our grandfather," I said. "The evidence may be peculiar, to say the least. It wouldn't stand up in court. But it tells the truth. Our grandfather was one of the Nine! The man we knew as XauXaz! Which, if you know your Primitive Germanic, means the High One!

"And the name he used when he visited Grandrith was Bileyg. That's Old Norse for One-Whose-Eye-Deceives-Him. Which is to say, One-Eyed!"

"What?" he said. Apparently, his reputedly wide and deep knowledge did not encompass Germanic linguistics. Or Germanic mythology.

"The man we knew as one of the Nine, XauXaz, must have been born in the Old Stone Age," I said. "I don't know how old he was. Perhaps 30,000. Perhaps 20,000. Who knows what his history was? At one time, he and two others, perhaps his brothers, who were also part of the Nine that then existed, went to lower Sweden. They were present when the Ursprache, the parent language of the Indo-Europeans, changed to what we call Common Germanic. The dialect that became the ancestor of all the Germanic tongues of today, English, High and Low German, Norse.

"In some way, perhaps because they had lived so long and knew so much, they became gods. Not actual gods, you know, but they were worshipped as such.

"What I'm saying is that XauXaz and Ebnaz Xau-Xaz and Thrithjaz—who died before we came— along—High, Equally High, and the Third, were the old Germanic male trinity, later accounted as brothers. And, by the way, Iwaldi, that dwarf, gnome, or whatever, was contemporary with them. And he ruled his people, who dug deep into the earth and lived underground.

"Common Germanic died out, of course, but the three continued to speak it among themselves as a sort of code. Sometime in man's history, they ceased to appear among men as gods. They shucked their role and retired to whatever identity the Nine required of them."

Caliban shook his head as if he were wondering about my sanity.

I said, "Our father got the elixir from the Nine. He was a Servant, as we are. As I was," I amended. "And then the same thing happened to him that happened later to us. The side effect of the elixir is to make the user mad, if only for a short time. Its effect is psychic, as well as physical. Something deeply disturbing, no matter how repressed, ruptures the surface, thrusts up from under. The particular form of the psychosis depends upon the character of the particular individual, of course.

"Take me, Caliban, or should I call you Doc, since I'm your brother? Take me. I had always thought my attitude towards killing was very healthy. And I'd always thought my attitude towards sex was extremely healthy. But somewhere in me was a linkage between the two. Something in me equated the act of coitus with killing, the thrust of the penis with the thrust of the knife, orgasm with *the bliss of the knife,* as Nietzsche called it.

"And take you, Doc. Brother. You have always, up until now, with one fatal exception, avoided killing. You never did it even to those most deserving being killed, if you could possibly avoid it. But you wanted to kill, Doc. And you equated coitus with killing. Down there, deep down there.

"And take our father, Doc. He went mad and was locked up in the castle. And he got loose and fled to London to hide in the big city. There his psychosis took the form of the grisly murders of prostitutes. Why, I don't know.

"He raped my mother. Which is why I was born. Later, he went to America. Something happened, the tide of evil reversed, siphoned off, as it were. He took the name of Caliban and devoted his life to good. Trying to make up in some measure for what he'd done in England, I presume.

"Note the name Caliban. Another name for a savage. Shakespeare's monster in *The Tempest,* and a literary archetype of the savage. An anagram of cannibal. It was to remind our father of what he had been.

"He raised you to devote your life to good. You were trained to become a superman of good. You were taught to hate evil and to fight it. But you were to love the evil-doer, not hate him. Hate the sin, not the sinner. Which is an extremely difficult, perhaps almost impossible, thing to do. This attitude has to lead to all sorts of conflict.

"You took a super-Boy Scout oath. You were reared by our father to be a physical and mental Ubermensch, though the development would not have been so successful if you had not been genetically superior. You have the bones and muscles of an Old Stone Age man because your grandfather *was* an Old Stone Age man.

"I suspect that our family is rather inbred, or at least has had more than a number of Paleolithic fathers and mothers. How do we know how many times Grandfather XauXaz, or his brothers, dropped in to resupply the archaic genes? Castle Grandrith may have been the Three's breeding farm.

"And you, Doc, like me and a number of others, were approached by the Nine. And you sold your soul, as we all did, for immortality."

"What soul?" Caliban said. The sneer was in his voice; his face had adopted its customary expressionlessness. But his green, gold-flecked eyes looked peculiar. I could not tell whether they were doubtful or murderous.

"A manner of speaking," I said. "You know well what I mean."

"You really think, then, that our grandfather, who may also be our great-great-grandfather and great-great-great-ancestor a number of times over, was the man-god known to the primitive Germanics as Wothenjaz and to later Germanics as Woden or Othinn or a dozen other names?"

"Yes," I said. "And I believe that the Nine are keeping the seat of our dead grandfather in the family. They made sure we would be trained to be what we are. Perhaps, I am their Wild Man of the Jungle candidate and you are their Man of the Metropolis candidate. It pleases them to pit us against each other. Perhaps, in the Old Stone Age, it was brother against brother in the ceremonial battle to the death for the chieftainship. Who knows? But they don't care who gets killed."

"I think you're trying to talk me to death," Caliban said.

Trish called, "Doc! Listen to him! He makes sense!"

"Not to me he doesn't," Caliban said in a low voice. "And even if he did, one of us has to die."

"I'm not fighting for a seat at the table of the Nine," I said.

He grinned slightly and said, "You're giving up?"

"I've eaten their shit long enough," I said. "I think our father decided that, too, and they killed him."

"I tracked down his murderers," Caliban said. The green-and-gold eyes seemed to pulse. "I did not kill them but I turned their traps for me against them, and they died. If I had to do it again today, I would kill them with my bare hands."

"How do you know they weren't agents of the Nine?" I said.

He had been inching forward now. He halted, and he shuddered. His bronze face, where it wasn't splashed with blood, had darkened with fury. His face twisted as if it were metal under great heat.

"You lie!" he screamed.

His penis rose so swiftly it looked as if it were being hauled up on a string. It swelled like a cobra, the blue veins pulsed, and the great red glans glistened.

I knew then that there was no talking him out of it. The fight was inevitable. I knew this deep down, and, perhaps, I had hoped deep down that it would take place. Whatever my true hopes, my penis rose also, though more slowly, and when fully erect, it looked pale and small against his.

He watched the organ swell and then he said, "I'm going to tear your balls and cock off, big brother!"

He sprang forward, swiftly as a tiger, and lashed out with one hand at my testicles. The other went up to catch whichever hand I extended for defense.

41

I intercepted the hand and without flinching, which he had hoped I would do so he could throw me off balance if he missed my genitals. He came up swiftly then, though I almost threw him over, because he was crouched to one side and so off-balance.

We were again in the stance we had had when on the bridge. He glared down at me, six foot seven against my six foot three and his 300 pounds against my 240. I am a big wide man, thick-boned as a Cro-Magnon, as I have said, and greatly muscled, but my proportions are such that I do not look like a shot-putter. Alone, with no other humans by me for comparison, I look more like the Apollo Belvedere, although somewhat more broad-shouldered and deep-chested.

Caliban's proportions were also such that he did not look so massively constructed if he stood alone. But next to me, he seemed to be muscled with pythons. And I'm sure that we looked to Trish like a male African lion straining against an American mountain lion.

For what seemed minutes, we strained against each other. Both of us were bleeding from a dozen wounds and profusely from several. We had become weakened by the loss of blood and the energy expended. Our breathing was labored.

We strove. And then, slowly, oh, so slowly, but steadily, his arms were pushed back. His eyes widened slightly, and he breathed more harshly.

The muscles of neck, shoulders, chest, and arms ridged. Blue veins pushed up the sweating bronze skin on his temples.

He bent forward and caught my nose in his teeth and bit. I jerked it out of his teeth, but it cost me a pain that seemed to run through my nose and split my brain. It shot down through the pit of my belly and down my legs, as if it were a streak of lightning. Part of it was torn off, and blood spurted.

Somehow, he jerked one hand loose and grabbed my testicles. It was done quickly, as savagely and powerfully as the swipe of a tiger's paw. Another sear of pain struck, like a spear head, between my legs. I screamed then, and I reacted half-unconsciously. We both were standing there with each other's ripped-off testicles in our hands.

Blood spurted from the torn skin and veins and arteries between his legs. I felt a warmth shooting down my leg but did not look down because that would have been fatal. There was not much time left before I became weak with shock and pain, and loss of blood.

I cast his testicles in his face and leaped. He dropped mine and tried to grab both my hands again, but this time I caught one of his hands and with the other made my own swipe. The penis, amazingly, was still huge and hard, though it was deflating. It twisted like a spigot in my grip; he screamed; I yanked with all my strength; the flesh tore like a piece of silk; the member, spurting blood at one end and jism at the other, was in my hand and before his face.

I dropped it; he stepped forward as if to pick it up. Then I was on his back and had a full-Nelson on him. He fell forward and crashed upon his face. The wind went out of him.

Despite this, he still had enough vitality to resist my pressure. His neck muscles became as hard as wood. I could feel my own strength flapping away, like a sick bat into the night.

Yet, my penis was still hard and throbbing. It was up against his buttocks, which also felt as hard as oak.

I applied pressure with my hands against the back of his neck in a surge, knowing that if he could withstand that, he might yet win. Blackness was closing in on the edges of my consciousness.

His skin began to gray, even as the bones of his neck creaked like a ship's mast against the force of the wind.

I heard, faintly, a cry of protest from Trish. Caliban grunted once as if he were trying to force something out from him. His neck bent, and then the bones snapped.

I spurted over him with only a vague awareness of it. The black rushed in as the fluid rushed out, and shortly thereafter I cared as little as Caliban about the world.

42

The awakening was partial and blurred. I felt some pain, though it was everywhere, but so little that I realized—later—that I was drugged. The lights overhead were high and hexagonal. Dimly, I knew I was in bed in the atom-bomb shelter.

"Clio," I said but could not hear myself say it.

A head, framed in a bronze halo, blacked out the lights. It was smiling and weeping at the same time.

"Trish," I said. "Where's Clio?"

Another head, haloed in gold, appeared beside the bronze.

It leaned down and kissed me.

"Go back to sleep, dear."

I obeyed.

When I awoke again, I was still drugged. The pain had increased, however. It was wired throughout my body but centered from beneath my penis.

I turned my head. I *was* in the shelter. It was 80 feet wide, 60 long, and 30 high. Portable screens divided it into rooms, with the exception of a cement-block cube which housed the fuel cells and the converters. The air system was based on that used in manned space craft. There were supplies enough to last us six months. I had been against building it because we were so seldom in England. Clio had insisted that we construct it, and now I was glad that she was so stubborn.

I had many questions, but I asked first, in a weak

voice, if she was all right. She told me to keep quiet and eat. She spoon fed me, and then I felt strong enough to put some questions to her. She began a lengthy account, during which, despite my intense curiosity, I fell asleep again.

On awakening the third time, I found Clio gone and Trish taking care of me. She said my wife had left the shelter to talk to the contractors about rebuilding Catstarn Hall.

I said, "I'm sorry, Trish. I tried to talk some sense into him. You heard me."

"I heard," she said. She shuddered. "I hope I never have to go through anything like that again if I live to ten thousand."

"Have you been contacted by the Nine yet?" I said.

She started and then said, slowly, "Yes. In the first place, we would have had worldwide publicity about this if the Nine hadn't pulled the strings of some highly placed puppets in the government. They clamped down on all reporters and police investigations, claimed security demanded it, and that was that. Oh, yes, the servants were told to be quiet, and threatened with severe penalties if they talked."

"The bodies?"

"We took care of . . . you . . . set up the intravenous and the blood. I didn't know Clio had had some medical training. Without her I'd have been lost. Then I drove like hell to Keswick and got Doctor Hengist, who is one of us. He'd already phoned to Whitehall before I got there. I'd phoned him I was coming. There were soldiers up here on the heels of the people from Cloamby and Greystoke."

"All those bodies," I said.

"The three of us worked like mules. We dragged every one of the bodies, except for those in the hall, of course, every one of the bodies outside and in here into a room in the castle and shut it up. That included dear old Jocko and Porky, too, but we'll give them a decent burial later, out on the hill by that big boulder. They'd like that."

There were tears in her eyes. For a moment, I did not realize that she was talking about the two old men.

"We washed off the blood as well as we could and covered up what wouldn't come off. Some high muckamuck is supposed to fly up here and make a complete report for the government, but he hasn't shown up yet. We'll tell him that a gang of criminals tried to kidnap us so they could force the location of the gold, which is nonexistent, of course, from us. We'll hint that the whole thing was a Communist plot. The only bodies for him to look at will be those in the crashed copter and in the ashes of the hall."

"What about the cars and the men on the road?" I said. "And the landing at Penrith, and so on?"

"We don't know anything about that."

She hesitated and then said, "We found out— we weren't officially notified—that one of the Nine is coming, too. One of Doc's friends dropped in— he's important enough to get through the military cordon—and he told us we're going to get a surprise visit."

"What about it? Why so alarmed?"

Clio entered then. I said, "What's so frightening about this visit from the Nine?"

"Who's scared?" she said.

"I've lived with you long enough to know you," I said. "Besides, I can smell the fear from both of you."

"Oh, Jack!" Clio said. "We were going to wait until you were stronger before we told you! But there's really not time now to put it off!"

Trish said, "Doc is alive!"

43

It was a shock, but I felt glad. Perhaps, now that he was alive, he would have felt the same sense of the madness drained off which I had experienced. The third time I awoke, even with the pain, I felt an exultation. This resulted, not from the inflooding of sensation but from the departure of a sensation. I *knew* that the physical linkage between my sexual behavior and killing was gone. It was as if I were a bottle uncorked and turned upside down and emptied of a black stinking decayed fluid.

The shock of being castrated by Caliban may have done it. And perhaps—I hoped it was so—the shock of what I had done to him had had a similar effect on him.

I would not be absolutely certain that I was back to normal until my testicles had regenerated. That should not take much longer than the month required after the ritual excision of one testis. And it should take much less time than the six months required to regrow my right leg below the knee. I had lost this when the RAF bomber of which I was pilot crashed after a mission over Hamburg.

Trish said that Doc was sleeping on a bed behind a screen at the other end of the room. He would live. That is, until the Nine found out he was not dead.

"Doctor Hengist could not believe that Doc was still breathing. He said that he would have to die soon. It was just as well, because the Nine would not let him live. Neither Clio nor I knew that the Nine had decreed you two must fight to the death."

Trish began to cry. She said, "It's wrong—evil —to have to murder each other. And it's hideously evil that the Nine can now say that Doc will have to be put out of his misery. Or that you two should have to fight again after you get back on your feet."

"I was weak once," I said. "I accepted the gift of immortality because the price seemed worth it. Not now. I intend to fight the Nine. But we have to be cunning until we are able to run."

"That's what Doc said," Trish cried, "when he was able to talk for a short time. Listen! Don't worry too much about losing the elixir. Doc has been working for thirty years on it. He couldn't get any samples of the elixir, of course, because the Nine controls it so rigorously. But he figured out that our tissues must be saturated with the elixir. Two years ago he cut off his own fingers and managed to isolate the elements of the elixir. He still hasn't been able to synthesize them correctly, but he says that it's only a matter of a short time until he will be able to do so."

"Is Caliban in good enough shape so that he could dispense with Hengist's services?" I said. "Could you and Trish take care of him, with remote-control advice from me? When I can get out of bed and take a look at him, I'll take over the active doctoring."

She nodded, and I said, "Very well. Wheel him into the room behind the fuel room. Hengist doesn't know about that, does he?"

Trish said, "I didn't know about it, either."

"When Hengist next comes, you tell him that Caliban died. He'll want to know where, because I am supposed to bring his head and genitals to the Nine."

Trish and Clio winced.

I said, "The Nine will have to be satisfied with what they can get. You tell Hengist that you two sunk Doc in the moat. If he insists that Doc be pulled out of the moat, then we're in for it. Knowing the Nine as I do, I imagine that they'll have to have positive evidence that he's dead. We may have to buy some time with an accident for Hengist or whoever acts as agent for the Nine."

"Oh, Jack!" Clio said. "*More* killings?"

"If we're going to resign from the ranks of the immortals, we will do it now," I said. "And we'll have to drop out of sight swiftly. You know that's increasingly difficult in this ever-narrowing world."

Trish and Clio left to wheel the sleeping Doc into the hidden room. An hour later, Hengist entered. He did not seem surprised that Caliban had died. Nor did he say anything about recovering the body. The next day, however, he notified us that the visit from one of the Nine had been cancelled. An agent, a Sir Ronald Hawthorpe, would bring me instructions and also interrogate me.

After he left, I tried to walk into Doc's room, but the pain between my legs discouraged this. I allowed Clio to wheel me in beside his bed. He was lying there with a stiff plastic collar around his neck. Clio had done a professional job in doctoring his broken neck. He was flat on his back and staring up at the ceiling. Tears formed pools with a deep golden-green bottom in his eye sockets, and tears ran down his cheeks. Trish was crying also, but at the same time she was smiling.

"He hasn't wept since he was a little child," she said. "Not even when his mother died or his father died, did he weep. He must have an ocean down there, and I thought it would never come. Oh, I'm so happy!"

If he did not stop crying, she would not be so happy. He could be suffering a complete breakdown, or he could be on the road to a healthiness he had never had.

I said, "Doctor Caliban, why are you crying?"

He did not answer. I waited a while and then repeated my question. After another long period of silence, he said, in a choked voice, "I am crying for Jocko and Porky and for the other wonderful friends I had. I am crying for many people, for Trish especially, because she loves me and I gave her almost nothing back. And I am crying most of all, and I cannot help it, for me."

Clio, always ready to be triggered with empathy, sniffled.

I said, "Then you must feel as I do, that you've suffered a strange sea-change, as it were?"

"I have," he said.

"Perhaps," I said, "we may be doing the Nine an injustice. Perhaps they knew that we would be all the better after having gotten through the effects of their elixir."

"I doubt it very much," Doc said. "They would not know exactly what the end-results would be. They must have gone through this themselves, though it's been so long ago they may have forgotten. You must not forget that they put us through hell before we met and that they ordered us to kill each other afterwards. No, they are evil, evil!"

Clio said, "But won't we go through something like that, too?"

"Nobody can say, except the Nine," I replied. "And they're not talking, of course. It may be that only those descended from the Old Stone Age people, those who have the genes for it, react to the elixir in this fashion. But we'll never find out. The question now, Doc, is something only you can answer, though I can predict what your answer will be, I believe. Are you prepared to give up the elixir and fight the Nine?"

"Trish said she told you about my experiments. I think we'll have the elixir ourselves some day. But whether we do or don't, I am no longer obeying the Nine. And he who disobeys, you know, is their deadly enemy."

I wheeled closer and took his hand. "They divided us, brother," I said. "But united . . ."

I did not feel brotherly, as yet, and I suppose he did not. But this was a man I could admire and respect and the best ally anyone could want. The odds were greatly against us, but if any two could put up a better fight, I did not know them.

Clio gave him another shot, and he was soon asleep. Trish stayed behind to watch him adoringly for a while. Clio and I returned to the room, where I slowly and painfully got back into bed.

Clio sat down and looked at me for a long time. Then she said, "Trish told me about you two."

"Oh?" I said.

My heart was beating faster than if I'd heard a leopard prowling in the African bush.

"When you two made love," she said.

"We weren't making love," I said. "We were loving each other. Fucking passionately and lovingly."

She reddened slightly. No matter how uninhibited her behavior, she still reacts to certain words.

"She said that nothing might have happened if you hadn't been so concerned about being crippled by your aberration."

"I did not explain to her why I was doing that," I said. "But she was essentially correct. Although I think the same thing would have happened even if I was not concerned about my aberration."

She did not go into a furious tirade or start weeping, as I had expected. She said, "The trouble with retaining complete youthfulness and its vigor is that a couple cannot grow old and fade away together. We're 80 and so should be weak and set in our ways and thoroughly accustomed to each other, like a wheel in a rut. A wheel that doesn't want to leave the rut. But we know each other to the last atom, and, while we love each other very much, we are youthful and we are beginning to want some variety. So . . ."

"So?" I said.

"So I think we'll have to have some variety now and then. The little vacations in the caverns provided that, but those are gone."

Suddenly, she stood up and bent over and threw her arms around me.

"What am I saying?" she cried. "I love you and only you! I really want no other man!"

She was sincere, and I loved her very much at that moment. I always love her, although there are some moments when the intensity is less. And, certainly, when I was in Trish, I was not thinking about Clio. Fairness is fairness.

She really did not want another man—as her permanent mate. But she was right. Immortality has its prices, and it is impossible to confine yourself to one mate forever if you have the vigor of youth.

This problem would have to work itself out whichever way it would go. At the moment, we had more vital business to attend to. Hawthorpe arrived that afternoon and, after some formalities, got to the instructions.

First, we must get Caliban's body up and remove the head and send it off to the Nine. Usually, the victor took the head himself, but since I would not be able to move for some time, that just could not be done. Hawthorpe would carry it to the Nine.

Second, I was to come to London as soon as I was able and not one second later. I would then be flown to Uganda and taken through the secret routes of the caverns. This time, I would not be blindfolded. After going through the ceremony of seating me, the Nine would hold a conference. This was the most serious meeting since 1945. Hawthorpe could not tell me much, but the discussion would be about the means used for solving the population problem.

The Nine did not intend to let the overcrowding and the pollution go on any longer. The only question was not when but how.

The Nine have a way with temptation.

For a minute, I visualized a world something like that into which I had been born but much better. The jungles and the savannas could return, and Africa would again have its millions upon millions of zebras, antelope, hippos, elephants, and its thousands upon thousands of leopards and lions. The human population would be few and scattered and living naked in thatched huts and fighting each other with spears. I would have vast areas to roam in. Perhaps, the gorilla could be saved from extinction, and if I could find just a few of The Folk left, their numbers could be increased to the point where they might become as numerous as they were 50,000 years ago.

It was a beautiful vision.

And, of course, it would have to be paid for, one way or another.

I might not like the payment.

In fact, I didn't like it.

Moreover, I would have to buy an entrance ticket with Doc's head.

I said, "It may take a few days before we can get Caliban's body up."

"Oh, no," he said quickly. "I have two men fishing for it now. I'll take care of everything."

"That's decent of you," I said.

"Not at all, just carrying out orders," he said.

If I tried to convert him to our side, I would be warning the Nine. It would be of no use anyway.

I said, "Come here, Hawthorpe," and when he was close enough I grabbed his throat with one hand and the top of his head with the other. He

was a big bull-necked man but squeaked like a
mouse before I twisted his neck. I then sent Clio
and Trish out after the other two. They called them
inside and shot them, and then dropped the weighted
bodies into the moat.

Both were shaken. Though they were old vet-
erans and cool enough in defending themselves or
attacking enemies on the alert, killing in cold blood
was new. I told them that they'd have more of that
before we were finished, one way or the other.

An hour later, after some difficulty in getting Doc
into the back of a station wagon, we drove off. I
stopped once before entering the woods to say fare-
well to the estate. I doubted that I would ever be
able to return. I looked at the castle, the ashes of
the Hall, the barns, garages, servants' quarters, the
broad meadows and the question-shaped tarn, the
woods beyond, and at the great boulder on the hill,
beside which rested the first Randgrith. *The old
man would sit when the two ravens returned*, the
local saying went. I knew now what that meant.
The old man, our grandfather, would never sit
because he was forever dead, and the two ravens
would not return.

Neither would I. Not for many years, anyway.

We drove away as the sun dropped behind the
High Chair. The soldiers on sentinel duty let us
through without delay. It would not be long before
the Nine knew that the three of us had gone, however. Doc was hidden under some blankets and
luggage. As soon as Hawthorpe failed to report in
as scheduled, the Nine would investigate, and they
would know that Caliban was still alive and with us.

Then the hunt would be on.

Hunter, beware the prey!

Before this is over, there may be more than one empty seat at the table of the Nine, and the world may be aware of its secret masters.

THE END

Postscript

Do you know who they are?

Since Homer and Beowulf—and doubtlessly before—storytellers have found for themselves a hero-figure, and have, with their audiences, discovered that just one story won't do, and a saga is born. The parallel between Homer and a long-running comic strip like *Gasoline Alley* is not often drawn, but it is a valid one. The hold of the continuing epic on its public is a firm one. People used to queue up to await delivery of the weekly papers in which they could find the latest chapter of a Charles Dickens novel. Ma and Pa Kettle had their countless thousands of faithful followers, and of course the success of a television series is based on this and nothing else.

The secret of the success of a saga lies in its reference to life—the very specific day-to-day, inside-the-skin life of the members of its audience. This is a matter of harmony or contrast; the narrative concerns itself meticulously with current and familiar events, like the Lanny Budd stories or the Forsyte Saga, or with events calculated to be exotic, like the legends of Bifrost or the Ring trilogy. (Dickens had the joyful genius of being able to do both at once.) Always, the most fascinating of all have been the stories which injected the superhuman into human events. This was the strength and magic of Homer—and also of The Shadow.

Batman's adventures in Gotham City are nothing less.

Which brings us, of course, to the marvelous (one wishes, sometimes, that a word had never been overused to the point of total dilution: marvelous they were, marvelous they are) pulp-magazine heroes and the almost endless sword-and-sorcery serial novels and their unforgettable, unconquerable protagonists. With all my heart I pity those who have lived their lives without having been injected with the enchantment of Northwest Smith or Hawk Carse, Tarzan, John Carter, Doc Savage, Conan the Conqueror or any of their swashbuckling colleagues.

Almost without exception, however, the serial epics of the last couple of centuries have been bowdlerized to an extreme, and almost inexplicable, degree. To explain my use of that word, I must digress and tell you about the Man from Mars who follows me around.

I've never gotten a good look at him, so I can't describe him accurately. What he is, however, is not as significant as what he does. He asks me questions. He asks me the *damnedest* questions. There's no special penalty involved in giving him wrong answers or no answers—except the pressure of the question itself. He's not selling anything in particular and what he asks may or may not reveal what he thinks is a right answer: I just don't know. But he keeps on asking questions that nobody else seems to ask, about all kinds of commonplace things and ideas. Why are our ground vehicles streamlined only where we can see them? Why is it I can walk, say, two miles down the boulevard howling curses, and/or punching a woman, but if I wear nothing but three yards of blue silk tied to my left forearm and carry a peacock feather, even if I walk sedately, I would be picked up in the first hundred and fifty yards? Why is it that most of our power plants are that category of machine called "heat engines," yet nobody seems to have designed one which can operate without a cooling system —that is, a device designed to dissipate heat? Why does society go to such extremes to protect the sacred life of an unborn child, and then send him off when he is seventeen to get his head blown off? Why, when the Health Department of a sophisticated modern city discovers an epidemic, and makes plans for a publicity campaign to stop it, does it find its funds cut in two? (The epidemic is venereal disease, but that isn't the answer—is it?) Anyway, he keeps on asking me these questions, and all too often I have to wag my head and say, well, sir, you see . . . uh.

One of his questions, then, is "Why don't your superhumans, your heroic fighters, leaders, battlers for good and against evil, so seldom have a sex life —or, indeed, sex organs?" Now, I don't know if Philip José Farmer has a Man from Mars like mine, but a book like *A Feast Unknown* is his riproaring answer—sure they have, and they refuse to be responsible for the misstatements of their bowdlerizing biographers. And if a man has been brought up by apes, he will eat like an ape and play sexually like an ape, and carry no burden of guilt for it, and will still continue to be a superman.

One of the most interesting aspects of this book is the absolutely direct and unconcealed connection

between sex and violence. Surely it takes no special-
ly trained perceptions to understand that the popu-
larity of violence in the popular media is invariably
a seasoning for sex, whenever it is not a substitute
for it. If Farmer says nothing else in a work like
this—and he says many other things—he makes it
clear that unlimited violence coupled with unlimited
sex is an unlimited absurdity. There is nothing in
the pattern he presents that shakes my basic con-
viction that people who get enough sex—and
enough is like enough food, enough water—cannot
be obsessed by it and will need no substitutes, including violence. This is the healthy, constructive
aspect of the new freedoms in sexual expression,
and long may they wave. Freely enough expressed,
described, and secured, human needs cease to be
preoccupations, and we can go on to other things.
I do not believe that violence is in itself such a need,
but is merely the manifestation of denial—denial
of food, of shelter, and of the phenomena surrounding procreation. This is the very core of the healthy
truth expressed in the slogan, "Make love, not war."

There is one other profundity which, under the
hyperbolic "chase" and the swashbuckle, Farmer
explores with great acuity, and this is the function
of the Nine—his name for something which has
preoccupied humanity since it could be called
human. It is the awareness of a controlling Presence
or Entity of immense resource, merciless power,
and a set of inexorable aims against which we
mortals (they, of course, are immortal) must be
tested. We are to be tested whether we understand
those aims or not, and to fail the tests is to incur
frightful punishments.

To identify this Power, to isolate its signs and symptoms, to recognize its agents, to comprehend its ends, and to assess its strength has been the basic chore of philosophers and theologians since the first of them, in his snake-fang beads, glared redly at an approaching thunderhead and clubbed a neighbor in an act of propitiation. Farmer, with his Nine, brings out an extremely important point: that perhaps the ultimate aims of such a power are functionally neolithic—which says two things: that it is in our blood and bone, and that it is hopelessly outdated—as good a description as any of the human predicament. It is gratifying to explain ourselves with naked apes and territorial imperatives. It is not wise to excuse ourselves with them.

Read *A Feast Unknown,* then, for its sprawling, brawling, shocking, suspenseful, hilarious self, and you will be well repaid in pure entertainment— which is true of all Farmer's work. True also, however, is that Farmer writes in symbols. His plays and his players are natural forces, natural people (by harmony and by contrast), and he is always questioning. He makes you recoil in horror and shock—but always in a manner that makes you ask yourself why you found it horrifying or shocking. He makes you laugh, and you wonder why you laughed; he makes you hope for certain outcomes, and you wonder why. He is, in short, continually asking you questions: questions about marital fidelity, questions about your fixed ideas about sexual practices, about violence, about prejudices—whether they involve eating worms or helping disadvantaged peoples, about clothing and hunting and

passports and gratitude and loving and atomic
weapons.

My God. I never thought to ask him. Maybe he's
a Man from Mars too.

Theodore Sturgeon
Sherman Oaks, Cal. 1969